DUTY AND l

The SS brotherhood and

By
Toby Oliver

Cover Design: CreateSpace
Published November 2016

ISBN-13:
978-1537475059

ISBN-10:
1537475053

With grateful thanks to David, Jill and Heather for their help and support.

We must all turn our backs upon the horrors of the past. We must look to the future. We cannot afford to drag forward across the years that are to come the hatreds and revenges which have sprung from the injuries of the past.

WINSTON CHURCHILL, speech at Zurich University

Chapter 1
The Millbank Lecture Theatre, London

It was a crisp, autumn evening as Sir Spencer Hall, the Head of MI5, slipped quietly into the darkened auditorium. He sat back and lit a cigarette. He was running late and had already missed most of the lecture. Spencer casually eased his gold lighter back into his hip pocket and gazed idly around the packed lecture theatre. Security was tight, but to the untrained eye, it appeared unobtrusive. The majority of the attendees would have been in blissful ignorance that the smartly suited men guarding the exits were a combination of armed MI5 and Scotland Yard Special Branch officers.

Since 1952, the biannual scientific conference had taken place in a different capital city. Ten years down the line, it was now the responsibility of the Foreign Office to host the latest get-together of the Western power's leading scientists. Although the various lecturers were caveated from revealing any top secret information, the one thing which could be guaranteed was the continued interest of the Soviet Intelligence Service.

The slight figure of Professor Bernard Zimmerman, a renowned guided missile expert, was conducting this evening's lecture. His presence in London had aroused considerable interest and resulted in several attempts by the KGB to infiltrate the conference.

During the final death throes of the Third Reich, Stalin's Soviet Union had been increasingly viewed by politicians in both London and Washington as the new enemy and the new military priority. Operation Paperclip was the codename used by the US intelligence and military to covertly track down leading German scientists to prevent them falling under the control of the advancing Soviet army. Since those dark days, the world had moved on, but was now paralysed by the Cold War and the long struggle for global supremacy pitting the Western powers against the Soviet Eastern Bloc, and the ever-present deadly threat of nuclear war.

Spencer's gaze continued to glide slowly around the lecture theatre before finally coming to rest on Zimmerman. Behind the thin, pinched features, and the kind pale blue eyes, lurked a tough, uncompromising personality. He wore a single-breasted, charcoal grey suit; it wasn't, Spencer noted, of Savile Row quality, but he still cut quite a dapper figure. The crisp white shirt was offset with an expensive blue silk tie looped into a Windsor knot, and the white shirt cuffs protruded fashionably below the sleeves of the suit. His hesitant, but flawless, English was delivered with an unmistakable thick German accent. Although his delivery was flat and almost expressionless, he still, somehow, managed to hold the undivided attention of his scientific peers.

Spencer's personal feelings toward Zimmerman were, at best, ambivalent, for the renowned scientist had once held the rank of Major in Himmler's deadly SS. He had worked alongside an elite group of scientists in the research and development of Nazi Germany's top secret V1 and V2 rocket development programme. During the dying days of the Third Reich, the work of Zimmerman and his colleagues had culminated with the launch of Hitler's weapons of mass destruction on the already decimated streets of London.

As the Allies advanced inexorably across Germany, another war had begun to take shape for the politicians on both sides of the Atlantic. They had foreseen another deadly conflict, the Cold War, with the Soviet Union. Scientists of Zimmerman's calibre were critical to the future of military development in the post-war era, and both the West and the Soviets were hell bent on exploiting their expertise.

Zimmerman had eventually been granted American citizenship in 1957, and, after an initial spell of working for the Army, now held a key role at NASA. The timing was interesting, as it was not until 1957, and the launch of the Soviet's Sputnik 1, America finally realised they were lagging behind the Soviet Union, and the German scientists working for the Kremlin had stolen a march on them.

The transition to life in America had not always been a smooth ride for neither Zimmerman nor his family. The occasional newspaper report would surface, and he'd be forced into the open to defend his war record, and especially his role in the SS. He employed the best lawyers money could buy to fight his corner, and Zimmerman's defence was always the same. For scientists of his standing, becoming a member of the Nazi Party, and then the SS, wasn't exactly open for discussion. In his case, it had been on the personal order of Reichsführer Himmler. Arguably, refusal to comply would have almost certainly ended in death. In fairness to him, Spencer had always accepted there was more than a grain of truth in Zimmerman's story. But, ardent Nazi, or not, he could not deny personally witnessing the terrible atrocities committed by the SS against the slave labourers working on Hitler's rocket programme.

Spencer drew heavily on his cigarette. His eyes through the haze of smoke were unflinching on Zimmerman as he gestured to his attractive young female assistant and asked her to place another slide in the projector. By the sound of things, he seemed on the verge of calling it a day. But, to Spencer's dismay, Zimmerman decided to throw the lecture open to the floor for a question and answer session.

Spencer resignedly glanced at his watch and slunk back into his chair. As he did so, he felt a sharp tap on his shoulder. He glanced up. His driver, Freddy Evans, leaned forward and said quietly, 'I'm sorry to bother you, sir, but Mr. Stein is waiting for you in the foyer.'

Thank Christ for that, he thought to himself. It gave him a valid excuse to leave. Spencer nodded, following Evans out of the auditorium.

Jack Stein was CIA and an old friend from the War. His six foot four figure was lean, just as it had been in his prime with the American Special Forces, neither had the soulful eyes, and the aquiline good looks women found attractive changed all that much over the years. In Spencer's experience, Stein rarely left anything to chance. As one of the CIA's top field agents, if he couldn't win you over with his charisma, he'd certainly win you over with his ruthless preparation and slickness. But, more importantly, they trusted each other, and in their game, trust certainly didn't come easily; it had to be earned.

As Spencer entered the foyer, Stein's face relaxed into a broad smile. He held out his hand in greeting. 'Sorry, Spence. I'm running an hour late.'

'Don't worry. I've only just arrived myself.'

Inclining his head toward the auditorium, Stein asked, 'I guess Zimmerman's still going strong in there?'

Spencer smirked. 'Christ, yes. I thought he was about to wrap things up, but he's only just thrown it open to the floor. I reckon he'll be at it for at least another hour, or so.'

Stein pulled a face. Like Spencer, most of it was way above his head. Besides, he'd had a long enough day already, and, only having just flown in from Washington the day before, was still suffering from jet lag. More to the point, he certainly didn't fancy listening to a bunch of eggheads prattling on about the whys and wherefores of rocket propulsion, or whatever it was.

Checking the expression on his friend's face, Spencer made a throwaway gesture. 'Believe me, there's no way I'm *not* going back in there.'

Stein visibly relaxed. 'Is the security okay?'

'It's tight enough. The theatre's been swept twice today.'

'Did you find anything?'

Spencer shook his head. 'We've had a lockdown on the place for a month. Trust me. It's clean as a whistle.' He glanced fleetingly across the foyer toward Stein's smartly suited CIA driver. 'Do you fancy a nightcap, Jack?' he queried in a relaxed, conversational tone.

Unusually, Stein found himself hesitating before answering. 'I'm staying with the American Ambassador and his wife at their place in Regent's Park.'

'Yes, so I've heard.' Knowing the Stein of old, Spencer guessed the arrangement didn't quite suit him. But, an invitation from Winthrop Alder, the American Ambassador, would have been a difficult one to refuse, or at least not without causing undue offence. Spencer eyed him speculatively. 'Is there a problem?'

'Heck no. It's just I have a meeting scheduled with Alder at 8.30, and I could do without a late night.'

'Christ, is that all?' Spencer remarked breezily. 'What is it, a brief?'

Stein smiled grimly. 'Yeah, something like that.'

'You can do that kind of stuff standing on your head, Jack.' He rubbed his hands together, pressed him again, and said expectantly, 'So what about it? *Do* you fancy a nightcap?'

They hadn't seen each other for a year or so; it sounded like a good idea. He figured a couple of drinks wouldn't hurt any, and they could catch up on old times. 'Okay, why not,' he relented.

Spencer smiled. 'Great!'

'Where are we going?'

'I was thinking of going back to my place.'

Stein caught the eye of his driver and told him about the change of plan, but guessed he'd probably overheard much of their conversation. An invite to Spencer's London base obviously had its advantages. As the Director General of MI5, the house was swept routinely for listening devices. They could at least relax and let down their guard, without having to worry the KGB might be listening in on their conversation.

As Spencer stepped outside the lecture theatre, a rather nondescript black saloon drew up to the curb. Unlike Government Ministers, he preferred travelling around London anonymously, and frequently changed vehicles through a dealership called The Spentar Group. The dealership was nothing more than a front, and was wholly owned by British Intelligence via a faux holding company.

There was a large military type seated in the front; beside him, was the equally tough-looking chauffeur, Freddy Evans. He kept the engine idling over, as his companion hurriedly jumped out and opened the rear doors, and allowed them to settle into the thick leather upholstery. He walked around the rear of the car, then signalled to Stein's guys along the road they were ready to move, before slipping back in beside Evans.

Spencer offered Stein a cigarette. He accepted. Stein had been trying to give them up recently. Not that he was back on them full-time, but every so often, he needed to cut himself some slack. The last two weeks had proved even more stressful than usual. The bi-annual scientific conference was much loved by Western diplomats and politicians alike, but, from a security aspect, it was becoming something of a white elephant.

The conference was increasingly targeted by the Eastern Bloc Intelligence Services. In the grand scheme of things, the consensus at CIA's Langley HQ and MI5 was it was tying up too much unnecessary manpower and resources to continue indefinitely. The trouble was, they still had to convince the politicians, and that was another matter altogether. Although Stein and Spencer continued carrying out their duties with good grace, the conference remained something of a non-negotiable political evil, something to be endured rather than embraced. Stein figured one way or another, he'd earned a drink and a smoke with an old friend, even one who happened to be Britain's top spymaster.

Even though the glass panel was closed between the rear and front seats, they both instinctively kept the conversation light, and mundane. As they drove from the lecture theatre and headed along the Thames, the last vestige of light had already gone, and below the darkened sky, a necklace of twinkling white lights illuminated the rather austere grey granite walls lining the embankment. It was a short drive to Spencer's impressive five-storey Georgian period house along Cheyne Walk, which came with uninterrupted views over the River Thames and Albert Bridge. It was a perk of the job.

In the cavernous room, which was part study, part library, Spencer handed Stein a large glass of bourbon, before slumping down on a worn leather armchair. Stein opted for the two-seater sofa opposite, and placed the cut glass tumbler to his lips, quietly savouring his first drink of the day.

'I get the feeling something's bothering you, Spence.' He waited for the catch. There had to be one. Friends or not, there always was.

'What do you make of Bernard Zimmerman?' came the blunt response.

Stein's eyes narrowed; it was a loaded question. 'What's there to know? He's one of the top men at NASA.'

'Yes. I understand in importance, he's considered to be second only to Wernher von Braun,' Spencer said equably.

'Hell, you know their backgrounds as well as I do. At the end of the war, it was a race against time. A case of "dog eat dog." Whatever way we look at it, the Nazi scientists were way ahead of our guys, or the Soviets. So, we fought tooth and nail, as did the British, to lift the best, before they had a chance to fall under Soviet control. Zimmerman was one of the Third Reich's leading players. At the end of the day, we struck lucky, but it could have gone either way.'

'I accept all that. Zimmerman was, and still is, a brilliant scientist, but put that aside, there's no escaping the fact, even before the war, his links to the fascists weren't just tenuous. He was a leading player. Let's face it; he's served both Adolf Hitler and several American presidents with equal skill.'

'Maybe, but Zimmerman's take on things is a little different. He freely admits he was a member of the SS, but joined out of necessity and not by choice.'

Spencer smiled noncommittally and took a gulp of his bourbon.

'Come on, fella. If the shit weren't about to hit the fan, we wouldn't be having this conversation, would we?'

'I guess not.'

Stein's voice was grave. 'Come on, out with it!'

'This is strictly off the record, Jack.'

Stein rolled his eyes. 'Don't do this to me, Spence! You know it'll end up getting messy.'

'Doesn't it always get messy?' He smiled.

Stein put on a polite face of inquiry, and downed his bourbon in one hit.

'Have you ever heard of someone called Helmut Schneider?'

'No, I can't say I have.'

Spencer offered Stein a re-fill; it would have seemed churlish to refuse. 'Schneider is a former Gestapo officer,' he explained, pouring Stein a fresh drink. 'During a mission behind enemy lines in October 1944, thirty-one members of the Special Air Service were captured in France.' Spencer handed him his bourbon. 'They were part of Operation Loyton.'

Stein recalled reading the security reports. The whole reasoning behind Loyton was aimed at boosting the local Resistance groups. Nearly half of the elite team who parachuted into France never came home. They paid a high price; there was a horrific attrition rate. It was a bloody guerrilla fight against some of the Third Reich's most die-hard fanatics. Some had died horrible deaths at the hands of the Nazis. By any standards, Loyton was a costly mission.

The Gestapo had tortured the captured troops, and subsequently, they were all executed. In the aftermath of the D-Day landings and the Allies advance toward the German border, the Führer had ordered his forces to make a last ditch stand. No quarter was given to the troops advancing toward the Fatherland. But, the cards were already heavily stacked against deep cover units, like the SAS.

As far back as October 1942, the Kommandobefehl or Commando Order, as it was known, had been issued on Hitler's personal decree. Any commando units encountered by German forces were to be handed over immediately to the Gestapo. The Order was regardless of whether they were in uniform or plain clothes all were to be considered spies. In essence, the Order went entirely against the Geneva Convention regarding the handling of prisoners of war.

Stein considered his reply carefully. His gut feeling was Operation Loyton hadn't been only business, but, somehow, personal to Spencer. It had proved to be a costly operation. 'So, what part did Schneider play in all this?'

'Schneider was directly responsible for not only torturing the SAS, but for executing every single one of them.' Spencer eased himself back down on the faded leather armchair, nursing a large, amber-coloured whisky, with a splash of water. When he spoke, his voice was thoughtful, measured. 'In my brother's case, he was pistol-whipped before being shot in the head by Schneider and kicked into a newly dug grave.' He added, with difficulty, 'Jamie was forced to dig his own grave.'

While Stein knew Spencer's brother, Jamie, had died during the war, up until now, he'd no idea he'd been murdered by the Gestapo. It wasn't something they'd ever discussed in any great detail. Whenever his brother's name had been brought up in conversation, the shutters had always come down. Although they were old friends, there were still times when Spencer remained very much a closed book. But, Jamie had always been a chink in his armour.

Stein looked candidly into his friend's face. 'For Christ's sake, Spence, why the hell didn't you tell me Jamie had been executed?'

He shrugged. 'What difference would it have made?'

Stein took a mouthful of the bourbon. He guessed there was little point in pressing him further. 'I still don't quite get where Zimmerman fits into all this?'

Spencer eased a pack of cigarettes out of his hip pocket and lit one. 'Schneider was picked up by the Soviets back in 1945, and ended up serving a stretch in prison. Well, more than a stretch.'

'Where was he?'

'Jamiltz Internment Camp.'

Stein pursed his lips together, letting out a silent whistle. Jamiltz was a notorious Soviet camp, where inmates were not permitted contact with the outside world. The regime was brutally harsh, and it became known as a silent camp. For several years after the war, the Soviet occupation authorities in East Germany denied its existence. However, Schneider's luck finally changed when the USSR eventually handed the camp over to the East German government.

'With a little help from his friends,' Spencer explained, 'Schneider finally managed to get himself back to West Germany.'

Stein looked at him with a hint of appraisal. 'Friends,' he queried warily, 'what kind of friends?'

Spencer drew heavily on his cigarette. He remained emotionless as he disclosed the next bit of information. 'One of them was Bernard Zimmerman.'

Stein shook his head 'I don't buy it. We've watched Zimmerman like a hawk. If he were involved in some Nazi escape network, we'd have picked up on him by now!'

'Are you sure?'

'Well, I reckon you're gonna tell me I'm wrong. What's happened?

'Schneider's turned up in London, under an assumed name.'

'When did he arrive?'

'Two weeks ago.'

'Why come to London, and why now?'

'He travelled back from Argentina a month ago to attend a family funeral in Austria. Unfortunately, for Schneider, his arrival in Vienna didn't entirely go unnoticed, and ever since, he's rumoured to have been on the run from Mossad, the Israeli intelligence service.'

Stein allowed himself a wry smile. 'I can see how that would focus his mind a little.'

'The duty rumour is he's trying to get himself out of the country and back to Argentina on a cargo ship from Southampton.' Spencer drew on his cigarette, and considered Stein thoughtfully. 'Schneider's passage to South America is being financed by your man.'

It took a great deal to rattle Stein, but the expression on his face spoke volumes. 'Goddamn it, Spence! Are you serious?'

'I'm afraid so.'

'You mean, he's helping to *bankroll* it?'

Stein still couldn't quite get his head around the idea Zimmerman was tied to some Nazi ratline, and, more to the point, had entirely outfoxed and slipped under the CIA's radar. Something had gone seriously wrong, but where? Questions would be asked at the very highest level, and heads would have to roll. But, he just couldn't fathom how the hell Zimmerman had managed to keep his links to the Nazi old guard secret. While he had no reason to doubt the soundness of Spencer's intelligence, it brought into question not only Zimmerman's position at NASA, but, more importantly, his ongoing Nazi connections had left him wide open to potential blackmail. Perhaps they were already too late; maybe the Soviets had already hooked him.

Stein shot him a cold, hard, questioning look. 'Are you sure about Zimmerman?'

'I have it on tape,' Spencer assured him. 'In fact, Schneider thanked him personally for putting up the cash.'

'Tell me something…' Stein said at length.

Spencer looked at him curiously. 'Go on.'

'Security has been pretty tight over the last few weeks, what with the Millbank Conference and all, so how in Christ's name did Schneider manage to get through British security?'

Spencer shrugged. 'Maybe he was brought across by private plane, or perhaps by boat from the French coast. Either way, it's pretty irrelevant how he arrived. The fact remains Schneider's here on our doorstep. In Nazi circles, he's still a highly respected war hero, rather than a war criminal. They'd move heaven and earth to help him escape back to South America. He's one of their own, a blood brother. As you can imagine, Schneider still has contacts in high places. You know how these Nazi escape organisations operate; they have a healthy support network. Right now, with Mossad on his tail, Schneider needs all the help he can get.'

'Are we sure about this Mossad connection?' Stein asked, shooting him a quizzical look. While he had no reason to doubt it, he wanted to know Spencer's view on the situation.

'Well, it wouldn't be the first time Mossad went after a high-ranking Gestapo officer, and where Schneider's concerned, he must be pretty near the top of their hit list.'

Stein held his gaze. While it sounded perfectly logical, and didn't dispute the Israelis wanted him dead, he had a gut feeling Spencer might be holding out on him. That British Intelligence was playing cat and mouse. Maybe he had something else on Schneider, and didn't want to come clean until he had concrete proof. But, it was just that; no more than a gut feeling. However, he'd known Spencer long enough to guess he probably had something else up his sleeve.

'Where did they meet up?'

'They first met at a cocktail party, hosted by Hans von Bitten, the West German Ambassador.'

Stein narrowed his eyes. 'Wasn't that the day after the Conference started?'

Spencer nodded. 'Von Bitten invited all the members of the scientific delegations attending Millbank.'

'Okay, so who invited Schneider?'

'I have my suspicions, but I really can't prove it.'

'Who do you reckon it was, then? You must have someone in mind.'

'I believe the invite came from one of the Embassy's security staff, Josef Frenzel.'

Stein pulled a face. 'Christ, is he still doing the rounds?'

Frenzel had managed to cover his tracks well. During the war, he worked for General Reinhard von Gehlen, Hitler's head of military espionage in Russia. With the defeat of the Third Reich imminent, Gehlen ordered his senior officers to microfilm their records on the USSR. They carefully packed the films in steel drums, burying them in secret locations scattered throughout the Austrian Alps.

Gehlen, along with Frenzel and a group of their fellow officers, voluntarily gave themselves up to the US Army Counter Intelligence Corps. General Gehlen had swiftly wasted no time offering up his services and, more importantly, his knowledge of the KGB and their clandestine activities to the US. The precious microfilms buried deep in the Austrian Alps provided an essential bargaining chip in helping the Americans take Gehlen's offer seriously. They bartered a deal, the Soviet records and his intricate network of contacts in exchange for his liberty and that of his imprisoned colleagues, including Josef Frenzel.

The high-risk gamble paid off, and Gehlen was eventually released from captivity and flown back to Germany. With American approval, he began his intelligence work, recruiting some of his former Nazi intelligence officers. Frenzel had been one of the first to be signed on. The so-called Gehlen Organization was to play a vital role subsequently in providing the CIA with reports on Soviet missile developments, supposedly provided by contact with German scientists captured by the Russians at the end of the war.

In April 1956, control of the Gehlen Organization was subsumed into the newly-sovereign West German Federal Republic. Gehlen was duly appointed Chief of the West German Intelligence Service. His transformation from enemy agent to a pillar of western democracy was now complete. With Gehlen's patronage, Frenzel moved seamlessly into a series of security roles, culminating with his appointment to the West German Embassy in London.

Before his arrival as Head of Embassy Security, Frenzel had already come under scrutiny from British Intelligence. While no-one could argue Frenzel wasn't wily, in

Spencer's opinion, he was far from the brightest on the block. He was often to be found drunkenly bragging to friends about covert meetings with former members of the SS and his close association with a secretive underground Nazi escape ratline called the *Schamhorst*.

'Schneider,' Spencer explained, 'was down on the Embassy's guest list as Professor Wilhelm Adler.'

'Has Schneider tried getting into any of the Millbank lectures?'

'Hardly. I guess, right now, he doesn't want to break cover too often. Would *you*?'

Stein smiled but didn't respond.

'The next time Schneider met up with your Professor Zimmerman was at Frenzel's apartment in Kensington.'

'You mentioned you had it on tape.'

'Frenzel's place has been wired since his appointment.'

'And he doesn't suspect he's being tapped?'

'He found a couple of devices we left around.' Spencer leaned forward and stubbed out his cigarette in a cut glass ashtray. 'Nothing major, only the stuff we wanted him to find. We've also managed to take over the apartment next door, so listening in isn't a problem.'

'What exactly have you got on tape?'

'Your man Zimmerman is helping to fund the *Schamhorst* network. Let's face it, he's certainly not short of a few quid or two. During the war, it came to light he had deposited a large amount of money in the Union Bank of Switzerland in Bern.'

Stein smiled dryly; it was even worse than he feared. 'Zimmerman was in good company then.'

In late 1944, the Office of Strategic Services, the forerunner of the CIA, had raised an intelligence report confirming information received in Bern, indicated accounts were being held at the Union Bank for Adolf Hitler by a German official called Max Ammann.

'But, how did we miss it?'

'Come on, Jack. Don't beat yourself up about it. We both know how things were. We did what we had to do, and fast. It's only recently we discovered a link to Zimmerman.'

Stein knew he was right, but it still stung that the full extent of Zimmerman's diehard allegiance to Nazism had somehow slipped under the net. Maybe his value at the time as a scientist had been the overriding factor. Perhaps it was better to turn a blind eye, rather than dig too deeply. Stein had no way of knowing. He'd spent the war embedded behind enemy lines. It hadn't been his call, his decision, to recruit the likes of Zimmerman and his German colleagues, but he's sure as hell inherited the fallout.

'If it's any consolation, it seems he's never officially touched any of the money, at least not for personal use. I can't help thinking it's ended up as being something of a poison chalice to him.'

Stein figured it wasn't much of a consolation.

'Think about it Jack. What would you have done in Zimmerman's shoes? I'd have lied through by teeth, if it meant escaping the Soviet Army. After giving himself up, he needed to sanitise his past and protest his innocence. To convince the Americans he'd been coerced into joining the Nazi Party.'

'You're right.' Stein shrugged. 'He certainly wasn't alone.'

'Your man covered his tracks well, very well. Zimmerman needed to keep a low profile. He needed to appear squeaky clean, at least until he was granted American citizenship. I could be wrong, but I guess, at that point, the CIA would have started to take their foot off the pedal and given him a little more leeway.'

Stein couldn't deny it.

'We believe he gave it another year, or so, before finally putting his head above the parapet to link up with his former brothers in arms, his first port of call was…'

Stein raised his hand. 'Don't tell me. Josef Frenzel.'

'It appears from day one Frenzel has been Zimmerman's go-between. Having listened to the tapes, it seems he's a signatory to Zimmerman's Swiss bank account. The fact Schneider now finds himself on the run is purely coincidental, but the first person he touched base with in London was Frenzel.'

Stein regarded him thoughtfully but kept any remarks to himself.

'From everything I know about Zimmerman, if he swallowed a nail, he'd shit a corkscrew.'

'I'm sorry, Spence, but you know I can't keep this off the record.'

Spencer gave him a long, slow look. 'At the end of the day, Professor Zimmerman's your problem.'

'So, what are you going to do about, Schneider?'

'I've waited a long time to reel him in. Jack, he's *mine.*'

Chapter 2
MI5 HQ, London

Jed Carter stepped out of the lift and made his way along the corridor, leading into the outer office of Sir Spencer Hall. His secretary, Dawn Abrams, was busily typing up a report from her shorthand notes. She glanced up as he entered the office and smiled briefly. Dawn was slim, brown-eyed, discreet, and totally loyal. She was warm and welcoming, but there had been the odd occasion when Carter had inadvertently crossed her. A late report or misplaced light-hearted comment, which had missed its mark, was bound to bring down the shutters. The brown eyes would flash angrily, and Carter invariably found himself apologising. In many ways, she was every bit as intimidating as her boss.

Dawn pressed the intercom on her desk. 'Mr. Carter is here to see you, sir.'

'Send him in,' was the sharp response.

Carter went through the adjoining door. Before closing it behind him, he hesitated. Spencer was not alone. The light streamed through the large sash windows, and the rhythmic ticking of a mahogany-cased grandfather clock seemed to fill the otherwise silent void. A stranger sat on Spencer's right. Jed Carter quietly closed the door and waited, until Spencer indicated for him to take a seat across the wide, green leather topped Victorian desk. As he took the chair, Carter curiously examined their faces.

'Jed, I don't think you've met Jack Stein before, have you?' His voice was casual, authoritative.

He'd heard a great deal about Stein, but had never met him in the flesh. If the talk was to be believed, he was every bit as hard and uncompromising as his boss.

'No, sir, I haven't.'

'Jack's an old friend of mine. He's over here from Langley for the Millbank Conference.'

Stein leaned forward and briefly touched his hand in greeting.

Stein's curious gaze was approving. Carter was young, too young to have served in the war. While not quite suave, he was dressed in a smart, dark suit and a pale blue shirt, with just a flash of large gold cufflinks. There was an indefinable brooding intensity in his expression which struck a chord, reminding him of his first encounter with Spencer during the dark days of the war in France.

The fact Spencer had assigned Carter to take on the case meant only one thing; Spencer considered him to be a star of the future. He exuded confidence, and, from what Stein knew, his progress from the elite Special Air Service to British Intelligence had apparently been seamless. He guessed Carter was something of a protégé and obviously relatively new to the espionage game. The Schneider assignment was a serious step up the ladder. Stein also liked how when he looked at them, it was almost a challenge.

In CIA circles, Jed Carter knew Stein was known affectionately as the "Silver Fox." While Stein's once dark hair might have turned gun metal grey, his reputation, like Spencer's, had remained one of untrammelled power within the intelligence community on both sides of the Atlantic.

'Have you finished reading the report?' Spencer asked him.

Carter handed a file across the table; a distinctive red cross and the caveat "TOP SECRET - UK EYES ONLY" was printed on the cover.

Spencer looked at him questioningly. 'Well?'

'Do you mind if I smoke, sir?'

'Feel free.'

Carter slipped a pack of cigarettes out of his pocket. He didn't allow it to show, but felt slightly in awe of both Spencer and Stein. He was unquestionably good at what he did, yet still felt he was possibly stepping slightly out of his league. Spencer offered his lighter. Snapping it shut, Carter said, 'I understand my casework is to be reassigned?'

Spencer's eyes held no expression, other than a piercing hardness. 'Is that a question or a statement?'

'Well, I'm not entirely sure. It was mentioned in passing by my section boss, but if it's all the same, I'd prefer to hear it from you, sir.'

'You've read the brief. Just how clear do you want me to make it?'

Carter drew heavily on his freshly lit cigarette. It was answer enough. His gaze glided thoughtfully toward the file. 'Whoever wrote up the brief on Schneider and Frenzel is pretty slick.'

Spencer didn't respond.

'May I ask who wrote it?'

'The agent's name is Joyce Leader.'

While it meant nothing to Carter, it wasn't lost on him Stein did a double take at the mention of her name.

'I thought you guys had closed her down after the war?' Stein asked, unable to conceal his surprise.

'We did,' Spencer explained, 'but as I've said before, Jack, no-one ever entirely leaves the Service.'

'Even so, from what you've said, Leader was never exactly the easiest of agents to handle.'

Spencer cast his friend a wintry smile. 'Maybe not, but when I found out Josef Frenzel was heading to London, I needed someone to get close to him, *very close*.'

'Yeah, I can see Leader would be kinda good at that.'

A quick, faint flicker of a smile crossed Spencer's face.

'Have you run it by Garvan?'

'Why should I?'

Stein pursed his lips together and raised his eyebrows.

The only thing Jed Carter knew, with any degree of certainty, was Garvan was the Assistant Commissioner of Scotland Yard's Special Branch. But, what was his connection to Leader, and why did Stein ask whether Spencer had run her involvement with him?

There was more than a hint of irritation in Carter's voice. 'So who is Joyce Leader? Hers is not a name I've come across before.'

Spencer leaned back in his chair and apologised. 'Joyce Leader was considered to be one of Britain's top double agents during the war.'

He arched his brows questioningly.

Spencer explained Leader had been born into a wealthy, Anglo-Austrian family of engineering manufacturers, whose political allegiance, or perhaps lack of it, to Hitler's

Third Reich had frequently brought them into conflict with the regime. Despite her father's obvious ambivalence, the family continued to prosper through their vast industrial outlets across both Austria and Germany, supplying armoured vehicles to the Nazi war machine. The family had also employed thousands of slave labourers in their factories, who lived or died at the whim of their guards.

Hitler had wanted to convey to the world the superiority of German engineering, and by default, the Leader family had been reluctantly drawn into Hitler's deathly vortex. Joyce always maintained that to protect her family from the increasing attention of the authorities, she had been co-coerced into joining the Abwehr, the German Intelligence Service. Whatever the real truth of the matter, after parachuting into Britain during 1941, her career as an Abwehr agent had proved to be somewhat short-lived.

Unbeknown to Berlin, British Intelligence had already been forewarned of her arrival by one of their established German double agents. She was swiftly picked up by the authorities, and placed under arrest at Camp 020, in Latchmere House, near Richmond, an interrogation centre for captured German agents in Britain. Anyone deemed unsuitable for use by British Intelligence faced either the firing squad or the hangman. It was a stark choice, but fortunately, for Leader, the interrogating officer decided she had potential. Having narrowly escaped almost certain death, she eventually found herself as a member of MI5's so-called Double Cross team.

The team's primary remit was to try and assess Adolf Hitler's plans. No easy task, but the Allied intelligence services knew it was vital to keep open the lines of communication with Berlin, both before, and after, the D-Day landings. By retaining contact with their Abwehr controllers, MI5's double agents played a crucial role in misleading Berlin about the Allies' intentions, while at the same time, gleaning vital intelligence from the German High Command.

It was an open secret Spencer had eventually come to admire Joyce Leader's undoubted skills as a spy. She was tough-minded, sharp-tongued, and throughout the war, her importance had increased steadily, not only in the eyes of British Intelligence, but, more importantly, also the Abwehr, who had never once doubted her integrity or the quality of her work. Spencer described her as an exceptional personality, and the fact he had re-opened her file for the Schneider case only served to reinforce his continued trust in her abilities. Even so, his decision had apparently taken Stein by surprise. What neither of them realised was the Schneider case was merely the icing on the cake. Spencer had actually reactivated Leader's file soon after Frenzel's posting to London.

It was an effort for Carter to keep the annoyance off his face. 'Why should we run her by Garvan?' he rasped. If he was expected to work alongside her, he had every right to know.

Spencer and Stein exchanged knowing glances. Carter guessed they didn't particularly care what he thought; it was on a need-to-know basis, and right now, he didn't need to know.

'So when can I meet her?' Carter asked.

'Probably tomorrow,' Spencer said cagily.

'How do you want me to play it with Schneider?'

'Play it?' Spencer repeated.

There was nothing to read in his boss's impassive face, so he pressed on. 'Whatever way you look at it, with Mossad on his tail, it's not going to be easy. I take it you don't want me to take him out?'

'If I did, I'd leave Mossad to do our dirty work.'

The glimmer of amusement on Stein's face did not go unnoticed by Carter. 'Does Joyce Leader know where he's hiding out?'

'Frenzel's been careful to keep him on the move. He's already had one or two close shaves.'

'You mean with Mossad?'

Spencer nodded. 'Frenzel is the lynchpin to the entire escape route. He controls the stuff we want, I want! But, he also happens to be the weakest link in the chain. Let's just say Joyce Leader has already done the groundwork by ensuring we've left him wide open.'

'Wide open?' he repeated curiously.

'To blackmail. How you use the information and damage Schneider is, of course, entirely up to you.'

Carter gave his boss a long, slow look. 'Why haven't they shipped him back off to South America? He's been here what, a week or more? What's the holdup?'

'My understanding is Frenzel has had a little trouble getting the cash up front. They've already had one aborted rescue plan.'

'What happened?'

'He was due to board an Argentinian cargo ship from Southampton, but at the last minute, the Captain upped the asking price. It was way over their original agreement, leaving Frenzel with something of a cash flow crisis.'

'I bet that went down well.'

Spencer smiled in bemusement. 'Like a lead balloon. Let's just say, the ship sailed for Buenos Aires without Herr Schneider on board.'

'Don't they have more than one tame captain?'

'A couple,' Spencer said, reaching into his desk drawer for a pack of cigarettes. 'The next one, Captain Juan Calero, is due in on Friday week.'

'Southampton?'

Spencer lit the cigarette and tossed his lighter back into the desk drawer. 'No, they've struck lucky this time. Calero's ship, the *Mendoza*, is offloading a shipment of beef at the Port of London.'

'I wouldn't have thought a ratline, like the *Schamhorst* would be short of cash. Its members' moved vast sums of money and gold out of Germany during the war?'

'Yes, they did, but over the last few years, we've closed down some of their European supply lines. Nothing major, but every little helps. More importantly, Calero has got wind of Schneider being on the run from Mossad.'

'Has he upped the price?'

Spencer cast Carter a wintry smile. 'With Mossad on his tail, wouldn't you?'

'I suppose so.'

Spencer drew heavily on his cigarette. 'It seems Juan Calero has trebled his usual asking price.'

'But, why not fly him out of the UK?'

'They could change his appearance and give him a false identity, but even so getting him through customs and crowded airports wouldn't be easy going. This way, he'll be picked up off the Argentinian coast from the *Mendoza* and taken directly to a safe house.'

'And what about Professor Zimmerman?' Carter asked, meeting Stein's gaze.

'What about him?' Stein came back to him.

'Joyce Leader's report says he's bankrolling Schneider's escape?'

'So she says.'

'Do we have proof?'

Stein smiled thinly. 'It's looking that way.'

'And if Zimmerman gets in my way?'

'You leave him to me.'

'It might not be that easy.'

Spencer automatically leaned forward across his desk. 'Zimmerman is the CIA's problem, not ours, do you *understand?*'

He guessed Spencer's decision wasn't exactly open for discussion.

Spencer inclined his head toward Stein. 'I think you'll find the CIA regard Zimmerman as their private preserve.'

Carter's expression remained deadpan. 'Private preserve or not, he's strayed into our territory.'

Spencer smiled. There were times when Carter could be an arrogant, argumentative bastard, but it was those very dubious qualities which helped make him good at what he did. Spencer placed both hands flat on the desk. 'This isn't a turf war, Jed. We need to work together, and, like it or not, there are certain niceties which we must observe with our American cousins.'

'So, where does that leave me?'

'I need Schneider, and I want him alive.'

Carter sucked heavily on his cigarette. 'Reading between the lines of the report, there's obviously a history between you and Schneider.'

A shadow crossed Spencer's face, before saying with characteristic bluntness, 'If you must know, he murdered my brother.'

Whatever answer Carter had expected it certainly wasn't that. Unusually, he found himself lost for words; it really didn't happen that often. Although he was well aware Spencer's younger brother, Jamie, was murdered during the war, he had no idea there was anything to link Schneider to what had, in effect, been a war crime. It made the prospect of taking on the assignment a whole different ball game. He felt suddenly decidedly uneasy. Was he merely just a means to an end, perhaps the fall guy, if things went badly wrong?

'I'd heard Jamie had been shot in France,' he said at length, 'but not the full story. While I was still serving with the Regiment, I'd heard rumours Jamie and twenty others were murdered in cold blood. The guys who survived Operation Loyton didn't talk about it much. Well at least not in any depth. But, from what I gathered, the Gestapo and the SS committed atrocities against our troops and the local French population.'

Spencer inhaled sharply. 'Yes, you're right. At least a thousand villagers were seized, and, along with some of Jamie's SAS colleagues, they were shipped off to concentration camps.' By now, his expression had closed down. 'Nearly half of those who had parachuted into France with him never came home. Some of the lucky ones, there weren't many, escaped to tell the tale. At the end of the war, the SAS sent a small team to investigate the fate of their missing men.'

'How did they get on?'

'It took years before they were able to track down those responsible for their deaths. The trouble was, the investigation team was never officially on the books. Being the SAS, they weren't afraid to push the legal boundaries, to do what they had to get results. The team ended up always getting themselves embroiled in ever increasing red tape.'

'So, what happened?'

'Without top cover, the investigation team went dark.'

'Went dark?' Carter queried.

'I help bury them in the War Crimes Investigation branch at the War Office.' Spencer stretched forward and stubbed out his half-smoked cigarette. 'Only a few people knew the team hadn't disbanded. Officially, its members were still serving with the Regiment. We finally decided to wind things up in 1957.'

'But, somehow, Schneider managed to slip the net?'

'He was the one that got away. In the dying days of the war, Schneider was swept up by the Soviets and served a stretch in prison. But, his friends from the *Schamhorst* network spent a great deal of money. They bribed some high-ranking Soviet officials and East German guards to get him safely back to the West, and eventually to Argentina.' A quick, faint trace of a smile crossed Spencer's face. 'If nothing else, I need to bring closure, not only for my own family, but to every family of those who died, and also to the men themselves.'

Spencer and Stein exchanged glances; it was probably time to call an end to the meeting. But, Carter held his ground; he needed to know exactly where he stood with Bernard Zimmerman. It was all very well for Stein to say he was the CIA's problem, but somewhere along the line, he'd probably cross paths with Zimmerman. The way things were stacking up, he wasn't even sure if Spencer had official government sanction for dealing with Schneider. He needed to know. Whatever way he looked at it, his neck was on the line. Carter waited for a response.

Stein imagined right now he was understandably daunted by taking on the assignment. The guy probably needed a little flexibility, a little reassurance they weren't going to hang him out to dry.

'The way I see it,' Stein said smoothly, 'is you follow Joyce Leader's advice. Just remember she's your link to the *Schamhorst*. Schneider is your main priority, and whatever else happens, we need to keep him alive. Now, that ain't gonna be easy; Mossad wants him dead, we know that. As for Zimmerman, well, as far as we are aware, he isn't on their hit list.'

'Where exactly does that leave me?'

Spencer said abruptly, 'Isn't it obvious?'

'No, not to me, it isn't!'

Stein cut across him. 'You can do whatever it takes to bring in Schneider; it's no big deal. But, if you do have to come down hard on Zimmerman, then let him know it's only a matter of time before we haul him in.'

Intelligence was a fast moving game; that was just the way it was, but Carter knew it wasn't set in black and white. There were always hidden layers. He had said as much. Zimmerman was a world-renowned NASA scientist, and the political fallout of his presumed association with the *Schamhorst* would cause seismic waves of controversy in Washington. They couldn't afford for the story to be made public. He was an integral member of the missile and space programme, and America's Cold War race for supremacy over the Soviet Union. Carter recalled seeing his name in the papers, and how he was described as the star turn at the Millbank Conference. However, the niggling feeling of being laid with the blame did not go away.

Spencer regarded him appraisingly. 'Don't worry yourself, Jed. I'll take the flak from the government. All I need is for you and Joyce to deliver Schneider and Zimmerman up on a platter.'

There was no doubt in Carter's mind. Come hell or high water, Spencer was on a single-minded mission to avenge his brother's death. To bring his murderer to justice, and Stein would do everything within his power to protect Zimmerman, or at least he'd do so until they returned to Washington to face the music.

Jed Carter knew he was viewed in the intelligence world as a mere minnow in comparison to sharks like Spencer and Stein. They were way out of his league. In spite of their reassurances, he still felt uneasy as to whether or not he was likely to be offered up as a sacrificial lamb in their deadly endgame.

Chapter 3
Bligh Street, South London

Helmut Schneider was heading back from the local shops with a small carrier bag. Before crossing the road, he looked both ways just to reassure himself he was not being followed. Two days earlier, Josef Frenzel had secured a short lease on a flat for him. By the end of the week, the plan was to move on again, this time to a different location in North London. The final details still needed ironing out, but there was no reason to believe it wouldn't go according to plan.

Since his arrival in England, they'd kept things tight. Communications between them were deliberately varied. They were either usually via a package dropped at the left luggage office at a main line station, a safety deposit box in Kensington, or by letter. Telephone calls were kept to a minimum, and then only if Schneider felt his life was in imminent danger.

As Schneider turned right into Bligh Street, he suddenly stopped dead in his tracks and immediately felt his pulse begin to quicken. There were half a dozen or so emergency vehicles drawn up along one side of the road. There was absolute chaos. Across, the street lay a pile of debris.

He swiftly took in the scene before approaching a bystander to ask what had happened.

'A gas explosion, mate,' the man said, inclining his head across the road.

Schneider instinctively followed his gaze and stared up at the block of flats. The residents had been evacuated after a massive explosion had rocked the entire building. Despite the enormity of the blast, just a single balcony and window had been blown across the street.

'Do you know if anyone was hurt?' Schneider enquired.

'No, I haven't seen them cart anyone out of the building.' The man suddenly lowered his voice. 'Or at least, they haven't yet, but I can't imagine someone wasn't seriously hurt, can you?'

Schneider looked up at the block of flats. 'I guess not. Do they know what caused it?'

'One of the firemen told me they think someone might have left their cooker on.'

Schneider took a sharp intake of breath. He somehow doubted it. Whatever caused the explosion certainly hadn't been the result of a gas leak. He'd been around too long to know the difference. The damage was too clean, too precise, and more to the point, it certainly wasn't coincidental. The balcony and window blown clean across the street belonged to the flat Frenzel had only just rented for him.

His gaze glided warily up and down the street. It had to be the work of professionals, and right now, he was nothing more than a sitting duck. Instinctively reaching inside his suit jacket, Schneider carefully eased a silenced handgun out of its holster slightly, just enough to click off the safety catch. There was no time to lose. Whomever had detonated the bomb wouldn't give up, and might still be in the area. He had to move, and move fast.

Schneider replaced the handgun and headed back out of Bligh Street, quickening his pace until he reached a red telephone box. He felt in his hip pocket for some change. As he picked up the receiver and dialled Belgravia 1899, his hands were shaking. It started to ring.

'Come on,' he hissed under his breath, 'answer the bloody phone!'

Eventually, Frenzel's voice came on the line. 'Hello.'

'It's me!' he rasped.

There was a slight pause, as Frenzel wondered why Schneider had risked breaking cover by calling him at his office.

'They're on to me!'

'What do you mean? What's happened?' he asked anxiously.

'They've blown up the flat, that's what's happened!'

'Are you okay?'

'If I hadn't popped out to the shops, they'd have taken me out.'

Frenzel hesitated before saying, 'I'll be there in ten minutes.'

'There's no way I'm hanging around here to let them pick me off!'

'So, what are you going to do?'

Schneider instinctively glanced over his shoulder. 'I'll head for the tube station.'

Frenzel could see the logic behind his decision. Mossad was unlikely to pick him off at a crowded area. 'Where do you want me to pick you up?'

'Embankment Station; it's only a couple of stops on the Bakerloo line.'

'I'll be there,' Frenzel assured him.

Schneider slammed the receiver down and opened the heavy door to the telephone box. He checked if the coast was clear, and allowed himself one last look toward the flats, before hurrying off in the direction of Lambeth North tube station.

Shit, he thought to himself. Somewhere along the line they'd managed to track him down. More importantly, Frenzel and the *Schamhorst* network had slipped up. There had already been one or two close shaves, but nothing on this scale. The only thing Schneider knew, with any degree of certainty, was his luck was likely to run out and soon.

**

MI5 HQ, London

Spencer enjoyed arriving at the office early; it allowed him time to get on with the routine stuff, before all hell broke loose after half past eight. The post-war intelligence world for him had never quite matched the high-octane existence of his life behind enemy lines. He knew Jack Stein felt much the same way. There existed between them the kind of unwavering, undying bond which could only ever be truly born out fighting for your life in the midst of battle, side by side.

The Cold War between the Soviet Union and the West was a constant state of political and military tension. It was a seemingly endless struggle for nothing less than global supremacy. The nuclear stalemate was of epic proportions, where the only assured outcome was Armageddon.

Since 1945, the Cold War era had dominated both political and intelligence policy, and as the Director General of MI5, Spencer had found himself fighting an increasing balancing act. By his own admission, he wasn't a natural diplomat, quite the reverse. For a start, he couldn't stand all the bloody Whitehall double talk. Stein had often expressed his surprise his old friend had managed to hold on to the top job for so long, and had even gone so far as to place bets Spencer wouldn't last six months. For, at heart, they were both field men, and although promotion brought its rewards, the downside was they'd both found themselves increasingly desk bound. To some extent, Spencer had learned to mellow with the passing of time. But, there was still a certain explosive aura about him he could never quite manage to shake off. Coupled with an underlying ruthlessness, both had frequently served to unnerve not only his intelligence colleagues but also many of his political masters as well.

Spencer had held down the job now for almost five years, but working at the behest of self-important politicians still didn't sit comfortably with him. To some extent, he had learned to play the game, to go along with it, the endless hoopla surrounding government ministers and their advisors. Over the intervening years, Spencer still hadn't quite managed to become a slick Whitehall operator. Generally, by the fourth meeting of the day, he'd almost lost the will to live, and was left wondering whether his appointment as Britain's spymaster was worth the endless internal battles which invariably entailed massaging the towering egos of government ministers.

The daily top secret situation reports, known as sitreps, by MI5, appeared to be pretty much standard. His eyes glided swiftly over the first page, before something suddenly caught his eye. It was a local police investigation, which had subsequently been followed up by Scotland Yard's Special Branch. The report was about an explosion ripping through a fifth floor flat on a rather nondescript block in a rundown part of London, just south of the river near Lambeth Bridge. The balcony had been blown clean out across the street. Although the blast had also taken out the living room window, there was relatively little damage inside the flat. Remarkably, no-one was hurt in the explosion.

As a precaution, all the residents had been evacuated. All in all, it had taken the emergency services about four hours before they decided it was safe enough to allow the residents back inside.

It was little short of a miracle no-one either in or outside the building had been injured from the falling debris. The initial report from the London Fire Brigade stated how explosions always take the path of least resistance, and in this case, fortunately, the easiest path was outside through the balcony. Despite the deadly force of the explosion, there was not thought to be any significant structural damage to the building. However, the next line suddenly jumped off the page at him.

"A plastic explosive device has now been determined as the cause of the blast."

As a consequence, the report was immediately handed over to Special Branch. Further enquiries confirmed the occupant of the flat was absent at the time of the blast. Such was the force of the explosion, they would have undoubtedly been killed. The name registered on the short-term lease was one Willem Cornelius, who claimed to be of Dutch origin. Since the explosion, there had been no trace of him. However, Cornelius was clearly an alias, as his name had recently appeared on a Watchers list in connection to the round the clock surveillance of Josef Frenzel. The so-called Watchers team was a mix of MI5 agents and Scotland Yard's elite Special Branch detectives.

Since Frenzel's appointment as security adviser to the West German Embassy, Spencer had detailed a Watchers team to tail Frenzel on a twenty-four hour basis. The cost of doing so was quite prohibitive. On paper, there were much bigger Soviet fish to fry in London, as opposed to tying up manpower on a former member of the Abwehr with links to the secretive *Schamhorst* network. Spencer had taken one hell of a gamble diverting much-needed resources. He didn't have either the authority or the necessary top cover from his immediate political boss, the Home Secretary, who was responsible for internal security, to sanction placing Frenzel under official surveillance, but he did it all the same.

Although it could be argued it was something of a technicality, it was an important one, for Spencer was still very much out on a limb. His decision had also required a certain amount of creative accounting by MI5's Finance Department, but then again, they were past masters at manipulating figures so the accounts looked better than would otherwise be the case. As a result, the Treasury had rarely questioned their financial returns.

For Spencer, Schneider's arrival in London, and more recently, Zimmerman, was the crowning glory. But, even so, if MI5 screwed up, was unable to deliver results, and allowed Schneider and the *Schamhorst* network to slip through their fingers, Spencer knew his position would eventually become untenable. At some point, he would need to explain himself, and questions would be asked. Why on Earth had he not briefed the Home Secretary that there was an active Mossad team operating in London? Why had he not provided a sitrep about Frenzel, Schneider, and the *Schamhorst* network?

It was a complicated situation. There had been many reasons, in Spencer's mind. The current Home Secretary, Chris Parker, for all his undoubted academic brilliance, was, in many ways, temperamentally unsuited to high office. Power without responsibility marked his tenure. He was considered a safe pair of hands in a government torn apart by internal feuds. As far as Spencer was concerned, government ministers came and went. During his incumbency, Spencer had already seen a change in Prime Minister and umpteen Cabinet reshuffles. In essence, Parker was someone the PM, Anthony Everett, could trust. At the Home Office, though, he didn't exactly inspire confidence. Parker had spent most of his life on the backbenches, heading up endless, and mainly, pointless committees, and generally trying to ingratiate himself with the Tory grandees.

Spencer was all too aware the Hawks in Whitehall would start circling and looking for blood, if he messed up. They would home in on the fact he'd circumvented the system for one reason, and one reason only to avenge his brother's death. It was only partially true, but Spencer knew his decision could potentially place him on the back foot, and he'd have to justify his actions.

In the grand scheme of things, it certainly wouldn't have been the first time he'd had to fight his corner. However, the Schneider case was personal, and, by default, made him vulnerable and open to criticism.

Spencer sat back in his chair, and thoughtfully linked his fingers behind his head. He needed to think things through. The Schneider affair was slowly coming together, but the sitreps were missing a vital link. In Schneider's shoes, he'd probably have broken cover and contacted Frenzel.

Spencer leaned forward and picked up the blue telephone from a bank of three.

His secretary answered. 'Yes, sir.'

'Dawn, I seem to be missing the latest sitrep from the Frenzel team.'

There was a slight pause down the line as she checked her in-tray. 'It doesn't appear to be here, sir.'

'Tell them to have it on my desk in ten minutes!'

Another pause indicated Dawn was most likely scribbling a note on her ink pad.

'Ask them to pass a copy to Jed Carter as well.' Spencer picked a pack of cigarettes out of the desk drawer. 'And while you're at it, put a call through to Jack Stein.'

Chapter 4
The Keogh Club, Hans Crescent, Knightsbridge, London

By the time Jed Carter arrived at the Keogh Club, it was warm outside, but the sky was glowering, threatening rain. A table was booked in his name. The Keogh had started life during World War II as an Allied Services Club, and much of its décor and contents were still well preserved. Unlike some of the more established clubs in London, women were allowed full membership, and, as a consequence, it had become an increasingly popular venue during the post-war years.

Inside, the bar area was all secluded lighting, with shaded lamps on the tables, and a selection of discreet seating areas, surrounding a large well-stocked bar. A heady mix of tobacco smoke and alcohol filled the place. Carter's first impressions were not entirely favourable. He'd been a member less than twenty-four hours, and had never visited the Keogh until now. Spencer had evidently pulled a few strings to secure his membership, but it all seemed a little too staid for Carter's liking. The faded flock wallpaper and carpets, and rather distressed furniture which had seen better days. It was in marked contrast to his favourite haunt, The Flamingo Club in Wardour Street, Soho, which turned seamlessly into "The All-Nighter" from midnight to dawn. The place pulsated to a wide range of acts soul, blue beat, pop, and jazz. The Flamingo had a broad social appeal, and was a preferred stomping ground for leading musicians.

Carter's gaze glided dismissively around the bar area. By the look of it, the Keogh's clientele was a pretty mixed bunch, but the majority were all of a certain age and heading on the wrong side of forty. There were one or two he recognised, a well-known reporter from the Tonight programme on the BBC and a junior Minister at the War Office, neither of whom were enjoying the company of their wives, but much younger and more attractive versions.

A waiter showed him to one of the secluded alcoves, but he declined a drink. Carter glanced at his watch; it was 7.25pm. He was running slightly early. He'd read the brief about Joyce, and had built up a mental image. Spencer described her as inscrutable, a mystery wrapped in an enigma. By nature, she was coldly calculating and invariably ruthless, but for some reason Carter couldn't quite fathom, was why, after all these years, she still enjoyed Spencer's trust in her abilities as a spy. What was it about her?

The brief had probably thrown up more questions than answers; he was curious. Leader's file had been closed for almost fifteen years, so why had Spencer now, of all times, decided to resurrect it. Back in the day, Leader had no doubt been at the top of her game, but fifteen years was a long time in the Service. She was out of date and no longer up to speed on current events, but, more importantly, during the war, she'd operated as a double agent.

At the time, he knew Joyce Leader had played a key role in helping persuade the Germans the Allies main invasion force would land at the Pas de Calais. The deception was so successful some fifteen reserve divisions were tied up near Calais, even after the invasion had begun at Normandy, lest it proved to be a diversion from the main invasion at Calais. The disinformation supplied to her Abwehr controllers had eventually paid significant dividends by not only aiding the success of D-Day but, in the process, helping to save countless lives.

Carter knew all that, but he still felt a certain amount of antipathy toward anyone who had parachuted into Britain during the war as a German spy. It didn't help any that, as a young boy, his mother had died at the height of the London Blitz during an air raid. The mental scars of that night were still painfully raw.

Carter had read Leader's file multiple times, cover to cover, in a desperate effort to uncover Spencer's motive. There were several current, top-flight female agents in the department. They were certainly much younger, and probably far more attractive than Leader, and could have easily snared Frenzel into a honey trap. It did not add up, or at least, it did not to Carter, and then he saw her. One of the waiters escorted her to the alcove.

Leader was taller than he expected, about five foot eight, according to her file, but with high heels, she seemed much taller, and possessed an almost cat-like grace. Joyce was wearing a figure hugging, navy coloured suit, accentuated by a blue and purple silk scarf. She was, he guessed, in her early forties, but looked much younger. She was extremely attractive, with blonde hair, pale skin, and enviable cheekbones. Joyce possessed all the self-assurance, tinged with just a touch of arrogance, which came from a woman who knew not only her worth but also knew her power over men.

Carter rose slowly from his chair and briefly shook her hand.

She flashed a smile in response and joined him in the alcove. 'So, what are we going to drink?'

'I'm easy,' he said.

A slight flicker of amusement crossed her face. 'I'm sure you *are*.'

Carter relaxed slightly. 'I'll have a gin and tonic.'

The waiter was still hovering in their forlornly lit alcove. Without hesitation, Joyce said, 'Make mine a double, but go easy on the ice.' Her gaze briefly followed the waiter across the bar area. She then opened her clutch bag and jiggled two Gauloises cigarettes from a slender gold case and proffered one to Carter. He thanked her. She gently patted her own into an elegant ebony holder before lighting it and glanced across the table at Carter. He had a stern countenance and a certain steeliness about him that discouraged flippancy. He sat with his arms folded in front of him. There was a brooding intensity about him she found intriguing, but by no means threatening.

'Do you think you're good at reading people?' she asked in her cut-glass English accent.

'I'd like to think so,' he replied in a relaxed, conversational tone.

'I take it you've read the brief?'

He shrugged his shoulders. 'Yes, from cover to cover.'

'Then you know, during the war, I grew from whore to Saint, all in a matter of a few years.'

Carter looked at her searchingly, but didn't respond. There was a certain haughty reserve about her he couldn't quite read. He watched curiously as smoke curled up from the tip of her freshly lit cigarette.

'Spencer suggested you might have a problem with my being on board.'

His eyes searched hers with a hint of appraisal. 'Why would he think that?'

She pursed her lips together, blowing out a cloud of blue-grey smoke. Before she could answer, the waiter returned with their drinks, and they thanked him. Somewhat grudgingly, Carter liked her self-assured style, and almost started to understand why Spencer appreciated her sharp, no-nonsense attitude. Leader was tough-minded. In many ways, she was a woman after Spencer's own heart, and would, under different circumstances, have undoubtedly made a deadly enemy.

Joyce took a sip of her drink. 'The trouble is you're far too young to understand what it was like.'

'That you were a Nazi agent?'

'I did whatever I had to do to survive. If I hadn't joined the Abwehr, I certainly wouldn't be sitting here today.'

'And, if things had turned out differently, and Germany had won the war, Britain would have ended up as a vanquished satellite state of the Third Reich.'

She caught the sudden sharpness in his voice. 'Then, I guess we wouldn't be having this conversation.'

Carter looked coldly across the table. 'What the hell is that supposed to mean?'

'Do you honestly believe I'd have survived the invasion?'

'You'd have had more than a fighting chance. Your Abwehr handler, Bernard Drescher, still trusted you. In fact, he believed you were Germany's top agent in Britain.'

The merest flicker of a smile crossed her face, but Leader's voice had an edge of exasperation. 'Long before Hitler's storm troopers marched down Whitehall, MI5 would have either liquidated me or exposed me as a double agent to Berlin.' She pursed her lips together provocatively, and a cloud of swirling grey smoke emerging from them. 'Think about it. Spencer was my British controller. If Hitler had invaded, then Spencer certainly wouldn't have gone down without a fight.' She paused and looked at him speculatively. 'He'd have made damn sure I had crashed and burned along with him! I wouldn't have survived a Nazi victory. I know you probably don't believe me.'

'I wouldn't say that.'

She met his gaze. 'He's actually been far mellower since the war.'

'You could have fooled me!' Carter snorted in disbelief.

Joyce smiled slightly, and began to twist and untwist her pearl necklace between her fingers, as if she was lost momentarily in some distant thought.

'And the Schneider Case?' he queried.

His question jolted Leader back; she fixed her eyes on him. 'What about it?'

'I might have missed something.'

She shot him a smile, with a pinch of mischief on her face. 'I'm sure you haven't?'

'I might be talking out of turn, but I was just a little surprised by Spencer's decision to reopen your file.'

Joyce rolled her eyes in exasperation. 'Are you?' She'd thrown the question out as a challenge. 'For Christ's sake, Jed, don't you *get it*? You're supposed to be the smart arse field agent. You work it out!' she snorted derisively.

Spencer had described him as fast thinking, professional, and someone who could make it to the very top; it was why he'd taken him under his wing. But, right now, she figured he still had a lot to learn. Carter should have played it differently. He needed to conceal his feelings better. At the moment, he couldn't quite manage to wipe the unmistakable hint of disapproval off his face. It was obvious to her he didn't relish the prospect of having to deal with an ex-Nazi agent.

The unexpected challenge in her ice-blue eyes wasn't entirely lost on him. Deep down, Carter was acutely aware he'd overstepped the line. At Joyce Leader's time of life, she certainly didn't need to justify or prove herself to anyone, least of all him.

At the end of the day, the Schneider Case was very much Spencer's personal fiefdom. Without any official political top cover, if things went wrong, they would both find themselves out on a limb. There might well be younger blood in the Department, but Leader's file had been reopened for one reason and one reason only. Josef Frenzel had worked for General Reinhard von Gehlen, Hitler's head of military espionage in Russia. As a former member of Nazi Intelligence, Frenzel was acutely aware in the dying days of the war, Joyce Leader was viewed by Berlin as one of their best assets. His appointment to the West German Embassy in London had made her the obvious choice to reel him in. It also helped Frenzel had a well-known weakness for women. Some of his more interesting scrapes had left him wide open to blackmail, and Leader was still a stunning woman, an ethereal beauty, who was not only stylish but could also turn heads. As she'd sashayed into the Keogh Club, Carter noted that every male gaze had followed her path across the bar to their alcove.

He was beginning to get why Spencer had needed to re-activate her file. The ice-blue eyes and long smouldering stare possessed an almost otherworldly quality about them. Having read the background reports on Frenzel, he guessed it probably hadn't taken her too much time to reel Frenzel into a honey trap. He also accepted Joyce had bravely placed her life on the line by going undercover.

Carter assumed she could have refused the assignment and blown Spencer's plans clean out of the water. But, for whatever reason, she hadn't. Joyce was fabulously wealthy and lived the high life in London and on the Continent, and had accepted Spencer's poison chalice. He knew there was a deep-rooted history between them, but even so, he still couldn't work out why she had accepted the assignment.

Carter had seen the photographs and listened to the tape recordings of her sometimes sordid meetings with Frenzel. In fairness to her, it really couldn't have been easy. He leaned back in his chair and decided he probably owed her an apology. He certainly had no right to be judgemental. It wasn't his place; what was passed was past. The only thing that mattered was their assignment to track down Helmut Schneider, before Mossad got a second chance to blow him to kingdom come. Outwardly, at least, Joyce appeared to accept his apology, but she wasn't exactly an open book, and there was no way of telling whether she had or not.

'When are you due to see Frenzel again?' he asked, hoping to dig himself out of a hole with her.

'This evening, after he finishes work at the Embassy.'

'Do we know where Schneider is hiding out?'

'I'm not sure,' she confessed. 'The last I heard he was holed up somewhere in East London. After the explosion in Bligh Street, Frenzel detailed one of his security team to mind him.'

'Do we know who it is?'

'A guy called Erhard Lange. Have you heard of him?'

'No, that's a new name to me. I'll check with Central Registry. We might have something on him. I can't imagine he's been at the Embassy long, otherwise his name would probably have crossed my desk by now.'

Carter signalled to the waiter and ordered another gin and tonic for Joyce and, this time, a whisky on the rocks for himself. As the evening wore on, she noticed the longer he sipped his whisky and the longer they talked, the more relaxed his body language became. Occasionally, he'd fiddle with the frayed upholstery on the arm of his chair. It was, she thought, almost a nervous gesture. She noted Carter rarely smiled, but when he did, it illuminated his face, and more importantly, he never spoke just to hear the sound of his own voice. A fact she found quite refreshing. In her experience, once a man had a captive audience, they loved nothing more than the sound of their own voice.

'I'd like to know your opinion on something,' he said.

Her eyes were appraising, and the expression unreadable. 'What about?'

'Wouldn't it be a damned sight safer if Josef Frenzel moved Schneider out of London altogether?' he suggested.

'Perhaps,' she answered cautiously.

'Then, why hasn't he?'

'The *Mendoza* isn't due to arrive at Surrey Docks until the end of next week. Frenzel toyed with the idea, but on balance, decided he needed to keep him within striking distance of the docks.'

'The trouble is he's also kept him within striking distance of Mossad.'

Leader shrugged indifferently. 'They've already chased him halfway across Europe. I don't think it's going to make *that* much difference, do you?' She drew heavily on her cigarette. 'It's a calculated risk; he needs to get it right, of course. You have to understand Frenzel is under immense pressure from the *Schamhorst* not to screw up again.' She passed him a mischievous smile. 'They don't exactly take kindly to failure. He's already messed up once by failing to get Schneider out of Southampton.'

'But, I understand that wasn't his fault.'

'Maybe not, but as far as their concerned, he should have had a contingency plan.'

'What about the *Mendoza's* Captain? Is he likely to up the price at the last minute?'

A brief, if somewhat ironic, smile flickered across Leader's face. 'I doubt it; you only shaft the *Schamhorst* once. They've put the word out, and if Calero values his life and wants to leave London alive, he'll take the money and run.'

'But, it isn't only Frenzel's old Nazi colleagues that'll be upset with him, is it?'

Joyce leaned forward and stubbed out her cigarette in the ashtray. 'What do you mean?'

'My understanding is General Gehlen wanted him to take his foot off the pedal in London and distance himself from the *Schamhorst* network.'

She agreed. 'Yes, he'd been playing fast and loose. He attended a neo-Nazi rally back in Germany.'

'Why wasn't he suspended?'

'He was reprimanded and threatened with suspension. But, you have to remember, Frenzel still has friends in high places, friends who look after their former brothers in arms.'

'It's still one hell of a risk sending him to London. If the Ambassador ever got wind of his connection to the *Schamhorst*, he'd be on the first available plane back to Germany.'

'Frenzel's well aware he's walking a fine line. But, in fairness to him, he did sever his links to the *Schamhorst*, that is, until Schneider turned up on his doorstep, begging him for help.'

'Can you ever sever links to the *Schamhorst*? Is it that easy?' he queried.

She offered a slight smile. 'No, it's a little like being a member of the Service. You'll find out for yourself, someday.'

He looked at her searchingly, not quite sure what she meant. So she explained, 'As you see, Jed, like me, you never really leave. If you do, well, Spencer told me once it's a little like being divorced. You might move on and cut the familial ties, but there's always an irrevocable link to the past which can never be entirely broken.'

'So is that why you're here?' he ventured.

She thoughtfully drew in her lower lip. 'It's difficult to refuse someone who once saved your life.'

'I would have thought by now you'd more than paid your dues to the Service.'

Joyce wouldn't be drawn. His first instinct was to press her further, but the flash of vulnerability had disappeared, and her expression grew impassive. She wanted the matter dropped; it wasn't important, and it wasn't why they were here. They needed to move on, to figure out how to take things forward.

Carter reached for his glass and took a gulp of whisky. 'What do you make of Frenzel?'

Joyce shrugged. 'He is what he is. I genuinely believe if it hadn't been for Schneider turning up on his doorstep, he'd have played it carefully at the Embassy. He's only too aware the Ambassador tried to block his appointment, but was overruled by the powers that be in Bonn.'

'You mean General Gehlen?'

'Not just Gehlen, but it was his influence that rubber-stamped his appointment.'

'Don't get me wrong; I understand, in his day, Frenzel was good and had all the makings of a top-notch spy. But, over the years, his constant womanising and loose mouth have made him a security risk. Why on Earth did Gehlen put him up for the job in the first place?'

'Call it a favour.'

Carter cast a long, slow look at her. 'It must have been one *hell* of a favour.'

'Apparently, while they were serving on the Eastern Front, Frenzel discovered a plot to assassinate him. From what I can gather, it was probably more by luck than judgement, but remember, at the time, Gehlen was Adolf Hitler's senior anti-Soviet spy. Stalin's security service tried to take him out, but somehow, Frenzel stumbled across the assassination plot and saved his life. He ended up being awarded the Knight's Cross, with swords for valour, by none other than Reichsführer Himmler.'

Up until recently, she had also believed, in intelligence terms, Frenzel was second eleven, a minnow, and in many ways, he still was. She'd certainly never heard of him until Spencer reactivated her file. But, the Knight's Cross, with swords for valour, was rarely bestowed, and would have given him a certain standing, not only amongst the SS, but the Nazi elite, and, in part, explained why Gehlen had readily rubber-stamped his appointment to London.

Joyce removed the butt from her cigarette holder and flicked it into the ashtray. 'So, how *do* you want to play it?' she asked coolly.

Carter guessed it wasn't so much a question as a challenge. He'd already crossed her once, and had no intention of souring things between them even further. He needed her on side, and it was pretty obvious to him Leader was well ahead of the game. She'd already successfully reeled Frenzel in, and had passed some high-grade material to MI5. To finally get a hook on Schneider and track him down, they'd have to use the photographs and the tape recordings they had on Frenzel. But, it was all about the timing, and with the *Mendoza* due to dock next Friday, time wasn't exactly on their side.

Leader glanced at her watch and slipped the ebony cigarette holder back into her handbag. 'I understand you speak fluent German.'

'The British Army sent me on a course.'

She looked sceptical.

'After leaving the SAS, I was posted to Berlin,' he explained.

'Undercover?'

'What do you *think?*' It was answer enough. 'Why do you want to know?'

'You never know it might just come in handy,' she said, fiddling around with the contents of her handbag. 'I have a proposition for you.'

'Go on,' he said warily.

'The Foreign Secretary is hosting a cocktail party for the conference delegates.'

'When is it?'

'Tomorrow evening. I just thought it might be a way of casually introducing you to Frenzel and Bernard Zimmerman, without arousing any suspicion. There'll be plenty of glad-handing, and you'll just be another face in the crowd. You know how things are at these events.'

She waited for a response. He took his time. According to Spencer, when faced with extreme danger, she had never once lost an iota of her coolness, but had also pointed out if Joyce had been in a team of one, she'd probably end up having a fight with herself. That said, Carter could see in spite of his initial reservations, she was not only cool-headed, but also a skilled operator.

On the surface, she seemed utterly indifferent as to whether or not he agreed to her proposal, and sat busily re-applying her lipstick. Deep down, Carter had an uneasy feeling she was starting to play him like a fiddle, and had effortlessly retained the upper hand. But, even so, he found himself agreeing the cocktail party sounded like a good idea.

Leader flashed him a flirtatious smile, and slowly placed the lid back on the lipstick. 'We'll have to use an alias for you, of course.' Her eyes suddenly glistened with amusement. 'I can see you as a Fred. Yes, what about Fred Tolly?' she suggested with a giggle.

Carter didn't quite share her amusement, but said equably enough, 'You can call me *whatever* you like.'

'I'll say you're a civil servant at the FO; they'll be two a penny tomorrow night, so Frenzel will hopefully be off his guard.'

'And how exactly are we supposed to know one another?'

She didn't miss a beat. 'Do you know John Eldridge?' Leader was referring to the Foreign Secretary.

'No, I do not,' Carter said flatly. 'I met him once, but only briefly, in Spencer's office.'

'Well, you do *now*,' she said briskly. 'He's an old friend of mine from way back.'

'Do you mean during the war?'

'Yes, he was a junior MI5 desk officer in the Double Cross team, his immediate boss was.'

Carter cut her off. 'Don't tell me. Spencer Hall.'

They were sparring with one another, playing cat and mouse. His invite to the Foreign Secretary's cocktail party certainly hadn't suddenly come out of the blue.

'Does Frenzel know about your friendship with Eldridge?'

She shrugged indifferently. 'What if he does? During the war, German Intelligence believed I was their top agent in Britain.'

Carter knew all that. 'Okay, but I still don't quite understand where Eldridge fits into it?'

'You have to read between the lines,' she said testily.

He took his time answering. 'Did they think you'd infiltrated British Intelligence?'

'Something like that. My Abwehr handler thought most of my insider knowledge came from pillow talk, you know, that I'd bagged a spy.' She smiled across the table at him. 'Well, actually several.'

'Including Eldridge?'

'Yes. It was a complete load of bull, of course, but it worked. The Abwehr never once questioned the intelligence I passed them. Spencer and the Double Cross team played a masterstroke, supplying me with the right material to fool the Nazi high command.'

Joyce slipped the lipstick back inside her handbag and snapped it shut. 'Tell me, how long have you been in the Service?'

'I left the SAS five years ago.'

'A mere baby then.' She smacked her lips together. 'Any regrets?'

'It's exceeded my expectations.'

His expression remained deadpan, so she threw back her head and laughed. 'You *do* impress me. A diplomat as well. You might have noticed diplomacy isn't exactly Spencer's strongest card in the deck.'

Her comment elicited a rare smile. 'Can you tell me something?' he asked.

'What is it?'

'Do you know a CIA agent called Jack Stein?'

She pulled a face. 'I can't say as I do, but the name seems vaguely familiar.'

It was hard to tell whether she was lying or not. 'It's just he asked Spencer whether he'd run it by Assistant Commissioner Garvan about re-opening your file.'

'Did he?' she replied blankly.

'Why would he do that?'

'I haven't a clue. Why don't you ask Spencer?' she suggested breezily, knowing full well he wouldn't.

Joyce picked up her handbag, smiled at Carter across the table, and made to leave, but then glanced back over her shoulder. 'The invite from the Foreign Office will be on your desk first thing in the morning.'

'Okay, I'll see you tomorrow.'

Joyce, once again, turned heads as she sashayed across the bar area. Even Carter grudgingly admitted she still looked incredible.

Chapter 5
Foreign Office Cocktail Party, Whitehall

Carter was longing for something to eat; he was running late and had missed lunch. The small bites available at the cocktail party were hardly likely to stave off his hunger pangs. As Carter was shown into the Durbar Court, he was greeted by a babel of sound. His gaze moved admiringly around the impressive four-sided court. The grandiose Durbar Court was all Ionic and Corinthian columns, a striking marble floor, and flickering lights. There must have been at least a hundred and fifty people talking in a variety of languages. The great and good of the scientific world had turned out in force to enjoy the hospitality of the British Government.

He was handed a glass of champagne, and, at the same time, a smartly dressed waitress appeared and offered him a canape. He winked at her and snatched several off the tray. Carter took his time scanning the crowd, swiftly picking up on Jack Stein deep in conversation with an elderly couple, but it was evident Stein had already spotted him. There was the merest hint of acknowledgement and a slight inclination of his head that completely bypassed his companions.

Carter was well aware Spencer wanted him to be his eyes and ears at the party, but more importantly, to meet the two men who could lead him to Helmut Schneider. Although official functions, like this evening, were sometimes glamorous, in Carter's experience, they were more often than not excruciatingly dull. He began to work the room with customary skill, occasionally stopping to pass the time of day with an old acquaintance or breaking the ice with someone hovering uneasily on their own. Carter made all the usual small talk before finally spotting Joyce Leader. He hung back a while, accepting another drink, but as he'd feared, the canapes seemed to be in pretty short supply.

Leader appeared to be listening to one of her two companions; Carter assumed it was Josef Frenzel. He had a deep, dramatic voice, and had his arm draped around her shoulders. He was lean and tall, the once handsome face now lined with wrinkles, and the blonde hair flecked with grey. Frenzel had a cigarette on the go, and through a screen of blue cigarette smoke, his limpid blue eyes were slightly glazed. Joyce appeared to be half listening to his banal chatter, as he let both his mouth and thoughts run free. At times, she looked faintly bored, but Frenzel was far too wrapped up in the sound of his own voice and self-importance to notice. Frenzel was obviously fascinated by Joyce, and appeared totally besotted by her.

Carter finally decided to break the ice, and went over to them. He extended his hand to Leader. 'How *are* you?' He smiled warmly. 'It's so good to see you again!'

She looked up at him with her trademark sultry gaze, her eyes peering up through her long lashes. She briefly took his hand and gave it a little squeeze. 'I'm so sorry. I know that we've met before. You must forgive me, but I'm rotten with names.'

It was all said so sweetly, so matter-of-factly. Whatever response he had expected, it hadn't been that one. Joyce was playing a blinder; he couldn't fault her performance. She was playing it cool and throwing her companions off the scent. Carter admired her style; he had to think quickly.

'It was last year,' he said, by way of explanation. 'You obviously don't remember me, but we attended a private supper party in Belgravia. In fact, I was sitting right *next* to you.' Under the circumstances, it was the best he could come up with.

She arched her brows questioningly.

'It was the Foreign Secretary's birthday party,' he prodded.

Joyce finally relented and put him out of his misery. A look of recognition suddenly crossed her face. 'Oh yes, I remember now. It's Fred, isn't it,' she hesitated, 'Fred Tolly?'

He inclined his head slightly. Why the hell she'd come up with the name of *Fred*, God only knew. It certainly didn't sit well with him. It was pure vanity, of course, and maybe that's why she'd chosen it, to burst his ego.

She turned to her companions and made the introductions. Tolly worked for the Foreign Office, she explained. Before he had time to take Frenzel completely in, she introduced him to another man. Pinstriped, slightly stooped, with owlish spectacles, it was Bernard Zimmerman.

'It's an honour to meet you, sir,' Carter said, shaking Zimmerman's hand. 'Aren't you one of the NASA delegates?'

'Yes, yes, I am,' he said softly, in his heavily accented English.

'How are you enjoying your stay in London, sir?'

After a pause, Zimmerman said, 'Everyone has been most welcoming.'

'Are you staying at the St. Philips Hotel?'

Zimmerman examined Carter's face. His gaze remained implacable as he checked out this interloper who was a tall, erect, slim man, immaculate in a dark suit, quite modern. Zimmerman guessed the tailoring was more Carnaby Street than Savile Row. It wasn't quite to the older man's taste. He suspected the Englishman already knew the answer to his question, but decided to play along with him, and said he was staying at the St. Philips Hotel.

'I've never been there myself.'

Leader cut across him. 'You really should; they serve the best cream teas in London.'

Carter looked at her candidly. 'You obviously speak from experience.'

Her face creased into a smile. 'You must join me sometime.'

'Is that an invitation?'

Before he had a chance to respond, Carter felt a sharp tap on his shoulder. He swung around; it was John Eldridge, the Foreign Secretary. Having achieved rapid promotion as a junior Member of Parliament, at the early age of forty-four, he was now a senior Minister in Her Majesty's Government. He'd long since proved himself a skilled politician, but had also retained close links to his former intelligence boss, Sir Spencer Hall.

For a period after the war, Eldridge had remained with British Intelligence, but after missing out on promotion, he had a huge falling out with Spencer. They discussed his long-term prospects, and in a fit of pique, he handed in his resignation. At the time, Spencer said it would be the making of him. He'd always known Eldridge would do well for himself; he had a quick mind, a hard head, a warm smile, and a cold eye. In fact, he was the perfect diplomat, and had proved himself to be an even deadlier politician.

They'd long since called a truce, and Eldridge admitted his resentment at being overlooked for promotion with the Service had forced him to re-evaluate his life. Since then, he'd never looked back, and was now enjoying huge success as a career politician. In a short space of time, Eldridge had become not only one of the most influential politicians in Britain, but also one of the most evasive and deceptive in the country. His former life with British Intelligence had helped him become a skilful Whitehall operator, adroitly cultivating personal contacts within the heart of Westminster.

'Tolly,' Eldridge said jovially to Carter. 'I thought that I'd find you here. You never could resist a lovely face!'

'No, sir, you're probably right.'

Eldridge planted a kiss on Leader's cheek. 'Where the hell have you been hiding yourself, Joyce?'

'I didn't think that I had, Johnny.'

His arrival appeared to impress Frenzel; in diplomatic circles, it was something of a coup to have the Foreign Secretary stop for a chat. He was aware of Eldridge's past with British Intelligence. During the war, his name was well known in German intelligence circles. Frenzel still believed Eldridge had once been a notch on Leader's bedpost, and his pillow talk had unwittingly supplied the Abwehr with Allied intelligence. It was a lie, of course; MI5's Double Cross system had been a game of human chess, one where Joyce and her fellow agents had walked a fine line between life and death. It had not only been a battle for supremacy between MI5 and the Abwehr, but had finally culminated with saving the lives of countless servicemen who had splashed ashore on the beaches of Normandy by deceiving the German High Command.

Eldridge nodded slightly toward Frenzel in recognition. Since his arrival at the West German Embassy, they had met socially at diplomatic functions, but it had always been fleeting, never more than a quick, polite acknowledgment. Eldridge turned his attention toward

Zimmerman and extended his hand in greeting. 'Have my office been in contact with you?' His voice was smooth, almost solicitous.

'Yes, they have.'

'We must get something in the diary before you return to the States.'

Zimmerman cast him a thin, wintry smile and apologised for not confirming a date with his staff earlier.

'I'm sure we can arrange something,' Eldridge said in a relaxed, conversational tone.

'Perhaps next week?' Zimmerman suggested.

'When do you fly out?'

'Saturday the 5th.'

'Good.' Eldridge smiled. 'I'll ask my diary secretary to contact you and see if we can arrange something.'

Zimmerman inclined his head.

A waiter handed Eldridge a glass of champagne; he thanked him before turning to Carter. 'I'd like to introduce you to a friend of mine.'

Carter looked at him questioningly, but kept his mouth shut and allowed Eldridge to steer him away. *What the hell was he playing at*? Joyce had only just introduced him to Zimmerman and Frenzel. The whole idea of his invite was to meet them.

'I'm sorry about that,' Eldridge apologised, leading him across the Durbar Court toward one of the main exits.

'Can I ask what's going on, sir?'

'I need to have a word with you in private; Jack Stein's waiting for us in my office.'

Carter eyed the Foreign Secretary warily. 'Has something happened, sir?' he persisted.

Eldridge reached the sweeping grand staircase. His patience was beginning to wear thin, and it showed. 'My dear boy, if it weren't important, I'd have left you back there with our German friends!'

It was answer enough, and Carter decided he'd better wind his neck in. Without another word, he dutifully followed the Foreign Secretary to his office.

**

Frenzel's gaze had briefly followed their progress across the Court, before saying to Zimmerman, 'So, what's all this about your meeting up with the Foreign Secretary?'

'They've been asking me all week,' Zimmerman said, with a long sigh.

'You've never mentioned it before.'

'Eldridge wants me to meet up with Professor Jones.'

'Maybe you should accept the invitation.'

'Who is this Professor Jones?' Leader asked innocently.

Frenzel looked at her indulgently. 'You surely *must* have come across his name during the war.'

She pulled a face and claimed she hadn't, or, at least, couldn't remember. It was a long time ago, she pleaded. Joyce knew full well that Reginald Victor Jones, or R V as he was known, on account of his initials, had been MI6's principal scientific adviser. Throughout the war, Jones had kept up an outward pretence of continuing his work for the Air Ministry as a cover.

He was a brilliant scientist in his own right, and had helped to organise the Millbank Conference. She'd only met Jones once, but remembered him as being a large man, broad-shouldered and over six feet tall, with a strong voice. Spencer maintained during the war, Jones had a disconcerting habit of usually being proved right. Although Jones had long since left government employment and returned to his first love, the world of academia, the Government had asked for his help in organising the conference.

Frenzel gently reminded her about him, and his crucial role in British Intelligence. Always the consummate actress, her features were giving nothing away.

'So why don't you want to meet him?' Joyce asked Zimmerman.

He smiled bleakly. 'We were old adversaries.'

'So were the Americans, but that hasn't stopped you working for NASA,' she said with her customary bluntness.

Zimmerman bristled defensively. 'That was a fait accompli.'

'But, it was one of your own making,' Joyce said provocatively.

'What do you mean by that?' he demanded irritably.

'If you hadn't given yourself up to the Americans, then you would have almost certainly been captured by the Soviets. At the time, I guess the Yanks were the lesser of the two evils.'

He looked through her, rather than at her.

Leader wrinkled her face. 'The prospect of a cold, second rate, state-owned dacha probably didn't hold quite the same appeal as the chance of a lovely home and the safety of American citizenship.'

'I think you'll find, Frau Leader, it was Dr. von Braun who engineered the surrender of his top rocket scientists, including me. We came as a package, along with our blueprints and test equipment, to the Americans. The Russian Army was closing in fast from the east, and we found ourselves under the direct command of the SS.' He cast her a cold, probing stare. 'By that time, we were nothing more than pawns.'

Joyce knew all about the slave labourers forced to work on Hitler's rocket programme, and how many of the Reich's leading scientists had finally thrown in their lot with the Americans. She'd first met him at the German Ambassador's cocktail party. Throughout the entire evening, Zimmerman had been careful to keep both his past and feelings under lock and key. But, now, the usually unreadable, kindly pale blue eyes suddenly flashed with anger. She'd managed to push all the right buttons; it was exactly the reaction Joyce had wanted to provoke.

'Von Braun had ten orders on his desk from the German High Command,' Zimmerman continued. 'Berlin was in chaos. Five of his orders threatened us with death by firing squad.'

'And the remaining five orders?' she asked.

He smiled tautly. 'We were damned if we did, and damned if we didn't. If we'd stayed at the rocket site, then, come hell or high water, we would have been lined up against a wall and shot! At the time, being taken prisoner by the Russians seemed almost as bad as extermination by the SS. It was nothing more than a matter of luck, Frau Leader, that we were swept up by the American troops, but, there again, they *were* searching for us. But, I'll be perfectly frank with you, if the Soviets had taken me prisoner, then I'd just have readily ended up working on their satellite programme.' Zimmerman drained his glass of champagne. 'I have only one moral compass, my work and my research.'

Joyce's initial instinct was to say more, to question him further about Peenemünde and the other test sites. About the slave labourers in their striped uniforms, who were expected to work until they dropped. Under the ever watchful eye of their SS guards, treatment was relentlessly cruel and harsh. But, she held back. Her own family weren't entirely without sin, and prisoners had worked in her father's factories. It was how it was. No questions were asked, and if they were, retribution was swift.

An uneasy silence followed, and it was Frenzel who decided to break it. 'One way or another,' he said smoothly, 'we were all in the same boat, Bernard. As you say, it was simply a matter of survival. It's all water under the bridge now.'

Zimmerman reluctantly decided to let it rest. There was simply too much at stake to risk antagonising her any further. Leader was an unknown quantity, and what's more, dangerously manipulative. But, for the life of him, he still couldn't quite fathom how his old friend had fallen as fast as he had for Joyce. She had a hold over him; it was obviously a sexual one. She was certainly attractive, but even so, his other lovers, and there had been many, had only ever been supporting players. This one was different, totally different. Zimmerman was acutely aware Joyce was not only admired by Frenzel, but by his former Abwehr colleagues, and, in particular, the *Schamhorst* network still appeared to hold her in high esteem.

Through no fault of his own, Zimmerman had found himself in a compromising position. The Millbank Conference had been in his diary for well over a year now. As an integral member of the bi-annual programme, he was one of the leading guest lecturers, personally invited by the British Government. Everything had gone according to plan. His initial lectures had been very well received, and he had almost begun to relax and enjoy being feted by his peers. That is, until his well-ordered world suddenly imploded when his old friend, Josef Frenzel, turned up unannounced at the St. Philips Hotel.

Security surrounding the conference was tight, and the CIA was keeping a watchful eye over their prized NASA scientists. In the foyer, Zimmerman had extended his hand in greeting. "You should have called," he'd grunted angrily. Frenzel had shrugged dismissively and suggested the phones were tapped.

His appearance was an unwelcome ghost from the past. He'd tried so long and hard to reinvent himself, to emotionally distance himself from his involvement with the Third Reich. But, Frenzel's appearance at the St. Philips Hotel had changed all that. They were having a drink at the bar when Frenzel dropped the bombshell that he needed his help, and the *Schamhorst* wanted to call in one last favour. At the time, Zimmerman had played it cool, but inside, he was panicking. For a start, he'd never even heard of Helmut Schneider, but his heart sunk even further when Frenzel explained he was a former Gestapo officer on the run from Mossad.

On joining the SS, Zimmerman had sworn a personal oath of allegiance to Adolf Hitler, "on your blood and your sword." The *Schamhorst* viewed it as a sacred, unbreakable vow. Long before surrendering to the Americans, Zimmerman already knew the writing was on the wall, and he had to escape the ruins of the Nazi Germany. As the Third Reich crashed around him, there was no way of knowing whether he would survive. He needed to save his family and to ensure their safety, and had used his contacts in the SS to open a Swiss bank account.

Neutral Switzerland was the favoured haven for Nazi bank accounts and safe deposit boxes; Swiss banks did lucrative business with the German Reichsbank and with individual Nazi officials. Zimmerman had funnelled a large amount of ready cash and gold into several secret accounts stowed away in Zurich and Berne. Its provenance nowadays wouldn't pass too much scrutiny. At the time, gold had generally come from two sources, the reserves of the central banks of occupied countries and from individuals in concentration camps. The fact he'd never touched the accounts was immaterial. The members of the *Schamhorst* had long memories. They had a list of everyone they'd helped, and their leading members. Zimmerman was at the top of that list, and no matter how much he wanted to erase his past, it had finally come back to bite him with a vengeance.

He began to fuss with his cufflinks. Joyce guessed it was a nervous gesture. She pulled out a pack of Kensitas cigarettes from her handbag, slipped one free, and placed it in the end of her ebony holder. Joyce decided to change tack and bring the conversation back to R V Jones. 'So, what *are* you going to do about Professor Jones?' she asked, flicking on her lighter.

'I'm not sure.' he said distractedly.

'It'll be difficult to refuse, at least not without causing offence.'

Frenzel agreed with her. 'Have you run it by the American Embassy?'

'Why should *I*?' he replied arrogantly.

Frenzel's expression hardened. He'd never personally warmed to Zimmerman. Like many scientists, he had a strong tendency to be arrogant, and had somewhere along the line forgotten he owed his former SS colleagues a debt of honour. The network needed his financial help to secure Helmut Schneider's escape to South America. The fact Zimmerman's reputation was potentially on the line wasn't exactly their highest priority. In fact, it wasn't a priority at all.

Chapter 6
The Foreign Secretary's Office, Whitehall

From the comfort of his spacious Whitehall office, John Eldridge handed out drinks to Carter and Jack Stein. He returned to the fully stocked drink cabinet, and rubbed his hands together in anticipation before deciding on a large bourbon and soda. Cigarettes were lit, and Eldridge's guests took up position in in comfortable Chesterfield style armchairs.

The Foreign Secretary carefully appraised the younger man. There was an underlying hardness about him that oozed an innate self-belief in his abilities. No doubt his service with the SAS had engendered enormous self-confidence and self-discipline, but there was a side to him touched with more than an edge of arrogance. He could now see why Spencer rated him as a star of the future. In many ways, it must have been almost like looking at a mirror image of his younger self.

Carter drew heavily on his freshly lit cigarette and looked thoughtfully at each of them in turn. 'So, gentlemen, can you me what this all about?'

Eldridge moved behind his desk and sat down. 'Yes, I'm sorry about dragging you away from the cocktail party, but I'm afraid we have a problem.'

'What kind of problem, sir?'

Eldridge sighed wearily. 'My dear chap, I'm afraid it's you!'

Carter felt his pulse quicken. He certainly hadn't seen that one coming. 'Me? I don't know whether to feel flattered or alarmed,' he managed to say evenly.

Patience wasn't precisely a virtue with Carter, and he'd rather Eldridge didn't beat around the bush. It was with some difficulty he managed to keep the irritation off his face, but he did.

Sensing his frustration, it was Stein who cut in. 'I'm afraid, Jed, you're in danger of blowing the entire assignment.'

Carter's expression closed down; he hadn't got a clue what Stein was talking about.

Eldridge leant back in his green leather chair and linked his fingers behind his head. 'We understand you called Scotland Yard this afternoon.'

It was a loaded question. 'What of it?' he answered warily.

'I believe you spoke to an old friend of yours in Special Branch.'

'Yes, Harry Webb.'

'Was there any particular reason why you called him?'

'I call him all the time.' He shrugged. 'We go back a long way.'

'Yes, so I'm led to believe.'

Carter took a sharp intake of breath; nothing would have pleased him more than to wipe the smug expression off the Foreign Secretary's face. 'I take it my phone call is recorded in the log?'

'You can never be too careful,' Eldridge said unnecessarily.

'If I had anything to hide, I wouldn't have called Harry from the office.'

Stein took a sip of his Haig whisky. He felt a degree of responsibility for Carter picking up the phone to a trusted contact in Scotland Yard. In Carter's shoes, he'd probably have done the same thing. Stein regretted questioning Spencer about reopening Leader's file with Assistant Commissioner Garvan. The answer had been left hanging in the air. He should simply have let it pass until Carter was out of earshot. It was too late now; the damage had already been done.

The transcript of the call to Detective Sergeant Webb had landed on Spencer's desk at 1600hrs. Stein's comments had naturally sparked his curiosity, but Spencer knew he probably wouldn't let it rest there. He could have delayed and hauled him in for a formal grilling at MI5 HQ, but why wait? Things were moving fast, and he couldn't afford Carter's snooping around to jeopardise the Schneider Case. The first real opportunity was the cocktail party, so he'd called in Stein and Eldridge to come clean with him.

'So, tell me, what did Webb have to say for himself?' Stein asked.

'Not that much.'

Stein arched his brows questioningly. 'He must have said something.'

'Only that he'd never heard of anyone called Joyce Leader.'

Stein and Eldridge exchanged glances; Webb was probably saying no more than the truth. Even so, they couldn't afford Carter a free reign to continue digging too deeply. Stein took a deep draught of his drink. 'During the war, Garvan was seconded to British Intelligence.'

'Yes, he was,' Eldridge piped up. 'I worked alongside him. He was bloody good, but, of course, it was never going to last.'

'Why not?' Carter asked.

'Garvan was a top-class detective, and still is. As you can imagine, it took him a while to fit into the Service.' Eldridge leant forward and flicked the ash off the end of his cigarette into a large, ornate cut glass ashtray. 'Then again, why wouldn't he feel like a fish out of water? After leaving the SAS, you must have found yourself in much the same boat, Carter?'

Jed cast him a rueful look. 'I guess at one time or another, sir, we've all found ourselves up shit creek without a paddle!'

Stein smiled to himself. Eldridge wasn't exactly renowned for having a sense of humour, and since his appointment as Foreign Secretary, had become hypersensitive to any inference he wasn't quite up to the job. Although hugely successful in the political field, it still somewhat played on his old insecurities that he hadn't quite made the grade and been promoted to the higher echelons of the Service. The fact his meteoric rise as a politician had taken some of his former colleagues by surprise still privately rankled with him. Even though he was now one of the most influential men in Britain, deep down, Eldridge continued to feel he still had to prove himself.

Perhaps Carter hadn't meant to cause offence by his seemingly innocuous remark, but his gut instinct told him Spencer's star of the future had delivered his barbed comments with deadly accuracy.

'Why did Garvan leave the Service?' Carter continued smoothly.

Edridge drew heavily on his cigarette, as if he were in dire need of a quick nicotine fix. 'You have to understand, Garvan was already something of a legend at the Yard, long before he came to us. Spencer persuaded him to stay on for an extra year or so, but it was only a matter of time before he jumped ship to head up Special Branch. Returning to Scotland Yard meant promotion and getting back on the career ladder. His close links with the security service naturally placed him in a unique position as he, so to speak, had a foot in both camps.'

Carter's response was clipped. 'Where exactly does Joyce Leader fit into the equation?'

Eldridge held his gaze. 'It's a little complicated, and delicate.'

'I don't doubt it, but why, after all this time of her being out of the game, should Spencer discuss re-opening her file with Garvan?'

Stein slightly smiled. Having raised the question in Spencer's office, he figured it was down to him to answer. He explained they had once been close.

When Carter replied, his voice was taut, but conveyed disbelief. 'Do you mean they had an affair?' His disapproval was evident.

'Yeah,' Stein said, through a swirl of smoke. 'It happened back in June '44. You've got to understand, after D-Day, things were slightly different. It's difficult to explain, but that's the way it was.'

The continued look of scepticism on Carter's face spoke volumes. Stein told him up until the invasion of Europe, there had always been a sharp dividing line. No matter how valued Leader was, she was still very much a double agent, and ultimately, an enemy of the State. There had been talk of giving her a clean sheet, but it was still on hold until after the cessation of the war.

'What exactly happened between them?'

Stein didn't quite know where to begin. In many ways, the relationship had rapidly spiralled out of control. In the run-up to the invasion, they had found themselves based in a large office in St. James's, which they'd dubbed the War Room. British intelligence officers had staffed it with a contingent from the American OSS intelligence agency. They'd worked long hours in an environment filled with clattering teleprinters conveying the latest intelligence reports to and from the various Allied Commanders. Within the War Room itself, there was a palpable sense of urgency mingled with a frisson of anxiety, for they knew the coming days and weeks would become increasingly crucial.

'They were very discreet,' Eldridge explained. 'A few rumours were circulating, but personally, I didn't pay any heed to them. To be honest with you, I just thought it was the usual typing pool tittle-tattle. You know, a bunch of the girls sitting around having a tea break, gossiping. It happened all the time, and most of it tended to be wide of the mark.'

'So when *did* you find out about them?' Carter enquired.

'Me, personally?'

Carter nodded.

'Not for some considerable time.'

'And Spencer?'

'Well, very little got past Spencer.'

'But, wasn't Garvan taking one hell of a risk?'

'Lord yes,' Eldridge snorted. 'Spencer was always utterly ruthless with anyone who stepped out of line and endangered the Double Cross.'

'Then why didn't he rein them in?'

It was Stein who replied. 'He did, but eventually decided to let it ride.'

'I just don't get it,' Carter snorted.

'I'm only guessing, but I think you'll find there were several reasons why he turned a blind eye. That doesn't mean to say Spencer didn't come down hard on them. For a while, both their futures were pretty much in the balance. You've got to remember, things were still pretty critical, and he needed Leader to keep up the pretence with Berlin. The Allies were clinging on to a foothold in France; we still knew there was a long, hard-fought campaign ahead of us.'

Carter's face remained devoid of expression. 'How long were they together?'

'For quite a while actually,' Eldridge chipped in. 'They played it pretty low key, but then again, they had to. As I said most of us didn't give any credence to the gossip. Besides, we were too bloody overworked and stressed out to worry about some ruddy office romance. Most of us were living on a diet of cigarettes and Benzedrine to keep us going. After the war, of course, Joyce was free to walk, so that gave them a little more leeway. That is, right up until Gavan was appointed to head up Special Branch. You see, it was the one role at Scotland Yard he'd always coveted.'

'So, what happened?'

'Given the choice, I think it's fair to say Garvan would never have given up on her. In fact, he wanted to marry her. But, Joyce was concerned it was just too complicated to continue. At some point or another, a security report would have landed on the Commissioner's desk, disclosing her past as a Double Agent. Deep down, she knew in the long term, it would never have worked out for him.'

'I can see that might have been a bit a deal breaker.'

Eldridge stubbed out his cigarette. 'The thing is, they're still close friends.'

'How close?'

'They're not sleeping together, Carter, if that's what you mean. Even so, we can't afford you to go blindly stirring up a hornet's nest at Scotland Yard.'

'There's something else I don't quite understand.'

A trace of exasperation crossed Eldridge's face. 'What's there to understand?'

'Well, I know for a fact Special Branch is already involved in helping us to track Schneider down. Now, whether their help has official sanction from the Home Office or not is neither here nor there. But, the one thing I *do* know is there is no way undercover Met officers would be working alongside MI5, without Assistant Commissioner Garvan's say so.'

Stein agreed with him. 'As the Head of MI5, Spencer was always going to share intelligence about Schneider. Why wouldn't he?'

Carter shot him a questioning look.

'Schneider's presence in the UK overlaps both their departments. Let's face it. It's not every day you have a high ranking Nazi war criminal on the run from Mossad. If there's likely to be blood spilled on the streets of London, then Garvan has every right to know. The explosion in Bligh Street might not only have taken Schiender out; it could also have killed or injured his neighbours. Who's to say it won't happen again.'

Carter accepted his point.

Stein rolled his cigarette thoughtfully between his fingers. 'It's also important to take into consideration Garvan is the lead of security at Millbank. The fact Professor Zimmerman has been dragged, apparently unwillingly, into bankrolling Schneider's passage back to South America hasn't exactly made his job any easier. As for Joyce Leader, re-activating her file was always going to be on a need-to-know basis.' Stein placed the cigarette between his lips and drew deeply on it before blowing out a plume of smoke. 'Besides, I imagine Leader probably already has enough on her plate without Garvan kicking up a stink behind the scenes.'

'Maybe, but surely it's only a matter of time before he finds out the truth?'

Stein pulled a face. 'Well, let's put it this way. Spencer wants to make sure her cover doesn't get blown, not even to Garvan.'

Carter kept his thoughts to himself, but reckoned it would be a tall order concealing her role indefinitely. There was another question bugging him, and it was one he couldn't quite shake free. 'I'm sorry but it's not adding up,' he said.

'What do you mean?' Eldridge asked him testily.

'I've read the background stuff about Schneider murdering Spencer's brother in cold blood. We know the case is deeply personal to him. I get all that. But, what I don't *understand* is, why the hell he doesn't have top cover for the assignment? What's that all about?'

Eldridge thoughtfully sucked in his lower lip. 'I guess you could say it's all about the timing, dear boy.'

His eyes swept swiftly over the Foreign Secretary's face. 'You'll have to explain that one to me, sir.'

'Have you met Chris Parker?'

He was referring to the Home Secretary, and more importantly, Spencer's immediate boss. As Head of MI5,

Spencer's remit was domestic intelligence, whereas its sister organisation, MI6, was responsible for external intelligence, and, therefore, reported to Eldridge and the Foreign Office.

In answer to his question, Carter said he was considered far too junior to have warranted an introduction to Parker.

Eldridge let out an involuntary chuckle. 'Trust me, it's probably a blessing in disguise. Let's put it this way. My esteemed Cabinet colleague has an eye on the future. He's due to retire before the next General Election. In recognition of his public service, it's almost a foregone conclusion he'll receive a peerage and a seat in the House of Lords. His wife, Clemmy, is deeply ambitious, and has always hankered after being styled "Lady Parker." Mind you, it'd take more than a *bloody* title to make Clemmy Parker a lady!' Eldridge reached into his desk drawer for a pack of cigarettes. 'You have to understand the Prime Minister views Parker as a safe pair of hands.'

'What's that supposed to mean?'

Eldridge pulled out a box of matches from the desk drawer and lit another cigarette. 'It means whatever happens in Downing Street has a ripple effect. Over recent years, the Tory Party has been riddled with bitter internal feuds. As you must be aware, two Government Ministers have recently resigned in protest at the PM's leadership; in fact, the whole thing has been a bit of a ruddy mess. Parker is viewed as a calming influence. As a result, Parker doesn't want to be seen to rock the boat and jeopardize his chances of a peerage. He really couldn't give a damn about Schneider, or anyone else. Right from the start, Spencer knew he'd never obtain official sanction to track Schneider down. It wasn't even worth running it by the old bugger. Besides, he'd have placed too many obstacles in his path. He's always been more of a hindrance than a help.'

'Are you telling me Parker has *no* idea what's going on?'

Eldridge pulled a face. 'It's all a little bit sensitive.'

'I take it that means he doesn't know?'

He leaned forward on the desk. 'The one thing Parker has always argued is no matter how high grade the intelligence might be, and look like a risk worth taking, if things go wrong, then a year or so down the line, some smart lawyer might just end up making it look like culpability on his part. Chris Parker is all about self-preservation, rather than national interest.'

Carter could appreciate the prospect of becoming embroiled in a controversial assignment, involving not only Mossad, the CIA, a Nazi ratline, and British Intelligence, would have been a complete anathema to the ever cautious Home Secretary.

'Where exactly does that leave you, sir?'

Stein smiled to himself; it took a lot of balls to tackle Eldridge head-on.

There was a slight hesitation to Eldridge's response. 'First and foremost, Carter, I'm a senior member of Her Majesty's Government. However, I'm not here in any official capacity, but solely as a friend to your Director General.' He took a long drag on his freshly lit cigarette. 'Let's just put it this way, if you screw up the Schneider Case, then I'll deny all knowledge of this conversation and that Sir Spencer Hall briefed me about it.'

'And if we I manage to pull it off, what then?'

As he held the younger man's unblinking gaze, a slow smile began to crease his face. 'Then it's a win-win situation.'

'You mean for *you*, sir?'

'Not just for me, Carter, but for all of us. I'll brief the Prime Minister that British Intelligence has not only prevented a war criminal from fleeing justice to South America, but we've also managed to tidy up a few other loose ends as well.'

'What kind of loose ends?'

'Well.' He smiled flicking his gaze to Stein. 'Josef Frenzel, for one.'

'Yeah,' Stein agreed, 'He's been kicking around the system for years. It'd be one way of quietly putting him out to grass.'

'Wasn't he a member of the Gehlen Organization?'

Stein nodded. 'During the war, he worked alongside Gehlen in the Soviet Union and surrendered to the U.S. Army Counter Intelligence Corps in Bavaria. You can imagine at the time, their knowledge and contacts inside the Soviet Union made them pretty valuable to us.'

'And what about now?'

'He's a busted flush,' Stein said.

'Why?'

'You must have read the reports?'

'All the same, I'd rather hear it from you.'

'When the Gehlen Organization morphed into the West German Intelligence Service, a hell of a lot of their employees came from the SS and their security police, the Sicherheitspolizei-SD. At heart, Frenzel is still a dyed- in-the-wool Nazi.'

'And what about Bernard Zimmerman? Is he still a Nazi at heart?'

Stein smiled tautly. 'If he is, then he hides it well.'

'But, he's bankrolling Schneider's passage to South America.'

'Maybe, but I guess he's under a good deal of pressure.'

'If he didn't want to get his hands dirty, why not just come clean and tell the CIA he'd been approached?'

Stein passed him a smile; it was pleasant enough, but closed. 'You could say, I'm still working on that *one.*'

The subject obviously wasn't open for further discussion.

'I'm flying back to the States tomorrow morning,' Stein continued.

Carter looked at him questioningly.

Stein raised his hand. 'I'll be back in London before the end of the conference,' he assured him. 'I can't call all the shots on Zimmerman alone. I need to discuss his future with Washington, and get a decision out of them before I return.'

Eldridge thanked Carter for his time. The meeting was clearly at an end.

He took his cue and stood up; they shook hands.

As he reached the door, Eldridge said to him, 'By the way, Carter, I forgot to mention to you. My staff had a meeting with Marcus Cohen, the Israeli chargé d'affaires, this afternoon. While we didn't quite read him the riot act, he was told we had it on good authority a Mossad team was operating on British territory, with the express purpose of eliminating Helmut Schneider.'

'What was his reaction?'

'He denied all knowledge; in fact, my private secretary said he made a pretty convincing defence of the Israeli position.'

'How, exactly?'

A slow, bemused smile crossed his face. 'Cohen argued if Mossad *had* been behind the explosion in Bligh Street, they wouldn't have missed their man.'

'Do you believe him?'

Eldridge shrugged. 'It has a certain ring of truth to it; you have to admit, Mossad's people are usually pretty slick.'

Although he was inclined to agree with him, he wouldn't be drawn, and reached to turn the door handle.

'I wish you luck, Carter; you'll certainly need it!' Eldridge said.

Carter paused a moment before slipping out of the office.

Chapter 7
Gliddon Road, Southwark, London

Schneider walked into the sitting room from the kitchen of his latest bolthole, slurping a cup of coffee. It was a rundown property in South London. Frenzel had secured a good rental price from the landlord, as the entire terrace was due to be demolished to make way for a block of flats. Erhard Lange, his bodyguard, was sprawled out on the sofa reading a newspaper. Schneider stood for a minute, lost in thought, before moving over to the window. He tweaked the net curtain and gazed moodily out of the window without actually seeing the grey fogbound skyline of London. Schneider took another sip of his coffee and glanced anxiously down into the street below. He looked both ways to reassure himself they were safe and not under surveillance.

'I'd rather you kept away from the window, sir,' Lange said, without looking up from his newspaper.

Schneider released the net curtain and began to pace up and down the room. He glanced at his watch. 'Your boss is running late.'

Lange's eyes shot toward the mantelpiece clock. 'Only by ten minutes,' he answered indifferently. 'If there were a problem, he would have contacted us by now.'

Schneider decided to keep his thoughts to himself. Frenzel had always been an unknown quantity to him. While he might need his help, that didn't mean he trusted him. His reticence was deep-rooted. As a former member of the Gestapo, Schneider had good reason to be wary of Frenzel.

In the latter stages of the war, Admiral Wilhelm Canaris negotiated an agreement, and joined the Resistance movement against the Nazi government. The German Intelligence Service used the Abwehr network to leak secrets and troop positions to the Allies. Canaris was eventually executed for knowing about the July plot to assassinate Hitler. The discovery of the Plot and Canaris' spy ring was to prove a crucial counter-intelligence victory for the Gestapo.

The fact Frenzel had served during the final death throes of the war working for General Reinhard von Gehlen, Hitler's head of military espionage in Russia, only added to his growing uneasiness. Frenzel's loyalties were seemingly a moveable feast. His moral compass ebbed and waned with alarming regularity. Having decided to pin his star to von Gehlen, he followed him into the service of the CIA. He then morphed again into becoming a pillar of the West German Security Service while maintaining his covert links with the Nazi *Schamhorst* network. Schneider's hatred of the Abwehr was ingrained, but he guessed it was probably a two-way street.

Schneider took another drink of his coffee and continued pacing the room. No doubt Frenzel had rated Erhard Lange, but Schneider was still undecided. On paper, his profile was exemplary. The son of a Waffen SS Colonel, his work and dedication to the *Schamhorst* had made him a leading member of the network.

While Schneider admired Lange senior's capabilities, behind the scenes, he was convinced his influence had probably helped ease young Erhard's path into the security world by calling in a few favours from the likes of Josef Frenzel. There was no denying Erhard looked the part tall, blond, and muscle bound everything you might want in a bodyguard trying to keep you alive. However, his relaxed, almost blasé, attitude did little to inspire confidence, or, at least, it didn't to Schneider.

'Tell me something.'

Lange glanced up from his newspaper.

'What do you make of Joyce Leader?' It was almost a throwaway line, but Lange sensed he was on a fishing trip for information.

'What about her?' he asked guardedly.

Schneider suggested she might have become a distraction.

'A distraction?' he repeated blankly. Lange figured it wasn't his place to comment, and said as much.

Schneider noted whenever Joyce was around, it was the only time Lange appeared to perk up and take any notice. He decided to let it rest, and anxiously re-checked his watch; Frenzel was now running fifteen minutes late. He was on the verge of moving back over to the window when the phone rang. Lange stretched out and reached for the phone on the small circular table beside the sofa.

'Hello?' he said, resting the newspaper on his chest. There was a pause. Lange sat bolt upright. 'Yes, sir, of course.'

As he set the receiver down, Schneider looked at him questioningly. 'Who was it?'

'Herr Frenzel.'

'Where is he?'

'On his way up. He called from the hallway phone downstairs.'

Schneider inwardly breathed a sigh of relief. His life was on the line here, and if Frenzel didn't deliver, he was nothing more than a dead man walking.

There was a tap at the door. Lange eased himself off the sofa and ambled across the room. 'Who is it?' he demanded, removing a pistol from his holster.

'It's me,' Frenzel said, knowing his voice would be instantly recognised.

Lange unbolted the latch-chain on the door. Schneider's expression registered surprise. The last thing he had expected was for Frenzel to turn up with Bernard Zimmerman in tow. Lange relaxed and let them in. Frenzel breezed into the flat. He was all smiles, full of himself. But, then again, Schneider mused, he was always full of himself. Even so, maybe it was a good sign Zimmerman was with him.

'I'm sorry we're running late,' Frenzel apologised. 'We were caught in traffic on the Albert Embankment.'

'I guess better late than never,' Schneider said, with the merest hint of irony.

Frenzel chose to ignore the jibe. 'It's been a long day,' he announced, rubbing his hands together. 'Have you stocked up?' His question was directed to Lange.

'Yes, sir. What would you like?'

'My usual.'

His "usual" was a vodka and tonic with no ice. Lange looked to Zimmerman.

'Whisky, straight,' he said, flatly.

Schneider drained his coffee. 'I'm fine.'

Lange disappeared into the kitchen to fetch the drinks.

'Do we have the money?' Schneider asked bluntly.

'Yes, we do,' Zimmerman said, in not much more than a whisper.

'But, have you secured the funds upfront for Captain Calero?'

'Relax,' Frenzel assured him. 'Everything is in hand.'

'Relax!' Schneider repeated. 'You've got a bloody nerve, Josef. I think you're forgetting it's my life on the line here!'

'Just trust me on this, will you?'

'I seem to remember you said the same thing last time round, and look what happened! I missed the passage to South America, and nearly ended up being blown to kingdom come by Mossad.'

Frenzel's face remained calm, but his eyes were unsympathetic. It rang through his mind it was a pity Mossad hadn't managed to take the bastard out.

Lange returned with their drinks. He really didn't want to hang around. 'I'll be in the kitchen, if you need me,' he said, beating a hasty retreat from the lounge.

Frenzel joined Zimmerman on the sofa. Schneider preferred to remain standing.

Zimmerman held his gaze across the room, and quietly, but firmly, steered the conversation back to the matter at hand. 'Gentlemen, let's just drop the pointless bickering, shall we! The way I see it, it really wasn't anyone's fault the previous plan failed. It was down to one thing, and one thing only, the Argentinian Captain became greedy and reneged on our agreement. No-one could have foreseen that happening.' Zimmerman took a sip of his whisky. 'My own contacts in the *Schamhorst* speak very highly of Captain Calero. He's someone they can do business with. They've assured me he won't let us down.'

'Let's hope they're right!' Schneider snorted dubiously.

He studied Schneider carefully before setting his glass down on a side-table and eased a pack of cigarettes out of his jacket pocket. He thoughtfully undid the cellophane wrapping and extracted one.

It suddenly crossed Schneider's mind he might have underestimated this gently spoken intellectual. The thin, pinched features and the deceptively kind, pale blue eyes masked a taciturn, uncompromising personality. He was all too aware Zimmerman was playing an extremely dangerous game. So far, he had covered his tracks well, very well. Then again, Zimmerman had to keep a low profile. One could well imagine how the unwelcome presence of a notorious, former Gestapo officer fleeing Mossad had been the ultra-cautious scientist's worse nightmare.

Whatever his personal feelings toward him, the promise to the *Schamhorst*, to the Nazi ratline, was one of total loyalty to the Brotherhood as a whole, and to every member thereof. The fact Zimmerman might personally disapprove of Schneider's actions during the War, and that he considered him a loose cannon, could not negate his moral responsibility to the *Schamhorst*.

Zimmerman lit a cigarette and discarded the spent match in the overflowing ashtray beside his drink. 'My understanding is Captain Calero is due to dock in London on time.'

'And the money?' Schneider pressed him again.

'The money was delivered by courier this afternoon.'

'A *Schamhorst* courier?'

Zimmerman nodded and drew deeply on his freshly lit cigarette.

'So, where is it now?'

Frenzel cut in. 'At a safety deposit box in West London. The plan is for him to collect the package tomorrow morning.'

Schneider looked at him questioningly.

'He'll drop it off here.'

'What time?'

'Midday.'

'How good is he?' Schneider probed.

'Good enough,' Zimmerman said sharply. 'Otherwise, I wouldn't be bankrolling your passage to South America!'

Schneider met his cold eye stare. He probably had a point and decided to change tack. He turned his attention back to Frenzel. 'Okay, so we now have the money, but how are you planning on getting me to the docks in one piece?'

Frenzel raised his hand. It was a valid question. 'When Captain Calero confirms the *Mendoza* has arrived safely in Surrey Docks, and the customs people have given the all clear, we'll set the ball in motion.'

Schneider seemed none too impressed. 'And how are you proposing to do that?'

'We have a vehicle lined up for you.'

'What kind of vehicle?'

'One which won't be questioned.'

Schneider rolled his eyes. 'Don't tell me; it's not a bloody hearse, is it?'

Frenzel threw back his head and laughed. 'Even *I* wouldn't do that to you, my friend.'

'I'm not so sure!'

'Just bear with me. I've decided there's little point at this late stage moving you on to another hotel or bedsit. This place is pretty low key and located close to the river. Once we get the nod from Calero, Lange will drive you to the docks and hand over the money.'

'And then what?'

'He'll deliver you safely on board.'

Schneider's eyes flashed angrily. 'And what about Mossad? It's not going to be that easy, Josef!'

Frenzel seemed unconcerned by Schneider's outburst, and answered equably, 'We never thought it would be. Let's just say, our plans have General Aurberg's approval. Need I say more?'

'The trouble is, Josef, I'm not quite sure what your plans are.'

'All in good time,' Frenzel assured him.

Schneider would have loved nothing more than to wipe the smug, self-important expression off Frenzel's face. But, under the circumstances, however much it might irk him, he figured he probably didn't have any choice, other than to play his game.

As they continued to bicker, Zimmerman looked pensively around the drab, sparsely furnished, sitting room. He could perfectly understand Schneider's frustration at being cooped up in a series of seedy bedsits and hotels, never quite knowing if his whereabouts had been discovered, or that every night might well be his last.

Much against his better judgement, Zimmerman had somewhat reluctantly agreed to meet Schneider again. Frenzel had called in one last favour and appeared keen to mollify his volatile charge. Frenzel had hoped the quiet, authoritative presence of the renowned scientist would help settle Schneider's understandable anxiety about the escape plan and whether they could actually pull it off. Zimmerman felt a frisson of sympathy for him. In some ways, they were in the same boat. Both men had been reluctantly drawn into helping Schneider. He was also acutely aware Frenzel had found himself under increasing pressure from both the *Schamhorst* and Schneider to deliver.

Zimmerman was also out on a limb and under pressure from the network. He'd made it clear from day one he would rather not complicate matters by becoming personally involved with Schneider. They had met briefly before, at Frenzel's flat and a cocktail party at the West German Embassy. However, it was one thing to bankroll the notorious former Gestapo officer's escape to South America, but with each meeting, he was forced to break cover. The ever cautious Zimmerman was concerned it was only a matter of time before the CIA or MI5 caught onto them.

As they pulled up in Gliddon Road, Frenzel assured him all was well, and they hadn't been tailed. He had little choice other than to take his word for it. But, he remained decidedly uncomfortable with the situation.

Even with the distance of time, the seemingly unbreakable links to the past had led to an endless spiral of complicity. Sitting in the dreary bedsit, the ruffled sensitivities of a war criminal didn't sit easily with him. However, Zimmerman knew he was still expected to fulfill his obligation to the *Schamhorst*. Deep down, he desperately wanted to break away, to forget the past and give his children the chance of a prosperous future in America, free from the sins of their father.

Schneider's sharp, commanding tones cut through his thoughts. He was still prattling on about the money and Captain Calero. Zimmerman admired Frenzel's patience with the self-important demands of his prickly charge. Zimmerman found himself looking at Schneider with a mixture of boredom and loathing. He embodied everything about the war and the Third Reich he had come to despise.

Times had changed, and although in his youth he'd been swept up in the enthusiasm and blind loyalty to the Nazi regime, his beliefs had long since ebbed. The horrors and atrocities of the past had begun to come back to haunt him. He had witnessed the most dreadful things imaginable that human beings can do to one another. There were the flashbacks and distressing memories, something he assumed the cold, ruthless Schneider was unlikely ever to be troubled with.

Over the last few years, Zimmerman had found his sleep increasingly disturbed; he'd wake up in a cold sweat, having relived some horrific incident of the past. It was invariably the same dreams; the pale, haunted figures of the slave labourers in their striped uniforms forced to work on Hitler's precious rocket programme. A prisoner beaten to death by an SS officer or savaged to death by a snarling guard dog. At the time, it was an everyday occurrence. To his eternal shame, Zimmerman had carried on his research, seemingly oblivious to the bestial horrors and treatment inflicted on those working at the top secret site at Peenemünde. Life expectancy had been limited, and countless numbers had died in appalling conditions.

Once again, Schneider's irritatingly sharp voice brought his mind back to the present. *What the hell was he droning on about now?* For some reason or another, he'd set his ire against Joyce Leader. Although Zimmerman had no time for her, Schneider seemed to have a serious down on the woman.

'How much does she know about our plans?' he was demanding of Frenzel.

It took every ounce of Frenzel's experience not to allow his anger to show. 'I'd trust Joyce with my life.'

'Then you're an even bigger fool than I took you for.'

His eyes swept swiftly over Schneider's face. 'What the hell do you mean by that?'

'I mean Leader isn't quite all she seems.'

Frenzel took a deep mouthful of vodka. Not for the first time, Schneider had been severely testing his patience. 'I think,' he said evenly, 'her war record speaks for itself.'

Schneider snorted derisively. 'Does it?'

'Why not just spit it out!'

'I'm surprised you didn't know there were rumours, serious rumours about your mistress during the war.'

'What kind of rumours?'

'After Admiral Canaris was arrested and taken to Flossenburg concentration camp, Himmler ordered an investigation into the activities of the Abwehr.'

It was old news. Frenzel interrupted and said testily, 'Just get to the point, Helmut, will you? As I remember, at the time, it was easy to be viewed as a traitor to the Reich. You could be strung up on a gallows for being a defeatist, or for just disagreeing with your local Nazi Party. If you have something on Joyce Leader, then what is it?' he demanded.

Schneider looked at him contemptuously. 'As you know, my good friend General Aurberg was close to Reichsführer Himmler. After the plot to kill the Führer, the Admiral's intelligence organisation was not only investigated but placed under the direct command of the Reichsführer. But, long before the attempt on Hitler's life, Leader's family were already under suspicion of disloyalty to the Third Reich. Her father had known Canaris for many years and shared the same traitorous political views.' Schneider set his empty cup down, and resumed pacing the room. 'Kurt Leader was as much a traitor to the Fatherland as that bastard, Canaris!' he thundered.

'So what are you implying, Helmut, guilt by association?'

Schneider stood looking down at him on the sofa. 'No, Josef, I'm not. I know by 1944,' he shrugged, 'maybe even before, she was working for the British.' Schneider folded his arms. 'Your pretty little whore's British codename was Borgia!'

A puzzled look of incredulity crossed Frenzel's face. At the time, it was believed much of her intelligence had derived from pillow talk, but the codename was a new one on him. He still seemed unsure whether to believe him or not. As a former Abwehr officer, Frenzel knew how complex and difficult things had been. On the Eastern front, his own staff had bravely worked undercover. He could imagine Joyce might well have been tasked to try and infiltrate British Intelligence. Whether she was coerced or did so willingly was obviously open to conjecture. He also had to take into consideration Schneider might well have old scores to settle, perceived past wrongs to avenge. But, there was a growing, nagging doubt at the back of Frenzel's mind maybe Leader was a plant. In spite of his inner turmoil, he seemed to handle the news well, or at least, he did so outwardly.

'But, where's your proof she was working for the British?' he demanded. The last thing he wanted was to give Schneider the satisfaction the news had rattled him.

'Some years ago, her name came up in conversation. Do you know Peter Wagner?'

'I can't say as I do.'

'He worked alongside her Abwehr controller, Drescher.'

The trouble was, Drescher was long since dead, and unable to corroborate Wagner's accusations.

By now, Schneider was on a roll, and had no intention of letting the matter drop. 'You have to ask yourself, Josef, is your whore still a British agent? *Is* she still working for them?'

Frenzel debated what to say but decided to remain silent.

'Does General Aurberg know you're sleeping with her?' he pressed.

He had to admit, it was a valid point, but one Fenzel had seen little reason to share in any great detail with the *Schamhorst*. That is, until now. Albeit reluctantly, he confessed he hadn't thought it necessary. There had been little reason to doubt her credentials, for Joyce was still well known in ex-Nazi circles.

'Then, may I suggest, Josef, you contact General Aurberg immediately. I've no intention of your whore jeopardising everything the *Schamhorst* and I have worked for!'

Zimmerman had heard enough of their constant sniping, and hurriedly drained his whisky. The long-held mistrust between Himmler's men and the Abwehr was entirely immaterial to him. As far as he was concerned, his job was done, and he said as much. While he wished Schneider good luck, his delivery was flat and devoid of expression. He inclined his head slightly and shook Schneider's hand before moving over to the door, but, as an afterthought, turned back.

'Forgive me, Herr Schneider,' he said.

The sudden formality wasn't lost on him.

Zimmerman decided to play Devil's advocate and asked, 'Can you tell me something?'

'Go on.'

'Is it true you were in the Jamiltz Internment Camp?'

Schneider guessed he already knew the answer. 'Yes, I was,' he replied sharply.

'Then, you were lucky to survive.'

Schneider couldn't deny it. Thousands of prisoners died. His luck, or so it was reported, changed when the USSR eventually handed over control of the camp over to the East German Government. 'Why do you ask?'

'It's just that I was wondering...'

'About what?'

'How did the *Schamhorst* manage to secure your release?'

'Two of my East German Guards were still loyal to the Reich.'

'Really,' Zimmerman said. 'I was under the impression they had accepted money in exchange for your release.'

Schneider held his ground. 'It wasn't quite like that,' he replied.

Zimmerman kept his thoughts to himself and opened the door. For a man with blood on his hands, more to the point, Soviet blood, Schneider's escape from Jamiltz wasn't just lucky; it was nothing short of a miracle.

Chapter 8
The Savoy Hotel, London

The following day, after visiting Schneider's rundown bedsit in South London, Helmut Frenzel found himself in the rather more salubrious surroundings across the river at the Savoy Hotel. Joyce adored the place, and had always considered it to be almost like a second home, living there on a semi-permanent basis. During the Second World War, the Savoy's management provided a subterranean air-raid shelter, for those guests who wanted it, in what had been the Abraham Lincoln banqueting suite. Upstairs, most people continued the dinner and dancing unabated while the bombs fell. But, somehow, the air of glamour and luxury was still maintained throughout the consecutive nights of bombing.

In the post-war years, the Hotel had changed, of course, but the one constant was Leader's continuing loyalty. The prices, in Frenzel's opinion, were exorbitant, but this was her world. She adored the atmosphere, the glitz of the sparkling crystal chandeliers, and ornate décor. Like her father, she was an inveterate gambler and spent most of her time in the various casinos dotted around London playing poker; some said she could have been a professional. Logical and analytical by nature, she loved the complexity and strategy involved with playing.

Joyce was old school, with an aristocratic background. From the moment he first met her, Frenzel had found himself slightly in awe. He had soon discovered she was quick of temper and liable to explode. But, Joyce was also full of life, and possessed an almost titanic appetite for drink, sex, and gambling.

Although her wealthy Anglo-Austrian father lacked any real political allegiance to the Führer, the family continued to prosper under the regime, supplying the Third Reich with much needed armoured vehicles for the Nazis' war machine. Even now, the family's industrial empire embraced holdings in companies involved in coal, steel, and their original vehicle production lines.

Long before they met in London, Frenzel was already in a rapidly deteriorating marriage. The relationship with his wife was, at best, volatile; it had been from day one. While they chose to lead separate lives, Inge had always refused to grant him a divorce and remained at the family home in Osnabrück. Their two sons were doing well; the eldest, Hans, was an engineer, and the younger, Wilhelm, was at university studying economics.

In hindsight, Frenzel could see his relationship with Joyce Leader was probably just too good to be true. Why would a woman, as stunning and sophisticated as she, find him even remotely attractive? In retrospect, Joyce hadn't appeared that interested, at first. He was vulnerable, of course, a prime target. He'd found her polite and cordial, but nothing more, or so she had made it seem. She was a challenge, blowing hot and cold by turns. A woman in complete control of her sexuality, Joyce knew full well how to use it to her advantage. But, that was what had made her so tantalising, and initially, so seemingly out of reach.

Frenzel had always enjoyed the company of women, and his loneliness had not only frequently placed him in potentially compromising situations, but had also left him wide open to blackmail. He'd had more than one or two close shaves where his career was placed on the line. But, more by luck than judgement, he'd always managed to narrowly escape total disaster.

Until last week, he had never seriously questioned their burgeoning relationship. For the first time in his life, he was genuinely happy. They were steadily spending more and more time with each other. For Frenzel, his feelings toward Joyce were the real thing, and he'd fallen for her hook, line, and sinker.

After dinner, they retreated upstairs to her spacious suite, with a spectacular panoramic view overlooking the Thames. Throughout dinner, Joyce had sensed he was on edge. By all accounts, his meeting yesterday with Schneider and Zimmerman appeared to have gone off without a hitch, and more importantly, the *Schamhorst* courier had arrived safely from Switzerland, with Zimmerman's money to bankroll Schneider's passage to South America. Frenzel had been pulling his hair out since Schneider had turned up unexpectedly in London. Although he expressed his relief the plan was finally coming together, he still seemed troubled. Up until now, he'd always relaxed in her company, but for some reason, tonight was different.

Joyce knew his current appointment to the Embassy was regarded as a step up in the security world, a godsend. However, Frenzel was acutely aware the Ambassador Hans von Bitten, a renowned diplomat, viewed Frenzel's appointment as something of an irreversable act. It certainly wasn't one which had sat easily with him. If rumours were true, and he had no reason to doubt them, after a few drinks, Frenzel could be a liability. The last thing he needed was a loose cannon operating at his Embassy. He didn't trust the man and had made his feelings clear, but higher authority had already agreed. Gehlen, the Chief of the West German Intelligence Service, had all but rubber-stamped his appointment.

Frenzel handed her a drink. It was an acquired taste, a mixture of gin and Dubonnet. Pouring himself a large Vodka on the rocks, he closed the drinks cabinet and sat on the sofa beside her.

Joyce reached out and gently placed her hands over his. 'What's wrong?' she whispered. 'You've been quiet all evening.'

Frenzel smiled, it was half in confidentiality, half in despair. He leaned forward, knocking the ash off his cigarette into the large glass ashtray on the side table and laid it on the engraved surround. He asked out of the blue, 'Who are you working for?'

Joyce continued to play it cool. She gave him a long, slow look. 'What are you talking about, Josef?'

'Why do you need to be armed?' he said, producing a Beretta from his jacket pocket.

God, she wondered, *what on Earth had happened?* She felt her heart begin to race, pounding ever more rapidly until her head felt fit to burst. Joyce assumed after she disappeared into the bathroom, Frenzel had quickly rifled through her handbag and found the slender Beretta. She shrugged indifferently. 'Since the war, I've always carried a pistol.' Her response was apathetic, before she added calmly,

'Old habits die hard, Josef, you of all people should know that.'

Frenzel cast her a puzzled smile.

'Come on,' Joyce chided him, taking a sip of her drink. 'Aren't you forgetting?'

He didn't respond.

'God, it was only the other evening you told me since the explosion at Schneider's flat you've carried one yourself.'

He held her gaze. 'That's a different matter.'

'Is it?'

'Tell me something.'

'Tell you what exactly?'

'Are you still working with the British?'

A look of incredulity crossed her face. 'You mean, working *for* the British?' she snapped back at him.

Frenzel picked up his cigarette from the ashtray. 'Shall we stop playing games with one another?'

'I would, if I knew what the hell you were going on about!'

'You betrayed us; you betrayed the Third Reich. You've spent years betraying those closest to you. There's nowhere left to hide, your secret's out, Joyce,' he announced grimly.

She stared back at him blankly, pulled a face and said, 'You've lost me, Josef!'

'Have I?'

Her thoughts were in overdrive, but still, Joyce managed to keep up the pretence. '*Please* don't tell me this is all Schneider's doing?'

The expression on his face spoke volumes.

'And you believe *him*?'

'Why wouldn't I?'

'For one, he's as twisted as a bloody corkscrew.' Her eyes narrowed as she tried to read his face. 'What exactly did he say to you?'

'Do you know the name Peter Wagner?'

It genuinely didn't mean anything, and she said so.

'He was a colleague of your Abwehr controller.'

'If Wagner had worked with Drescher, I'd have known about him. Besides, security was tight, and if Drescher was unable to receive a transmission, I was pre-warned and his deputy, Erik Fruehauf, stood in for him. If this Wagner character had been a member of the section, I'd certainly have known about him!'

'It was Wagner who told Schneider about you. That you'd betrayed the Fatherland!'

She waited for a response, but none was forthcoming. Deep down, Frenzel desperately wanted to believe her, but the situation was already out of his hands. A quick phone call to General Aurberg concerning Schneider's accusations was enough to seal her fate. They simply couldn't take any chances.

'Can't you see? He's lying to save his own skin!' she persisted.

Frenzel held her gaze. 'Give me a reason, why should he lie?'

'Oh, come on, Josef, do I really have to spell it out for you?'

'I guess you do.'

'When did you start trusting the Gestapo, especially a bastard like Schneider?'

Frenzel reluctantly admitted she had a point. The old enmities of mistrust between the Abwehr and the Gestapo still existed. For the most part, they remained unsaid, but they existed all the same. On a personal level, he found Schneider opinionated, impatient, and arrogant. In fact, on a day-to-day basis, he found him a complete nightmare to deal with.

'For Christ's sake, Josef, you've never liked the man! He's nothing more than a bloody paranoid schizophrenic!'

'Maybe, but, in my shoes, what would you do. How can I be sure he's not telling the truth, then what?'

Her eyes flashed with anger, and she said defiantly, 'So where's his proof, other than this Wagner character I've never even heard of?'

'I understand Drescher was a relation of the Führer's spymaster, Admiral Canaris.'

'Yes, he was the Admiral's cousin.'

Frenzel rolled his cigarette thoughtfully between his fingers. 'Drescher was lucky to have escaped with his life.'

Joyce cast him a puzzled look. 'He was loyal to the end.'

'You would say that.'

'I've no reason to lie.'

'But, we all know Colonel Drescher was under investigation.'

She rolled her eyes. 'After the attempt on Hitler's life, we were all under suspicion. It's just the way it was. You know how Reichsführer Himmler and the Gestapo worked, guilt by association, *even you.*'

He couldn't exactly deny it. At the time, as a member of the Nazi intelligence service, he was fair game.

Joyce detected the uncertainty in his eyes and continued, 'Things could have turned out very differently for you, Josef.'

Frenzel raised an enquiring brow. 'I don't know what you mean.'

'Aren't you forgetting something? Your *own* boss, General Gehlen, was one of the few conspirators who managed to avoid detection and survive. If he'd been caught, well, there's every chance you'd.'

He abruptly interrupted. 'But, this isn't about me!'

In all fairness, he really couldn't fault her line of defence. The trouble was, Schneider had already sown a deep-rooted seed of doubt in his mind. While his proof might not be cast-iron, he had come up with one or two tantalizing snippets of information. Most of it centred on her work for German Intelligence during the latter stages of the war. She was one of the few remaining British-based agents Berlin had still trusted, but, in hindsight, her reports concerning the Allies' main area of attack was focused on Calais and not the Normandy beaches. They were, at best, misleading. Who knew, perhaps they were *deliberately* misleading.

He didn't doubt Joyce could explain it all away. At the time, her intelligence had seemed sound enough; she'd have certainly no reason to doubt it, nor had the German High Command. The Third Reich was in turmoil, fighting for its very existence. But, the one serious doubt in Frenzel's mind was whether she had aided Drescher to mislead not only Berlin but also leak secrets about troop positions to the Allies.

The actual situation was far more complicated, of course. Joyce soon began to realise, whatever half-truths or suspicions Schneider had managed to plant in his mind, they were both fortunately still unaware of the true extent of the Double Cross System, and the fact British Intelligence had actively run and controlled the German espionage system in the UK. It was something at least, but not much. Joyce knew she was rapidly running out of options.

'Tell me, my dear, did you know this Suite is packed full of surveillance equipment?'

She looked completely taken aback. 'Are you being serious?'

He smiled at her somewhat lamely. 'You and your MI5 friends really have done a rather good job at stitching me up, haven't you?'

'I know you probably won't believe me, but I swear to God, Josef, I've never betrayed you or the Fatherland!' she protested.

He breathed deeply. 'Sadly, Joyce, it's a little too late in the day to start plea bargaining. Oh, and if you were wondering about your people, I've had the Suite swept clean, but then again, I assume you already guessed we had!'

'Why would I?' she said definitely.

Joyce took a sip of her drink and began to realise something was wrong, very wrong. The bastard had spiked her drink, and she was starting to lose control. A wave of nausea suddenly swept over her entire body. She couldn't focus properly, and watched helplessly as the glass tumbled out of her grasp onto the floor. Its contents spreading in a dark stain on the plush carpet.

He looked on impassively as Joyce tried struggling to her feet, but her legs gave way. She started to lose consciousness and collapsed vulnerably onto the floor. He couldn't quite believe it had come to this, but he was under orders, and there was no other way. In her day, Joyce had been a top field agent and knew how to handle herself. Frenzel hadn't wanted to take a chance of her cutting up rough. Whether Schneider's accusations were true, or not, were, for the moment, immaterial. The *Schamhorst's* primary concern was delivering Schneider to South America.

Chapter 9
Bennett's, Chelsea, London

Jed Carter arrived at Bennett's for breakfast, and was shown to his table in the dining room. He was a little surprised Joyce Leader wasn't there to meet him. In the short time he'd known her, Joyce had always been a stickler for punctuality. They'd met on a couple of occasions since their first meeting at the Keogh Club, once at his office and then for lunch at Fortnum and Mason in Piccadilly.

The waiter hovered solicitously beside the table as Carter briefly inspected the breakfast menu. However much he might want a full English breakfast, there was no point in ordering before she arrived. Somewhat reluctantly, Carter ordered a pot of tea.

The waiter inclined his head deferentially. 'For two, sir?'

Carter snapped the menu shut. 'Yes, for two, thank you.'

'We have a selection of newspapers.'

'I'd like *The Times* please.'

As the young man snaked his way back through the tables, Carter reached into his jacket pocket and checked his leather bound diary. It was more for reassurance than anything else that he hadn't misread the timings. The dining room was busy, gently illuminated by four beautiful crystal chandeliers and laden with rich wood panelling. Carter kept an eye on the main entrance; there was a steady trickle of diners, but still no sign of Joyce.

The waiter swiftly returned with a silver salver and a neatly folded newspaper. 'Would sir like to order now or wait a little longer?'

'Could you bring me some toast?'

The young man took out his notepad. 'Do you prefer jam or marmalade?'

'Both.' Carter smiled. 'I have a sweet tooth.'

'Do you have any particular preference?'

'As it comes, thank you.' Carter again glanced toward the main entrance and began reading the newspaper. By 9.30, he'd had enough, and was starting to become seriously worried. Most of his toast had remained uneaten. He settled up the bill for his meagre breakfast and headed to the reception desk.

'May I use the phone?' he asked the smartly dressed girl behind the counter.

'Yes, sir, of course, you can,' she said, turning the phone around toward him.

In all, Carter made two calls. When he couldn't raise an answer from Joyce's suite at the Savoy, he contacted MI5. Spencer's secretary, Dawn, answered. 'Good morning,' she said briskly.

'It's Carter.'

There was a slight pause on the line. 'Is anything wrong Jed?'

'I need to speak with the boss.'

'He's tied up in a meeting with the Chief of Staff.'

'It's about Borgia.'

She was still known to the Department by her wartime codename. Dawn instinctively knew it was serious. 'Hold on a minute. I'll interrupt their meeting.'

As he waited, Carter mouthed a silent apology to the receptionist. The girl flashed him a broad smile. She was in no rush to be rid of such a handsome stranger. His slick, well-tailored suit bulged with muscle bound arms. It was just a pity he wasn't a regular at Bennett's. To her mind, the place could do with a younger, smarter set, rather than the usual mix of crusty politicians, businessmen, and wealthy widows.

Spencer eventually picked up the receiver in Dawn's office. 'What's all this about Borgia?' he queried.

'We'd arranged to meet for breakfast at Bennett's.'

'And?'

'I've been waiting for at least an hour, and she still hasn't turned up. It's not like Joyce at all.'

'No, it's not,' Spencer said thoughtfully. 'Have you called the Savoy?'

'Yes, sir.'

'Right, I'll ask Dawn to get over to the hotel and start checking things out.' Spencer glanced across the office at the wall clock. 'I'll meet you at the Savoy at about 10.15.'

Carter figured it wasn't so much a question as a command, and replied he'd take a cab and wait for him outside the hotel.

Spencer set the receiver down and turned to Dawn. 'Do we have last night's surveillance reports?'

She moved around the desk and sorted through the in-tray. 'They're here, sir,' she said, handing him a classified file.

Spencer looked her in the eye. Dawn was not only good at her job and totally discreet, but she also managed to juggle her role skillfully, while keeping abreast of the constant daily changes. She had her finger on the pulse of MI5's workload, and had become the lynchpin to the successful operation of his own role.

'Have you read the reports?' he asked pointedly.

'Not in any great detail, sir.' Dawn shrugged.

He smiled slightly and perched himself on the edge of the desk, and opening the file and searching for the latest sitreps on Josef Frenzel.

For the Director General's Eyes Only

Vehicle: Black Mercedes – (Diplomatic) CD Plate departed Embassy at 1440 hrs. Chauffeur – identified as Boris Baumann – passenger – backseat – Josef Frenzel.

1505: St. Philips Hotel, Westminster. Subject – Josef Frenzel enters hotel.

1536: Leaves accompanied by Professor Bernard Zimmerman. Vehicle heads south. Birdcage Walk to Parliament Square. Heavy traffic encountered due to a serious accident on the Embankment (North Side) Emergency Services in attendance. Traffic diverted.

1625: Contact lost with subject car due to the above accident.

His expression hardened. Accident or not, Spencer wasn't too impressed with the report. He closed the file and handed it back to Dawn. He already knew the answer, but asked all the same. 'Did you know they'd lost contact?'

Spencer could read her like a book. There was no point in denying it; she confessed she did. 'It wasn't their fault,' she said defensively. 'They did manage to pick up Frenzel's whereabouts later.'

'Really,' he smiled tautly, 'but how much later?'

'If you check the file, sir, I think you'll find it was about 1900hrs.'

He didn't say, but it was probably better than nothing, but not that much. It still smacked of incompetence. 'Where did they find him again?'

'The Savoy Hotel.'

'But, we already knew they were booked in to have dinner together?'

'Yes, sir,' she confessed lamely.

'Who was in charge of the surveillance team?'

Dawn knew it was a loaded question. Spencer was well aware she was engaged to the senior officer in charge of the detail. 'Jim Jarvis,' she said unnecessarily.

'When did Frenzel leave the hotel?'

'It was just after midnight.'

'Was he alone?'

'Yes, sir. He was picked up by his driver.'

Spencer didn't mean it unkindly but said, 'You know you could do a whole lot better for yourself than Jarvis.'

The trouble was Dawn suspected he was right. The annual confidential reports landed on her desk, she was also well aware he considered Jim to be a second eleven player. He was never going to be a top flight operative. She loved him all the same, and at the end of the day, what did it matter? He was kind, gentle, loyal, everything, in fact, a woman wanted in a man. It was her decision, her choice, and hers alone.

Dawn knew his advice was well meaning, but deep down, it still rankled. Not that she would ever admit it to Spencer, but she'd occasionally found herself questioning whether Jarvis's interest wasn't quite all it seemed. Maybe, he simply viewed her as nothing more than a means to an end, a chance to wheedle his way into the inner sanctum of MI5.

Spencer looked at her, almost indulgently. 'Do me a favour, will you?'

She looked at him quizzically.

'Tell your boyfriend, if he messes up and loses Herr Frenzel again, he'll be lucky to end up checking passports at Dover!'

Dawn looked at him bleakly, but didn't respond. She folded her arms tightly around the file. 'You mentioned something about wanting me to visit the Savoy?'

'I'd like you to speak with the reception staff and Joyce's maid to see when they last saw her. Don't make too much of it. The last thing we need is to start raising alarm bells. I'll meet you there later this morning; I shouldn't be too long.'

'Yes, sir.'

Spencer turned and headed back to his office. He depressed the door handle, paused, and glanced over his shoulder at her. 'Contact the car pool, and tell Evans to have my car ready at the front door for me.'

She nodded. 'I'll phone down immediately.'

Chapter 10
Gliddon Road, Southwark, London

Joyce hurt like hell. A sharp throbbing pain pulsed inside her head. Her mouth was parched. She forced her eyes open to find herself lying on a rickety camp bed, and instinctively made to move, but found her wrists and ankles were bound tightly. It ran through her mind it could have been worse; at least she hadn't been gagged.

'*The bastard!*' Joyce cursed, and momentarily closed her eyes again. She needed to take stock, to focus, and allow her training to kick in. She took a sharp intake of breath, opened her eyes, and allowed her gaze to glide slowly around the stark, unfamiliar room. In the centre stood a battered table and Windsor chair which had seen better days. Beside the door was a large galvanised bucket, it briefly crossed her mind maybe she was expected to use it as a toilet. Wherever she was, it certainly wasn't the Savoy. Motes of dust floated aimlessly in the shafts of light shining through a dirty sash cord window. There was a large London plane tree outside, shiny leaves wet with rain and its bark flaking off in small patches to expose new bark underneath.

God knew how long she had been here. Nor had Joyce any idea she was sharing Schneider's safe house. Frenzel had drugged her, but even so, it really couldn't have been easy removing her from the hotel undetected. But, what she couldn't understand was, why he hadn't killed her there and then? It didn't make sense. For some reason, Frenzel needed to keep her alive. It might only be temporarily, but there had to be a reason. As she lay helplessly on the bed, it crossed her mind they probably didn't want to run the risk of having a body on their hands. Well, at least not until Schneider was safely on his way back to South America.

Occasionally, she tried to loosen the cords binding her wrists, but doing so only served to chafe her skin red raw, and the painful welts began to bleed. Eventually, Joyce managed to wriggle herself toward the edge of the camp bed and sit upright. There were dark lines of exhaustion under her eyes. Right now, she figured her only chance of staying alive was Jed Carter becoming worried she hadn't shown up for breakfast at Bennett's. Joyce was realistic enough to know the chances of Carter managing to track her down alive were almost non-existent. It was only a matter of time before Frenzel returned, but how long would she have to wait, trussed up, feeling utterly helpless?

Try as she might to control it, a wave of panic suddenly swept over her, for Joyce knew, at some point, it was inevitable Frenzel would have her killed. The *Schamhorst* would demand it; she already knew too much about the escape plan, and was a potential liability. Frenzel would no doubt delegate the task to his faithful lackey, Erhard Lange. After all she'd gone through during the war, she certainly didn't want to die like this. More importantly, Joyce didn't want to die here, in this sordid, grubby little room.

Joyce momentarily shut her eyes; she desperately needed to clear her thoughts of fear and panic. There was no point breaking up and giving Frenzel and his cronies the satisfaction. She needed to dig deep and protest her innocence. If they killed her, then they'd have a dead body on their hands, and it'd be an encumbrance. No, they'd wait until Schneider was safe aboard the *Mendoza* before killing her. She had a little time left, but not that much.

Even though her thoughts were still hazy, Joyce tried concentrating to recall the events of last night in detail. But, it really wasn't easy; she was still suffering from the after-effects of being drugged. The memories returned in snapshots and fractured conversations. Frenzel had mentioned a Peter Wagner? But, if he'd worked alongside her German controllers, she'd have known all about him. Joyce was intrigued. Was he a figment of Schneider's twisted mind? Perhaps not, but instinct told her Schneider was playing a double-edged game. Maybe he was hiding something? Had he been afraid she was getting too close to Frenzel, or had he genuinely managed to discover the truth? There was simply no way of knowing, but one thing was sure, Schneider's enmity had sealed her fate.

Joyce vaguely remembered coming around and being manhandled into the boot of a car. Through a drug filled haze, her eyes had temporarily flashed with terror. She had desperately wanted to cry out, to beg Lange not to close the boot, but even if she'd had the strength, her pleas would have fallen on deaf ears. Lange slammed the lid shut, plunging her into a horrifyingly small, black void. *So this was it*, she'd thought, *would they torch the car or leave her to suffocate?*

The engine had juddered into life; her heart was racing out of control. Joyce recalled trying to reach out toward the catch on the inside of the lid, but the sedative must have kicked in again. The next thing she remembered was being carried up a flight of stairs. It must have been to this room, and then everything went black, as she drifted again into unconsciousness.

Joyce opened her eyes, and in frustration again tried to free herself, but as she did so, she heard footsteps and the sound of floorboards creaking. Joyce instinctively held her breath and waited. A key was placed in the lock; there was a click, and the brass door knob turned. Framed in the doorway was Josef Frenzel. He stared at her for a moment, looking through, rather than at, her. He closed the door, and without speaking, pulled up the Windsor chair in front of the camp bed. His eyes narrowed, and she found him looking at her with icy detachment. It was Joyce who broke the silence between them.

'What are you going to do with me?' Her voice was clipped, expressionless.

Frenzel was in no hurry to answer. He calmly reached into his jacket and retrieved a pack of cigarettes. He slipped one between his lips and flicked on his lighter. 'We'll be moving you later today.'

'Where to?'

'To the basement. Lange's clearing it out as we speak. The landlord's been using it for storage.' His eyes roamed toward the window. 'We can't have you slipping your tethers and making a bid for freedom.'

She raised her tightly bound wrists. 'I'm not exactly Houdini.'

'I wouldn't put anything pass you, my dear.' He drew on his freshly lit cigarette.

'How did you get me out of the hotel?'

He smiled a sad, almost cynical, smile. 'Lange bundled you into a laundry basket; we had a car waiting at the delivery entrance.'

It was something. At least she now knew how they had managed to spirit her out of the Savoy.

'I have to confess, Joyce, my first instinct was to kill you last night.'

'So, why didn't you?'

'Orders.'

'Orders?' she repeated curiously.

Frenzel sighed wearily. 'I was persuaded, for the time being, you were marginally more valuable to us alive than dead.'

She managed to conceal her surprise, and looked at him with a hint of defiance. 'You mean *Schneider* persuaded you?'

'It wasn't his call,' he said grimly.

'Whose call was it?'

Frenzel looked slightly rattled. 'The General.'

She arched her brows questioningly.

'General Dieter Aurberg,' he responded.

Joyce gave him a puzzled smile. She knew Aurberg headed up the *Schamhorst* network, however his involvement not only surprised but alarmed her. Recently, Aurberg had become something of an international spokesman for the entire post-war, neo-Nazi movement. Up until now, she had assumed Frenzel's paranoia about her past had been stirred up by Schneider and Schneider alone.

There was one thing she knew for certain; if Frenzel didn't manage to extricate Schneider from London, not only would the *Schamhorst* seek revenge, but his position at the Embassy would be fatally compromised. Ambassador von Bitten was respected by the West for covertly providing the Allies with vital information throughout the Second World War. If Frenzel's involvement with a Nazi ratline came to light, then von Bitten wouldn't hesitate to place him on the first available flight back to Germany, his career and reputation utterly destroyed.

Joyce gave him a long, slow look. 'I can't, for the life of me, think why General Aurberg would be interested in me.'

Frenzel pulled deeply on his cigarette and blew out a cloud of blue-grey smoke. 'I'm sure you don't.'

'Are you going to tell me?'

Frenzel crossed his legs and sat back in the chair, and regarding her thoughtfully. 'Does the name "Borgia" mean anything to you?'

Joyce looked at him with a mixture of fear and defiance. 'Yes, of course, it does,' she said matter-of-factly.

'I understand on good authority "Borgia" was your British codename.'

'Does this come from Schneider's mysterious friend, Peter Wagner?'

He pursed his lips together and exhaled a plume of smoke. 'Do you deny it?'

Deep down, Joyce knew her only hope was to come out fighting. 'Surely to God you aren't seriously accusing me of being a traitor to the *Fatherland*?'

'What do you think?'

She rolled her eyes. 'If Schneider ordered you to jump, you'd ask how high! Don't you see, he's still pulling your strings?'

'This isn't about Schneider. It's about your treachery!'

Joyce scoffed. 'You simply don't get it, do you!' she snapped angrily.

Frenzel arched his brows half questioningly, half in surprise. He admired her spirit. Even now, she still wasn't willing to go down without a fight. 'I don't know what you're on about,' he said, somewhat nonplussed.

'Do you actually know what I did during the war?'

There was a slight pause. 'You were an Abwehr agent operating in Britain.'

'Think about it, Josef. You were a member of German intelligence yourself, you still are. So, you must understand how it was. Things were very different; failure wasn't an option. I worked bloody hard to gain the respect of Berlin; it didn't just happen overnight!'

'I'm sure it didn't,' he said evenly.

She looked at him sharply, but there was nothing to read in his expression. 'How do you think I managed day in and day out to pass on so much high-grade intelligence?'

Frenzel inhaled deeply on his cigarette. 'Ah, *my dear*, therein lies the rub. You see, I'm not entirely sure,' he chortled and smiled almost mockingly at her.

Joyce knew she needed to fight back and perhaps sow a tiny seed of uncertainty in Frenzel's mind. Joyce suspected he still felt a glimmer of affection for her. But, he was hiding it well.

'You know how it was,' she persisted. 'We obeyed orders, and we never questioned them.'

Frenzel kept his thoughts to himself, but there was no denying, at their level, failure to follow orders would have resulted in certain death. Even his own mother, Minna, served a week's prison sentence for being late for work two days running, after the RAF had bombed Delmenhorst and severely damaged their home. Her punishment was washing the stone steps of the local prison from top to bottom, then starting over again for twelve hours a day.

He listened in silence as Joyce pleaded her case. How she had been expected to foster contacts within both the British military and industry. To use any means to extricate information. To bed them, and, if necessary, blackmail her honey trap victims into revealing even more vital snippets of intelligence. As the war progressed, so did the increasingly insatiable demands of the German High Command.

Joyce paused; there was seemingly genuine reproof in her eyes. 'Do you honestly believe I could have achieved all that without becoming a double agent? Drescher needed me on the inside, to lull British Intelligence into thinking I was working for them. I had a lucky break.'

'You mean bedding John Eldridge.'

She smiled slightly. 'He was young and surprisingly naive. As far as Drescher was concerned, it was a major coup to bag an MI5 agent.'

He answered non-committedly, 'I can see it would be.'

'Right up until the bitter end,' she said passionately, 'I continued to pass top secret intelligence to Drescher and Berlin.'

'But, were you playing fast and loose? That's the question, my dear. In my shoes, what would you do? What would you think?'

He had a point, but she still continued to plead her innocence. Joyce was not only playing for time but also banking on the fact her wartime Abwehr handler, Bernard Drescher, was dead. There was really no-one else left, or so she hoped, to refute her story. The only fly in the ointment was Peter Wagner, but she didn't know who the hell he was.

Frenzel wanted, needed to believe her, but his thoughts remained unspoken. 'You have to understand, my dear, like yourself, I'm merely obeying orders.' He smiled lamely. 'The *Schamhorst* finds itself in a very awkward situation.'

She continued to look at him defiantly.

'How can we know for sure you're not still working for British Intelligence? Until Schneider turned up unannounced on my doorstep, I certainly didn't travel around London with a firearm. Former agent or not, I really wasn't expecting to find a Beretta hidden away in your handbag. More to the point, Joyce, it's General Aurberg's call and not mine. It's out of my hands.'

'Nothing changes, does it,' she said, casting him a rueful smile. 'They'll always be as thick as thieves, sticking together like glue.'

'I know exactly what you're thinking, Joyce, but trust me, it really isn't like that. Aurberg and Schneider might go back a long way. We all know they were close friends during the war, but the General's decision has nothing whatsoever to do with their past friendship. It's more to do with Sir Spencer Hall.' He breathed deeply, and began to play with the cigarette between his fingers. 'We all know he has his own agenda, his own reasons for wanting Helmut Schneider dead.'

Joyce feigned ignorance, and professed she didn't know what he was talking about.

'It doesn't matter,' Frenzel said, without interest. 'We simply can't afford to take chances.'

Joyce had given it her best shot, but realised that whatever Frenzel may or may not personally believe, General Aurberg's decision was final.

Chapter 11
The Savoy Hotel, London

A black taxi pulled up outside the imposing entrance to the Savoy Hotel. Carter paid the cabbie, and automatically checked out the four vehicles parked along the narrow street near the entrance of the theatre. As yet, there wasn't any sign of Spencer's ex-commando driver, the bearlike Freddy Evans. He decided to wander the short distance back to the corner of the road overlooking The Strand and wait there for them. The rush-hour traffic was slowly dying down, but there was still a steady stream of double-decker buses pulling up and discharging passengers on their way to work at the numerous shops and offices in the busy surrounding area.

Carter lit up a cigarette and pulled his jacket collar up against biting autumnal breeze. As it happened, he didn't have to wait too long before he caught sight of Spencer's familiar racing green Rover as it did a sharp right turn across The Strand toward the hotel. Spencer liked to ring the changes and used a variety of vehicles from MI5's large car pool; his preference was something that wouldn't stand out, but this Rover was a particular favourite of his.

As Evans drew into the curb beside Carter, he smiled through the windscreen in recognition. Evans switched off the engine, jumped out of the car, and opened the rear door.

'Haven't seen you for a while, Jed,' he said.

'No, I've not been into the office recently. You could say the boss has been keeping me on my toes,' Carter answered non-committedly.

Spencer alighted from the car and paused to straighten his overcoat. 'We shouldn't be too long,' he said to Evans.

'Okay, sir. I'll sit tight here.'

'Just make certain you don't get another ruddy parking ticket,' he chuckled.

'Bloody parking wardens,' Evans grunted. 'Like sodding little Hitlers all of 'em!'

'Yes, Freddy, but just don't go hitting any more of them. Otherwise, I might not be able to swing another assault charge with the police.'

'Don't you worry about me, sir. I've learnt me lesson.'

'I hope to God you have, Freddy. It cost me several bottles of Scotch last time around to convince the Met to drop the charges.'

Behind Spencer's back, Carter winked at Evans before following Spencer inside the hotel. They walked through the foyer and straight to the lifts. On the fifth floor, Spencer headed the way down a long corridor on the plush, blue carpet to Joyce's palatial suite. He produced a set of keys from his overcoat pocket and unlocked the door. It opened on to a large, tastefully decorated, high-ceilinged living room.

Carter quietly closed the door behind them and took his time taking in the strangely eclectic mix of antique and modern furniture. To his mind, it shouldn't have worked, but somehow, it did. There was the usual debris of life, books and family photos. His gaze was finally drawn to the original artwork lining the walls. He was certainly no art expert, but guessed they were probably worth a small fortune. On an MI5 officer's salary, he'd have been lucky to have afforded to buy one of the smaller gilt frames without going into serious debt.

Spencer noticed his interest. 'Everything, including the furniture is from her private collection. Joyce has been a permanent fixture at the hotel for so long the management allow her to do more or less as she pleases.' As he eased himself out of his overcoat and slung it over the back of the sofa, there was a knock at the door. 'That'll be Dawn,' he said, without missing a beat.

Carter managed to hide his surprise well, but he couldn't imagine why Dawn had been dispatched to the Savoy. It seemed like overkill, or, at least, it did to him. He went over to the door and let her in. She smiled briefly in greeting and breezed past into the living room.

'How did you get on?' Spencer asked.

'I checked with the reception staff; no-one's seen Joyce since last night. There was nothing out of the ordinary, other than she reported a broken tap in the bathroom.'

'Did they say anything else?'

'No. Well, at least nothing worth mentioning.'

'Have you managed to speak with her maid yet?'

'Lord, yes, but you know what Hetty's like. I could scarcely get a word in edgeways. She turned her bed down as usual at seven-thirty. By that time, Joyce was already downstairs having a drink at the American Bar with Frenzel. That confirms the report from the Watchers team; they saw them arrive a little after seven.'

'They don't suspect anything's wrong, do they?'

'No,' Dawn confirmed. 'At least, I don't think they do. They know me well enough by now. Joyce and I have been friends for years. Besides, we have lunch here at least once a month.'

Carter realised maybe, in the future, he shouldn't be quite so quick to judge, at least not where Spencer was concerned. As a familiar face, Dawn's presence at the hotel had been low key, and less likely to arouse suspicion amongst the staff.

She cast Spencer a rather uneasy smile. 'I didn't make a big deal of it. After all, it wouldn't be the first time Joyce had taken herself off on a whim, would it?' Her eyes suddenly started filling with tears. 'You know what she was like. It was usually Monte Carlo,' she sniffed, 'followed by a postcard saying wish you were here, knowing bloody full well I was stuck in the office with.'

'With *me*!' Spencer said, with a deadpan expression, before swiftly turning his attention back to Carter. 'Will you take a look around the suite, Jed?'

'Yes, sir.'

'You can leave the living room to me; Dawn can show you around the rest of the place.'

She took her cue. 'The door on the right leads straight into the bedroom,' she said, crossing the room. He followed her.

Spencer waited a moment before moving over to an ornate Victorian pedestal desk. The suite had been under constant surveillance since Joyce had bravely agreed to take on the assignment. It was a win, win situation, or so it had seemed. British Intelligence could glean vital information, while at the same time provide Joyce with immediate backup, if Frenzel unexpectedly cut up rough.

But, last night, all of Spencer's heartfelt assurances and plans to keep her safe had failed. Something had gone drastically wrong with the operation. As he searched the room, his mind tumbled back to the war. When he first met her, it had been evident, beneath all the bravado, she'd been scared witless and full of self-doubt. He'd given her a lifeline, a chance to become not only a double agent but also a way of surviving the war. It was a lifeline which had eventually saved the lives of countless Allied servicemen.

Spencer picked up the phone off the desk and unscrewed the receiver, inspected the microphone, and carefully replaced it before heading to the Picasso hanging over the faux fireplace. He lifted the frame and then purposely returned to the centre of the room, pulled up a chair under the chandelier, climbed on the seat, and checked the surveillance equipment.

Everything was starting to fall into place. Spencer paused a moment, gathering his thoughts before returning to the desk. He sat down gathered up the paperwork scattered across the leather bound worktop and systematically searched through it. There were a couple of gilt-edged invites, a letter from her sister in Germany and countless shop receipts. He then proceeded to open each of the drawers in turn. He pulled out her diary and began methodically working his way through it. There was nothing out of the ordinary, but he hadn't expected there would be. Someone as experienced as Joyce would never have committed anything incriminating to paper.

Hearing Carter and Dawn talking quietly outside the bedroom, he glanced over his shoulder toward them and called out, 'Did you find anything?'

Carter re-joined him. 'Well, it's pretty obvious someone's on to us. I don't know about the living room, but the rest of the surveillance equipment appears to have been either cleared out or sabotaged.'

'It's the same in here,'

'Do we know exactly what happened here last night? Surely to God, the Watchers team must have realised something was wrong. They knew she had dinner downstairs and returned to the suite with Frenzel about half nine.'

Spencer closed the diary and placed it back in the drawer. 'Apparently, the team leader thought it was a glitch, a technical fault,' he said reflectively. 'In fairness, it's not the first time we've had an issue.'

'What did they do?'

'Well, that's just it. Nothing.' Spencer said sharply, 'other than relying on eyeball contact to clock Frenzel leaving the hotel.'

'Who was in charge?'

Spencer's gaze came to rest briefly on Dawn. 'Jim Jarvis.'

Carter pursed his lips together. He wanted to let rip about Jim's rank incompetence, but unusually decided to err on the side of caution, and diplomatically kept his thoughts to himself. But, things were not looking too bright for Jarvis's future in the Service. After Frenzel's driver managed to give him the slip, he was already on borrowed time.

'Dawn, do you mind waiting downstairs in the car?' Spencer asked her. 'I shouldn't be too much longer up here.'

In fairness, she seemed almost relieved to be stood down. She loved Jim dearly, but knew his career was effectively over. He'd probably be moved to some mundane pen pushing Civil Service job, something more suited to his skills. She couldn't discuss it with him, but she guessed even Jim must have grasped he didn't have a long-term future with the service.

Carter waited until she'd left the room before saying, 'It's not my call, sir, I know, but I can't afford to have Jarvis screwing anything else up. I need someone to watch my back, someone I can trust!'

While Spencer sympathised with him, time was not on their side. He would deal with Jarvis in due course, but right now, he needed Carter to take him under his wing and see the Schneider Case through to the bitter end. Even Carter couldn't deny Jarvis was pretty handy with a gun, and had initially earned his spurs in the Service as a sniper. Maybe he was promoted too quickly, or maybe he just wasn't cut out to be a field agent. The system was usually pretty slick at weeding out the wheat from the chaff, but just occasionally, someone slipped through the net and was found wanting. Up until now, Jarvis's record had been quite exemplary.

It was evident to Carter whatever Spencer's views were, he didn't have the time to dissect the rights and wrongs of Jarvis's performance. Carter had no alternative other than to accept Spencer's decision; it was final and not up for discussion. He also couldn't help wondering whether Joyce had slipped up somewhere along the line. Perhaps she'd simply been out of the game for too long, or Spencer had expected too much of her.

'We could be missing a point here, sir,' Carter suggested.

Spencer stood up from the desk and looked at him expectantly.

'We're automatically assuming Frenzel is behind her disappearance, but there could be another explanation.'

'Like what?'

'It could be down to Mossad?'

'I think you'll find, Carter, Mossad's involvement in this caper is something of a red herring.'

His expression registered surprise. 'I know the Foreign Secretary was hedging his bets about an Israeli hit squad being on Schneider's tail, but.'

Spencer held up a hand. 'There is a hit squad, Jed; it just doesn't happen to be an Israeli one.'

'Who then?' Carter queried.

'You've read Schneider's file,' he said, almost as if it was a challenge. 'Think about it; there's always been a question mark about his escape from East Germany.'

'Well, I know, but if I remember correctly didn't the records confirm the *Schamhorst* bribed his prison guards and two high-ranking Stasi intelligence officers?'

'I know on paper it looks pretty watertight. General Aurberg personally signed off a small fortune from the ratline funds to secure his release. Aurberg would have moved heaven and earth to see Schneider walk free. Only hard line Nazis ended up in Jamiltz Internment Camp. It tended to be a one-way ticket to oblivion; old scores were settled, and more importantly, Schneider had blood on his hands, Soviet blood. You've been in the Service long enough now to know the

Kremlin would never have allowed someone of Schneider's standing to walk away Scot free. Money talks, that's true enough, but ask yourself: how did Schneider survive inside the camp for so many years? Jamiltz was controlled by the Soviet intelligence service; they enforced a total isolation policy. No-one was legally charged with war crimes; they simply disappeared. The others, well, death was primarily down to a combination of starvation and disease. Thousands of prisoners died at Jamiltz, but Schneider survived *and* escaped? It doesn't add up.'

'The story goes that his luck changed when the Politburo handed the camp over to the East Germans,' Carter suggested.

'And maybe pigs can fly.' Spencer smirked. 'Of all his Gestapo colleagues at Jamiltz, he's the only one to have escaped. Now, he could have got lucky, but I doubt it. As for the rest, they were eventually shipped off to Siberia.'

Carter knew what he was getting at. That Schneider had agreed, either in desperation or under duress, to spy for the Soviet Union. His escape from Jamiltz, aided by the *Schamhorst*, was the perfect cover. Aurberg and his cohorts would have been none the wiser. In fact, it would have been utterly unthinkable Soviet Intelligence had turned their esteemed colleague into a communist agent.

Carter understood all that, but still decided to play Devil's advocate and suggested, 'But, we can't rule out the *Schamhorst* didn't play a blinder and called in a few favours from behind the Iron Curtain. The *Schamhorst* has very deep pockets, and if they managed to bribe the right people in East Germany, say, old comrades in arms, then they could have lifted him out from under the Soviets' noses, without their knowledge.'

Although he accepted Carter had a valid point, it was evident Spencer not only remained unconvinced but possibly had something else on Schneider, something irrefutable. If he did, Carter guessed he wasn't quite ready to share it.

'So what you are really saying is, if Mossad is out of the equation, then who wants Schneider dead?' Carter pressed him.

'Do I really have to *spell* it out to you?'

'The way I see it, sir, it could go one or two ways. Either General Aurberg has discovered his friend has jumped ship, or Schneider has fallen foul of his KGB spymasters.'

Spencer took his overcoat off the sofa and shrugged it back on. 'What's your gut instinct?'

Carter took his time answering. 'Moscow?'

'Okay, so where does that leave us now?'

He was being tested; he knew that. Spencer wanted to know what he'd do, what his next move would be. His priority was Schneider, that much was a given, but Joyce Leader's disappearance had not only thrown a spanner in the works, it could also jeopardise the entire investigation.

Whether Frenzel had a hand in it was still very much open to conjecture, but he was certainly the last person to have seen her at the Savoy. Whatever way you looked at it, Frenzel was the lynchpin to both Leader's whereabouts and Schneider's passage to South America.

Carter's initial reaction was, in the grand scheme of things, Joyce was expendable, and they should focus the entire operation on preventing Schneider from boarding the *Mendoza*. In his view, she was probably already dead anyway, so why waste the manpower on trying to track her down. He spoke his mind, but suspected Spencer had his own agenda, and it didn't quite fit in with his own rather clinical assessment of the situation.

Changing the subject entirely, he said unexpectedly, 'I'd like you to take Jim Jarvis under your wing.' Carter's expression closed down immediately, which prompted a flicker of amusement from Spencer. 'I know what you're thinking.'

'Do you, sir?'

'You'd rather take him out, and so would I, but it's a little late in the day to be arguing the toss.' Spencer took his time buttoning up his overcoat. 'You've got to trust me on this one, Carter.'

'What exactly do you want me to do?'

'Stick to Frenzel like glue.'

'You mean take over the surveillance team?'

'Lock, stock, and barrel. The one thing we know is Frenzel is a creature of habit and enjoys the rather seedier side of London.'

'Strip joints?'

'To be precise, Soho Strip joints, Shepherd's Bush Market for cheap end prostitutes. You name it, he's been there. The rougher, the better. But, ever since Joyce managed to hook him, let's just say he hasn't paid for sex.'

'So, if he's not buying sex, what does he do?'

'He still likes to sink a few drinks at the Anaxos Club in Greek Street. You know the type of place. The hostesses wear low cut tight fitting dresses, and make-up piled on with a trowel. It's become something of a ritual with him. He regularly drops in after work, usually about five-ish. Give me a call at the office, if he turns up there this afternoon.'

'And then what, sir?'

'You're to meet me outside, Carter, that's what!'

As Spencer made his way out of the hotel, he felt a deep sense of guilt about reactivating Joyce's file, but hurriedly stifled it. He needed to keep a level head. Emotion only muddied the waters, and this was no way to run an operation.

Chapter 12
Federal German Republic Embassy

Jed Carter was dropped off at the end of the road and headed toward a parked grey Ford Cortina. He opened the driver's door, placed his right arm on the roof and leaned forward. Jim Jarvis was at the wheel.

'Move over,' he said, sharply.

'You're running late, Jed!'

'To hell I am, just shift your bloody arse over, will you!'

Jim held his cold, probing stare. There was a moment's hesitation before he gave in to the senior officer's command and shuffled across to the passenger seat. Carter climbed in beside him and closed the door. Carter eyed the other man briefly. He was dark haired, about five foot eleven, with hazel eyes; his features were too narrow to be considered handsome. God only knew why Dawn was so infatuated with the ruddy man. Maybe it was nothing more than envy on his part? Carter let the thought go. Analysing Dawn's love life wasn't a priority. In fact, it wasn't a priority at all, at least not right now.

'Any sign of Frenzel?'

'Not since lunchtime.'

'Where did he go?'

'He popped into Barkers on Kensington High Street, and bought himself a pair of trousers and a rather snazzy striped silk tie.'

'And then what?'

Jarvis shot him an irritated glance. 'He returned to the Embassy. It's all in the log,' he added defensively.

'Yeah, well, I'm glad something is!'

Jarvis looked at him sharply. 'What in hell's that supposed to mean?'

'It means if you weren't so tasty with that sodding PPK, I'd have refused to work with you!'

Jarvis passed him a weary, somewhat cynical, smile. 'Well, whatever way we look at it, Jed, that's really not your *call*, is it?'

'You're living on borrowed time with the Service; even you must realise that, Jim?' If he did, he kept his thoughts very much to himself. 'So, what happened last night at the Savoy?' Carter pressed.

'You must have read the report.'

'But, I'd rather hear it from the horse's mouth. You were in charge of the surveillance op. What went wrong?'

'We thought there was a technical hitch,' Jarvis explained. 'We've had a couple of temporary blackouts before.'

'How many?'

'Two.'

'When and where?'

'Shortly after the equipment was installed, we had a half hour break in transmission at the hotel.'

'And when was the second time?'

'At Frenzel's flat in West London. It was down to a power cut.'

'What, on both occasions?'

'No, the break at the Savoy was due to a loose connection, but the tech staff soon fixed it.'

'Only last night wasn't down to a power cut or a loose connection, was it?'

'We weren't to know that,' Jarvis said reflectively.

A silence fell between the two men as Jarvis stared unseeingly through the windscreen. He knew full well he'd screwed up, but he didn't need to hear it, least of all from Jed Carter. It was one thing to be balled out by the boss, but Carter was a young, arrogant so and so, who was relatively new to the business, and it rankled with him.

'When you eyeballed Frenzel leaving the hotel, you should have checked to see if Joyce was safe.'

He didn't respond.

'For Christ's sake, Jim, it's standard procedure. We've not only lost valuable time trying to find out what happened to her, but, also, our surveillance equipment was sabotaged. For Christ's sake, we've been left playing catch up.'

'I could have blundered in while they were together, but I'd only have ended up blowing the entire assignment. It was my call, and I'll have to live with it!'

'You might well have to live with it, Jed, but Joyce may well have paid with her life!'

Jarvis really didn't need telling that he'd screwed up.

'When you eyeballed Frenzel leaving the hotel, didn't you think to check on her?'

'My priority was to keep tabs on Frenzel.'

It took every fibre of his control not to allow his anger to show. 'Okay,' Carter managed to say evenly, 'so who else, other than her maid, Hetty, had access to the suite yesterday?'

'The maintenance staff. There was a problem with the plumbing.'

'Did you check them out?'

'Of course! The snag was listed on the hotel's worksheet.'

'I don't care what was on the ruddy worksheet. Did you run it by the building manager?'

'I didn't bother,' Jarvis admitted, albeit reluctantly. 'At the time it all seemed above board.'

'I can guarantee whoever entered the suite wasn't employed by the hotel unless, of course, they have surveillance experts on their books!'

Jarvis folded his arms defensively. The hazel green eyes regarded him warily. 'I guess whatever way you look at it, Jed, we're bloody stuck with one another.'

Carter opened a pack of Player's cigarettes and offered one to Jarvis. He figured it was probably time to call a temporary truce between them. They might have got off to a bad start, but he needed his support, regardless of what had happened.

Jarvis hesitated before accepting the proffered cigarette. Carter handed him a box of matches, apologising that his lighter was out of fuel. Jarvis smiled slightly and struck the match to light it.

'Before you ask,' Jarvis added, flicking the spent match into the dashboard-mounted ashtray, 'we have every exit to the Embassy covered. But, if things start kicking off on

Friday morning when the *Mendoza* arrives at the docks, then we'll end up being stretched pretty thin on the ground. I've put in a request for extra backup from Special Branch.'

'Have you heard anything from the office?'

'Not yet.'

'They'll need to come up with something pretty smartish.'

'I hope so, Jed,' he said, taking a draw on his cigarette. 'Otherwise, we'll all be up shit creek without a paddle!'

'Maybe we will,' he answered, placing an unlit cigarette between his lips. Jarvis returned the box of matches. 'Thanks.'

Carter imagined the decision hinged on Spencer having a deep and meaningful conversation with Assistant Commissioner Luke Garvan. For a start, he'd need to come clean about reactivating Joyce Leader's file and how MI5 had failed to protect her. It certainly wouldn't be an easy call, and no doubt Spencer had stalled doing so for as long as he reasonably could. But, within the next twenty-four hours, he'd have to take the bull by the horns and explain to his old friend exactly what had happened, and that he'd let Joyce down.

Spencer desperately needed not only extra undercover Special Branch officers, but also the help of Garvan's numerous contacts in the Port of London Authority, without delay.

**

At 1810, four hours after Carter had joined the surveillance team, the call came through from the team covering the rear of the building. Frenzel had been spotted leaving the Embassy in a chauffeur-driven Mercedes. Jarvis replaced the receiver on the console. Carter started up the Cortina and let the engine idle until the black Mercedes swept past them. To lessen the risk being spotted, he waited a moment. Ideally, he needed to keep at least two cars between them.

'Call the Office,' Carter said, pulling out of the curb. 'Let them know we're on the move.'

Jarvis reached for the receiver. 'He'll be heading to the Anaxos Club.'

Chapter 13
Anaxos Club, Greek Street, Soho

Spencer Hall pushed open the door, entering the Anaxos Club, followed by Carter. Across the bar, Josef Frenzel was sitting by himself, a haze of blue smoke rising from behind his newspaper. Spencer paused for a moment, marvelling at the gaudy décor; it was all red flock wallpaper and peeling gold paint. The low, golden lighting, did little to hide the grubby, seedy interior. The Anaxos was in dire need of a complete overhaul. However, if rumour was to be believed, its staunchly loyal clientele had resisted not only a lick of paint but any attempt by the owners to modernize the Club.

Someone was playing and singing at the piano, and had gathered a small audience. As Spencer had described to Carter, the waitresses were dressed uniformly; typical Soho Club hostesses low cut tight fitting dresses and heavily made up. The girls were all very young and attractive. The laws governing hostesses in Soho were very strict. They were forbidden to solicit punters during opening hours. However, if they managed to drum up some private business, it was deemed to be the girls' affair and not the Club's. If the proprietors were found taking a cut of their earnings, they ran the very real risk of being closed down by Westminster Council and the Met Police.

Spencer turned to Carter. 'Get the drinks in, will you.'

Carter reached for his wallet. 'What are you having?'

'A double scotch on the rocks.'

'Do you want me to join you?'

'Yes,' he said sharply, and headed across the Club.

Frenzel was far too involved with his newspaper even to notice their arrival. Perhaps he'd grown complacent. In the past, he was never quite this cavalier, or careless. Right now, Spencer needed to start reeling him in and applying the pressure. If it wasn't already too late, he might just be able to save Joyce Leader's life.

Spencer's rich, velvety voice cut in on his reading. 'I thought I'd find you here.'

Frenzel half-turned in his chair. 'Ah, Sir Spencer, what a pleasant surprise!' he said, barely managing to conceal his horror. 'I've never seen you here before.'

'No.' Spencer smiled. 'To be honest with you, I can think of any number of places I'd rather sink a few drinks than the Anaxos Club.'

'So what brings you here?' he asked warily.

'Business, my dear Josef, business.'

Frenzel set his newspaper down, and waved to the chair opposite him. Spencer took his cue and sat down. 'Would you care for a drink?'

'No, thanks. I've already ordered.'

Frenzel caught a glimpse of Jed Carter standing at the bar. He instantly recognised him as the tall, young good looking man Joyce had introduced as Fred Tolly at the Foreign Office Cocktail Party. Whatever his real name was, he doubted it was Tolly. Maybe Schneider had not been that far off about Joyce Leader working for British Intelligence. In which case, by now, she'd have stacked up a whole raft of incriminating evidence against him. If Leader was a plant, then MI5 had already discovered his involvement with Schneider and the *Schamhorst*. In the past, he'd sailed close to the wind, but this time, it looked like his luck had finally run out.

'What about your man over there?' he said, gesturing toward the bar.

Spencer briefly followed his gaze. 'He can take care of himself.'

'I'm sure he can. Will he be joining us?'

Spencer felt the other man's eyes examining him carefully. 'I hope so, Josef. I've just ordered a large scotch on the rocks.'

Frenzel's watchful eyes held Spencer for a fraction of a second. The all-powerful Director General of MI5 didn't make social calls to someone of his standing. Spencer's unexpected appearance at the Anaxos Club could mean only one thing: his days at the Embassy were numbered. Frenzel's thoughts were beginning to spiral into freefall.

Spencer's gaze glided irritably across the club toward the woman playing the piano. She was singing a melody of songs from latest hit musicals. She had a mop of dyed, jet black curls and a well-lined face, which could, at best, be described charitably as lived in. The traditional, heavy make-up of a night club hostess looked faintly absurd on a woman in her mid to late sixties.

'Who is she?' he asked.

'A friend of the owner.'

'Does she do requests?'

'Why don't you ask? What would you like her to sing?'

'I'd like her to stop that bloody caterwauling.'

Frenzel's expression froze. He didn't quite know how to respond.

'She can't hold a tune to save her life!'

'Rosie's very popular here.'

Spencer arched his brows. 'You do surprise me.'

Carter brought the drinks over from the bar and joined them at the table. 'I don't think there's any need for introductions, is there?' Spencer smiled coldly at Frenzel.

He returned a rather forced smile which lifted to his cheeks and crinkled his eyes. 'I'm sure you're well aware we've already met. Fred Tolly, isn't it?' Frenzel mumbled.

Carter nodded and said, 'Good to see you again, sir.'

Knocking the ash off his cigarette into the glass ashtray on the table, Frenzel took a sharp intake of breath. 'Shall we just drop the niceties and get down to business, gentlemen?'

Spencer took a large swig of whisky before reaching down for the leather briefcase beside his chair. He opened it, searched inside, and handed over a plain brown envelope. His face remained calm, but the eyes were glacial.

In Spencer's experience, he'd always struck him as a man of few words or at least few worth remembering. There was a moment's silence. Frenzel's anxious voice broke it. 'What's this?' He again looked at the envelope, and raised his eyes nervously.

'Why not open it and see?'

Frenzel hesitated before slitting open the envelope. He pulled out the contents; his eyes carefully ran over them. There were several pages of transcripts, either taken at his flat in Kensington or the Savoy. He hurriedly skipped through the pages. There was no need to read everything in minute detail; he'd already gotten the gist of the report. In the past, he'd always been able to bluster his way out of seemingly impossible situations. But, this time, Spencer had well and truly trumped him.

Frenzel's pulse suddenly began to quicken as he shuffled through the explicit photos taken with a hidden camera of him and Joyce Leader. He guessed this was just a taster of things to come. As he stared down at the photos, his mind was in turmoil. So far, Spencer hadn't mentioned Schneider, but he was probably just playing with him, keeping him on edge. 'What are you going to do with all this?'

'That all depends.'

'Depends?' he repeated warily.

Spencer thoughtfully toyed with the whisky glass between his hands. 'I've found your Ambassador, Hans von Bitten, always plays with a straight bat.'

Frenzel had heard the cricketing term before. 'Yes, he's a good man,' he conceded. 'An honourable man.'

Spencer inclined his head toward the brown envelope. 'Yes, he is. You've got to admit, there's more than enough stuff in there to send you packing back to your wife and family in Osnabrück.'

That thought had already crossed his mind. Thus far, Spencer was stating no more than the bloody obvious.

Carter intervened, 'Given von Bitten's strict security guidance for his Embassy staff, we were just a little surprised the man who drafted the rule book ended up contravening his own advice.'

Frenzel somewhat reluctantly accepted it was a point well made. He assured Carter there was really no need for him to spell it out, but he did so all the same. Embassy officials were required to clear visitors to their private homes with their security staff or British diplomatic protection, preferably both. The latter was mainly staffed by Luke Garvan's Special Branch officers, but not exclusively. There was also a number of British Intelligence officers embedded within the setup. By inviting Professor Zimmerman and then Joyce Leader to his flat, without prior clearance, Frenzel had bypassed strict

Embassy procedure. As the head of security, he'd not only left himself wide open to blackmail, but his position had now become completely untenable.

'We've compiled a report for the Ambassador,' Carter continued smoothly.

Spencer gave him the nod; he'd signed it off before leaving the office.

'There's nothing criminal about your actions naturally, but in the wrong hands, it could be seen, let's say, as a kind of impropriety.' Carter paused to take a sip of his beer. 'A series of late-night visits to your home, without prior consent. You know how these things look in the press … rumours of a senior Embassy official embroiled in a potential scandal.'

'But, only if the rumours were leaked to the press,' Frenzel came back at him.

Carter shrugged indifferently. 'These things happen, Herr Frenzel, but as you know, von Bitten is a stickler for rules. We also have to take into consideration the sensitivities of our American friends. Zimmerman is their man; he's supposed to be here in London on official business and not some bloody Nazi reunion.'

Spencer cut in; he didn't want him going too far, at least not just yet. 'The report is, how shall I say, very much the sanitised version of events.'

Frenzel narrowed his eyes questioningly. 'I'm afraid you've completely lost me.'

'Have I?'

'What do you mean by the *sanitised* version?'

'Well, that all depends on upon how this pans out, but, as things stand, I don't think we need to bother the Ambassador, not just yet, with all the sordid little details, do we?'

Frenzel still played dumb; he didn't quite know what else to do.

'The trouble is, I still have a feeling you've really no idea Helmut Schneider has played you and your friends in the *Schamhorst* like a fiddle.'

He was dismissive. 'Really, I would have thought you of all people could have come up with something a little better than that.'

'So, you do not deny your involvement with Schneider then?'

'Why waste time? Anyway, I guess it's probably a little too late in the day for denials. But, please, don't insult my intelligence by accusing him of being a traitor. Besides, Sir Spencer, I'm well aware you have a particular interest in my old friend.'

'That's beside the point. Whatever way you look at it, Schneider's a war criminal.'

'He was obeying orders.'

'Orders or not, he seemed to take particular pleasure in killing defenceless women and children.'

'I know where this is going,' Frenzel grunted. 'Lieutenant Jamie Hall wasn't exactly defenceless, though, was he? Your brother was a member of the SAS and a trained killer.'

Spencer gave him a wintry smile. 'Jamie didn't deserve to be tortured, forced to dig his own grave, and then shot in the back of the head by Schneider any more than anyone else.'

Frenzel folded his arms sighing. 'You have your own agenda; I know that. But, please, spare me this endless merry-go-round of false accusations. I don't deny in the past I've had my differences with Schneider, who hasn't? I'll admit, he's not the easiest of people. But, I still owe a debt of honour to the *Schamhorst*; it's just the way it is. When the call came through Schneider was on the run from Mossad, however much I might have wanted to, I simply couldn't turn my back on him.'

'But, that's just it, Josef,' Spencer said, with the merest hint of a smile. 'You see, it's not Mossad after his blood but the KGB.'

Frenzel rolled his eyes. 'You won't let up, will you? The British and Americans have been circulating these tired, old rumours for years. The trouble is, Sir Spencer, no-one gives them any credence, at least not any longer. It cost us a great deal of money securing Schneider's release from behind the Iron Curtain. But, even so, it was money well spent. As a former member of the Gestapo, he warranted both our support and allegiance.'

Spencer took his time answering. He calmly eased a pack of cigarettes out of his hip pocket, carefully unwrapped the cellophane, scrunched it up, and placed it in the ashtray. Carter offered his lighter; Spencer thanked him. Frenzel suspected the wily old bastard had something else up his sleeve, but what? He was a little surprised he hadn't mentioned Joyce, so far.

Spencer took a long drag on the cigarette before deliberately blowing a swirl of grey smoke in Frenzel's direction. 'What do you know about Schneider's sister, Anna?' His manner was clipped, almost perfunctory.

Frenzel considered his reply carefully. 'She died during the Russian advance.'

'Anything else?'

'Only that she was raped by Soviet troops and died of her injuries.'

'And what about the rest of the family?'

'They perished in a bombing raid.'

'You mean Anna's children?'

Frenzel nodded. 'Yes, along with their grandparents. It was a terrible time for all of us, more so for Schneider.'

'Why?'

'I, at least, had the opportunity to surrender to the Americans, rather than be swept up by the Russians. Schneider, on the other hand, wasn't quite so lucky.'

'No, I suppose not. He ended up in Jamiltz Internment Camp. There were what, forty, fifty thousand prisoners?'

Frenzel shrugged indifferently. 'I've no idea.'

'The trouble is, there's a serious flaw with Schneider's story.'

Frenzel regarded him thoughtfully. 'Whatever it is, I have a feeling you're about to enlighten me.'

'Well, for a start, Anna and her family are very much alive and well, living in East Berlin.' Spencer leaned forward, and reached for his glass on the table. 'Now, you have to ask yourself, Josef, why on Earth wouldn't he have told you the good news about his baby sister?'

Frenzel looked candidly into the hard, toughened face. *Was Spencer lying to him? Spinning yet another, endless web of lies and deceit?* No, for once, the British spymaster was telling the truth.

'How long has he known about Anna?' he asked bleakly.

'Long enough.'

Spencer explained after being taken prisoner and fearing summary execution, Schneider had initially assumed the identity of a dead Wehrmacht Major. Six weeks later, his luck was to run out, when the Major's commanding officer came across him in the Camp, and not only recognised Schneider, but was infuriated he'd stolen his fallen comrade's identity.

Schneider was temporarily removed from Jamiltz and ended up being interrogated by the KGB. Having been outed by a senior Wehrmacht officer, he figured there was little point in denying the accusations. He'd all but given up, and had prepared himself for the worse. If he was lucky, it would be death by firing squad, but that decision was entirely in the hands of the Soviet authorities. It was a decision he'd taken himself a hundred or more times before. There was blood on his hands, his captors' blood. He expected no mercy, nor sought it.

Day after day, he was threatened with execution and deprived of sleep, food, and water. Schneider knew all too well how it worked. They were slowly grinding him down, asking about his actions on the Russian front, the atrocities, and the killings. His interrogators considered him arrogant; it was partially correct, but his demeanour also acted as a mask. Once or twice, it fleetingly crossed his mind many of his victims must have felt the same sense of hopeless deprivation, pain, and hopelessness. But, it was short-lived.

Schneider had begun to lose track of time, and demanded his tormentors just to get it over and done with. He'd told them everything he knew; he'd nothing else to give them. They didn't listen to him, but he hadn't expected them to, and then, without warning, he was moved from his cell and taken up to a sparsely furnished office. He was kept standing until a smartly suited, middle-aged man entered. He remembered his interrogators instantly sprang to attention and saluted the stranger. It was soon afterwards Schneider realised the powers that be in the Kremlin had decided to spare him, but it would be at a terrible cost.

He had a choice, but refusal to accept their offer would have far-reaching consequences. The stranger, Feliks Volkov, was the KGB's top man in East Berlin. Volkov had done his homework well. He turned up the pressure. Every man had a price, a breaking point, and this was Schneider's. They'd found Anna and her children, alive, living in Dresden. Initially, he refused to believe them point blank. Admittedly, things had been confusing during and after the fall of Berlin, but a close friend had reported their deaths to him. Why now should he believe them? Volkov produced photos; it looked like Anna, but he remained unconvinced. As for the children, they were adults now, and there was no way of knowing if it was them or not.

Volkov was patient, cunning, and shrewd. He bided his time, and two days later, Anna was brought to the prison, along with the children. They had a tearful reunion, and Anna told him although the family were all severely injured, her eldest, Peter, had lost a leg, thankfully, they had survived the bombing. With her husband long dead on the Eastern Front, she decided to stay, but suffered at the hands of the invading Soviet troops. At that point, she didn't need to say any more. The tears streaming down her face spoke volumes.

Frenzel was unable to contain himself any longer and butted in, 'So, after everything that happened to his sister, are you seriously telling me Schneider agreed to spy for the Russians?'

Spencer shrugged. 'What would you have done in his shoes? Volkov used Anna and the family as leverage, a way of turning the screw. Schneider knew the score. Volkov had made it quite clear. If he failed to play their game, his beloved little sister might well have survived the war, but she was unlikely to survive his refusal to work for Moscow. Volkov's plans were entirely faultless; he used Stasi intelligence officers, who'd once served the Third Reich, to contact the

Schamhorst, and say they'd discovered Schneider's whereabouts at Jamiltz. The rest, as they say, is history.'

He was still doubtful. 'Are you sure about all this?

'Because, Josef, almost two months ago, Feliks Volkov defected to the West.'

Frenzel's expression dropped with incredulity. He still couldn't quite get his head around the fact Schneider, of all people, had betrayed everything they had believed in.

Spencer continued, 'For the time being, we're keeping Volkov under wraps. Further down the line, the government will want to make some political capital out of his defection. The Soviets will kick up a stink, but that's part and parcel of the game, the endless point-scoring, and one-upmanship against the other side. Next year, it could be one of ours.'

It all seemed credible, but Frenzel still bided his time. 'It's one thing for Feliks Volkov to smear him, but talk's cheap.'

'Volkov was merely the icing on the cake. A while back, the Americans started to take an interest in Schneider.'

'You mean, in Argentina?'

'Amongst other places, yes. At one point, using an alias, Schneider was making regular visits to New York to meet a Soviet contact. He also cultivated numerous business interests. By all accounts, he was quite successful. He traded legitimately in engineering parts; in fact, he's established himself as a leading advisor to the Argentinian government.'

Frenzel gave him a faint flicker of a smile. 'Now, let me see. Would these engineering parts have anything to do with the arms trade?'

Spencer returned his smile. 'Your friend, Helmut Schneider, has his finger in many pies, none of which stand up to too much scrutiny.'

'So tell me, Sir Spencer, how has my dear friend managed to upset his Soviet spymasters?'

'Well, now, that's the million-dollar question. We believe he's probably been syphoning off Soviet funds and lining his own pockets. I'm still waiting on a report from the CIA about the investigation. Let's just say, whatever he's done, Schneider is a dead man walking.' Spencer stubbed out his cigarette. 'Now, that just leaves one more question, Josef.'

Frenzel eyed speculatively and breathed deeply. 'I suppose, in our line of business, there always has to be a punchline.'

'We can play this one of two ways, Josef.'

'Can we?' he asked dubiously.

'If you deliver Schneider to us, then you might just be able to come out of this mess with some semblance of credibility.'

'Are you blackmailing me?'

'I wouldn't exactly call it blackmail, Josef; we already have more than enough to send you back to Germany. But, it's entirely up to you how we play it. We could just tell von Bitten about your naughty little tryst with Joyce Leader. It wouldn't go down too well, but he wouldn't necessarily be surprised you couldn't keep it in your pants. Or, we could take it up a notch or two further, and reveal the full extent of your involvement with both the *Schamhorst* and Helmut Schneider.' Spencer smiled slightly. 'So, my dear, Josef, which is it to be?'

'Nothing is ever quite that simple, though, is it?'

Spencer leaned down and picked up his briefcase, resting it on the table. 'I'm afraid you'll have to run that one by me. What are you on about?'

'Well, I'll need to contact the *Schamhorst*. I can't just bail out of everything, not just like that, or, at least, not without General Aurberg's approval.'

'We don't have time,' Spencer said sharply.

Frenzel evaluated Spencer's demeanour. He had to ask the question, but was afraid of the answer. 'Just what do you know about our escape plan?'

'Enough.'

'But, how much do you have on us?' Frenzel braced himself before asking, 'Do you know about the *Mendoza*?'

'What do you *think*?'

'Then, I don't know what I can do to help. The ship's due to arrive at Surrey Docks tomorrow morning. The Captain will be expecting payment upfront.'

'If Schneider doesn't turn up, then it solves your problem.'

Frenzel shook his head. 'No, no, it doesn't quite work like that. We've come to an arrangement; we've used this captain before, and will no doubt use him again in the future. The fact Schneider might not turn up is neither here nor there. To keep his silence, he'll still demand payment.'

'Well, Josef, that's rather more your problem than mine. We can either do this the easy way or the hard way. Are you going to give us Schneider, or not? The choice is entirely yours.'

'I can't promise anything. Can you give me a couple of hours?'

Spencer assumed he probably wanted to contact General Aurberg before committing himself. He returned the brown envelope and its contents to his briefcase. 'Call my colleague with your decision.'

Carter retrieved a pen from the inside pocket of his jacket, and scribbled a telephone number on the back of his beer-stained, cardboard placemat, handing it across to Frenzel. He glanced at the card before placing it into his overcoat.

'I can be reached on that number at any time, day or night,' Carter assured him.

Frenzel nodded, and said stiffly, 'Thank you.' He watched Spencer snap the briefcase shut and make to leave.

'There's one other thing.'

Spencer glanced at his watch, sighed, and said with a hint of resignation, 'I'm sure there is. What is it?'

'The photos, the transcripts,' he said, inclining his head toward the briefcase. 'She's still very good.'

Spencer stared back at him blankly. 'I'm sorry, you've completely lost me.'

'Your agent.' Frenzel pressed him.

'My agent?' Spencer repeated blankly.

'Yes, Joyce Leader.'

'I assure you, she's *nothing* to do with me, Josef.'

Frenzel let out a deep-throated chuckle. 'Now, give me some credit. Even *I* know Leader was a British agent during the War.'

Spencer appeared indifferent. 'There's no point in denying we recruited her. Why would I? Don't get me wrong, she was dependable enough, but Leader's only real loyalty was arguably to the Abwehr, and in particular, to her handler, Bernard Drescher. Whether you wish to believe me, or not, is entirely up to you, Josef.'

'Come on, are you seriously expecting me to believe you didn't set me up with her?'

'Why would I? I didn't trust the bloody woman during the war. So what makes you think I'd do so now?' He lied convincingly. Spencer stood up from the table. 'I'm not sure what kind of yarn Schneider, or whoever, has been spinning about her, but you're way off the beam. I won't deny we wired your flat; you were fair game.' He shrugged. 'But, as far as employing a has-been like Joyce Leader? Forget it,' he said with a throwaway gesture.

'What about her suite at the Savoy? It was full of listening devices.'

'Yes,' Spencer said dismissively, 'why wouldn't it be. You were practically living at the ruddy place. I wanted to have a hold over you, Josef; that's why!'

Spencer had taken not only Frenzel but also Carter by surprise. Whatever way anyone looked at it, it was a convincing performance.

As Spencer headed back across the bar, Carter hurriedly came to his feet, and said to Frenzel, 'Give me a call.'

He held his gaze steadily. 'Don't hold your breath, Mr. Tolly.'

'You're already in the shit, and you know it! Schneider's betrayed you and your friends in the *Schamhorst*, and everything they've ever stood for. For what it matters, and I'm only guessing, he's probably also betrayed one of the Reich's most successful spies.' Carter waited to gauge his reaction. He wasn't disappointed. Frenzel's expression closed down. 'Am I wrong?' he asked.

'Goodbye, *Mr. Tolly* or whatever your name is. Don't keep your boss waiting.'

Chapter 14
MI5 HQ, London

'Jarvis was right about one thing, sir.'

Spencer looked at Carter. 'Was he?'

'He's put in a request for more manpower.'

'Yes, so I've heard,' he said non-committedly.

'If Frenzel doesn't come up trumps, and there's no guarantee he will, then we'll find ourselves out on a limb. We don't have enough teams to cover all of Surrey Docks.'

As a flicker of irritation crossed Spencer's face, Carter realised he'd overstepped the mark. 'I think, Carter, that's called stating the fucking obvious! Just concentrate on doing the day job, and I'll do mine! Understood?'

Carter found himself mumbling an apology. He was beginning to discover it paid to keep both his mouth and brain in gear. He watched Spencer head back down the corridor. The self-assured, rolling gate possessed an indefinable commanding presence. Carter figured his boss was probably already one or two steps ahead of him. Maybe he should have kept his thoughts to himself, but he'd felt compelled to ask all the same. Without additional Special Branch officers and the help of the Port of London authorities, they were facing an uphill struggle in securing Schneider's arrest.

**

An hour later, Assistant Commissioner Luke Garvan walked into a small private dining room. Spencer rarely entertained, but when he did, his venue of choice was usually the select ambience of the Naval and Military Club, or as it was otherwise known, the In and Out Club from the prominent signs on the building's separate vehicle entrance and exit gates in Piccadilly. A quick phone call and a little gentle persuasion had secured Garvan's attendance.

The familiar tall, loose-limbed figure dressed in a smart, pinstriped suit paused in the doorway, his gaze roaming thoughtfully around the oak panelled room. If he was surprised to find Jack Stein seated beside Spencer, he didn't allow it to show.

Spencer rose and extended his hand in welcome. 'Thank you for coming at such short notice.' He half turned toward Stein. 'You know Jack, of course.'

Garvan inclined his head, as they shook hands. 'I thought you'd flown back to the States?'

'Yeah, I did, but only for a couple of days. I needed to get back to London for the end of the Millbank Conference.'

As Garvan joined them at the table, a waiter hovered attentively, and presented them with the menu. 'Your usual, sir?' he asked, addressing Spencer.

'Make it two bottles of the Chateau Artois, will you? Thank you.'

They deliberately kept the conversation light until the waiter returned with the wine; then, they ordered dinner.

With the door closed on them, Garvan looked across the table at Spencer. 'In my experience Spence, where you're concerned, there's no such thing as a free meal. What are you after?'

'Am I *that* transparent?'

'You've always been that transparent.'

'Jack had to fly back to Washington for advice.'

'So, what's that to do with me?'

Stein cut in. 'I take it Spencer's been keeping you up to speed about Zimmerman's involvement with Schneider and the *Schamhorst* network.'

It was a given; Garvan said he had.

'Then you must know it's political dynamite.'

'Yes, I'm sure it is.'

'I needed a decision.'

'About what?' Garvan queried.

'I needed to know how they wanted me to play it. The Administration can't afford a large-scale, public scandal. So, you won't be surprised Washington wants us to bury the story.'

'I'd be more surprised if they didn't.'

'We can't allow this God awful mess to break in the Press. Can you imagine the coverage, the headlines? Leading NASA scientist is still...' Stein hesitated slightly, searching for the right words.

‘Is still batting for the other side,’ Garvan offered.

‘Well, fella, that’s one way of putting it.’

‘Am I wrong?’

Stein allowed a slow smile to cross his face. ‘Nah,’ he conceded. ‘You’re not wrong.’

‘What’s next?’

‘We’ll ship him back Stateside, and quietly retire him.’

‘Ill health?’

Stein nodded. ‘You know the script, a few well-placed editorials, and we announce with much regret blah-blah, Professor Zimmerman has been forced to stand down due to ongoing health problems. The fact the old bastard will end up living to be ninety-five is irrelevant. By that time, there’ll be another President, another generation on Capitol Hill, who won’t give a shit.’

‘They might not give a shit, but I guess they still wouldn’t want Zimmerman’s connections with Schneider and a Nazi ratline coming back to haunt them in the future.’

‘You’re right; it’s not exactly in the Nation’s interest to make that kind of stuff public.’

The conversation lulled, as the waiter returned with their starter course. Garvan unfolded his linen napkin, and waited until the door closed on them. ‘So, that’s Zimmerman taken care of, but that’s not why I’m here, is it?’ he said, shooting the question at Spencer. ‘We could have swept the Zimmerman stuff up in a report.’

‘It isn’t anything major. I just need more manpower at Surrey Docks,’ Spencer said.

Garvan raised his brows. ‘Nothing major?’ he repeated. ‘Christ almighty, Spence.’

‘Can you spare anyone?’

‘Quite frankly, no, I can’t. As it is, I’ve already gone out on a limb for you. You know full well I don’t have permission from the Commissioner for this Schneider business, and if I start pulling officers off other cases, he’ll come down on me like a ton a bricks.’

‘It’s important.’

‘When isn’t it?’ Garvan scoffed.

Right now, he was not prepared to make any promises he might be unable to keep. Things were difficult enough at Scotland Yard; they were already fully committed to providing first line security cover for the Millbank Conference, including two visiting Foreign Ministers, who had tagged along for the ride. Garvan had alerted Customs about the *Mendoza's* arrival; he'd called in a few favours, without going into too much detail about Schneider. His opposite number in Customs had promised his men would be all over the *Mendoza* "like a rash." It was no more than a delaying tactic, but it would buy them valuable time.

'What's this really all about, Spence? Talk to me.' Garvan pressed.

Friends make for the worse enemies, and right now, Spencer desperately needed to keep Garvan onside. His decision to cajole Joyce out of retirement had not been one he had taken lightly. Since the war, they'd remained close friends, but however difficult that decision had been, Spencer never allowed his personal feelings to cloud his professional judgement.

'I've managed to back Frenzel into a tight corner.'

Garvan didn't look up, and began toying with the food on his plate. He'd heard that line so many times before. 'You mean, you've blackmailed him?'

Spencer stretched back in his chair. 'Blackmail is such an ugly word.'

Garvan held his gaze across the table. 'But, you've managed to screw him, am I wrong?'

'Well, let's just say, I got someone else to do my dirty work for me.'

'Who?'

Spencer took a large slug of wine. 'Actually, it's someone we both know rather well.'

Garvan continued to hold his gaze. 'Really, go on. Tell me, who is it?'

There was a protracted pause while Spencer summoned up the courage to confess. 'If you must know, I've re-activated Joyce Leader's file.'

Garvan's mood changed in a moment. 'You've done what!' he blasted back at him.

'Now, Luke, just hear me out, will you!'

'Why the hell didn't you mention this before to me?'

'For a start, you'd never have agreed to my involving Joyce. Besides, it wasn't your call to make in the first place!'

'Tell me something. When you turned up at Scotland Yard, asking for help to track Schneider down, had you already discussed the case with Joyce?'

'Believe me, I didn't force her into anything.'

Garvan remained unconvinced. 'I just can't believe you've done all this, without saying something. Here I am, watching your back, and you do this!'

'Listen, if there'd been any other way.'

'Just spare me the bloody explanations. What's the point?' he rasped angrily.

It wasn't lost on Garvan, as Stein and Spencer exchanged glances. He had a distinct feeling something was going on. They were still holding out on him. He tossed his crumpled linen napkin angrily on the table. 'Come on, just spit it out. What's happened?'

It was Stein who answered. 'We don't know where she is.'

The colour drained immediately from Garvan's face. 'What the hell do you mean she's gone missing? What in God's name went wrong? Didn't you have her under surveillance?'

He listened in stunned silence, as Spencer explained how Joyce had disappeared from the Savoy. However, much they tried to put a positive spin on the situation, Garvan knew only too well the chances of finding Joyce alive were still, at best, minimal. He set his knife and fork down, and pushed the plate away; his appetite had faded. Garvan drained his glass; Stein refilled it for him. He fought hard to keep his temper in check. They were both trying to gauge his reaction, to see how the land lay, for, without his help and contacts at the Port of London Authority and Customs, Schneider might still manage to slip through the net.

'How did they get on to Joyce?' Garvan demanded. 'Where did the information come from?'

'Guilt by association,' Stein suggested.

'You mean with Bernard Drescher?'

'Not only Drescher. You know how things were. After the assassination attempt on Hitler, as far as the Gestapo and SS were concerned, the Abwehr was tainted.'

Garvan looked to Spencer. 'What do you think?'

'It doesn't matter what I think. Our only hope is in convincing Frenzel that Joyce was only obeying instructions, and was ordered to infiltrate British Intelligence.'

'Do you think he'll buy it?'

'I'm not sure,' Spencer confessed. 'But, the way things stand, Frenzel's our only realistic hope of finding Joyce alive.'

Somewhat reluctantly, Garvan found himself agreeing with Spencer's assessment. Their hands were tied. He didn't need either of them to spell it out. Under normal circumstances, Garvan could have put out a general call at Scotland Yard or placed a missing person article in the Press. But, if some astute journalist linked Joyce to Josef Frenzel, they would end up having the Press circling like hungry hyenas looking for a great headline. "*Missing woman involved with a high-ranking German Embassy official.*"

By default, the West German Ambassador would also find himself embroiled in a potential scandal. Questions would be asked, not only in the National Press, but also in the House of Commons. Spencer's primary concern, however, was not the sensitivities of either the Ambassador or Downing Street, but ensuring Schneider was brought to justice.

The assignment had always been high risk, but it was a risk Joyce had been willing to take. She knew all too well that one slip-up, one mistake was all it would take for her world to implode. Maybe they were already too late, but Spencer refused to give up all hope. It was his responsibility to either save her or die on his own sword. But, judging by the deadly expression on Garvan's face, he'd probably take matters into his own hands.

Spencer was only too aware he'd made a bit of a hash by telling Garvan. He'd probably come across as too uncaring and matter-of-fact. It certainly hadn't been his intention, far from it. But, words had failed him, or, at least, the right words.

Chapter 15
Ponsonby Street, Westminster

Carter closed the front door of his flat, and tossed a set of keys into a silver dish on the hall table. He glanced up, momentarily studying his reflection in the mirror, and rubbing his chin. He needed a shave, but it would have to wait until morning. Carter wearily loosened his tie, and started to head into the kitchen when the phone rang. He stopped dead in his tracks, and swearing silently under his breath, retraced his steps back to the hall table and picked up the receiver.

'Yes,' he barked tiredly.

'I'm sorry to disturb you, sir,' came the familiar tones of Mary, an MI5 telephonist.

He relaxed slightly as he visualized the attractive, young Mary. He really should get around to asking her out. 'There's no need to apologise,' he said, his voice softening.

'Herr Frenzel is on the phone for you.'

Carter's pulse quickened. Having already resigned himself Spencer's gamble was probably unlikely to pay off, he was surprised Frenzel had responded so quickly. 'Put him through, will you, Mary.' He waited. There followed a series of clicks before Mary came back. 'I have Herr Frenzel for you, sir.'

There was another click. 'Hello,' he answered.

'Good evening, Mr. Tolly,' Frenzel responded.

'Do you have something for me?'

'Mr. Tolly, you have to understand what I have to say is *private*.'

'What exactly do you mean by private?'

'I need to speak to the organ grinder and not the monkey.'

Carter found himself taking a sharp intake of breath and hesitating. If he screwed things up now, the one given was Spencer would never forgive him. He needed to play it carefully. 'You have to understand I'm not sure if I can arrange a meeting at such short notice with Sir Spencer.'

'Listen to me, Mr. Tolly. If you want to bag Helmut Schneider, then that's the deal.'

'The way I see it, you're not exactly in any position to start negotiating!'

There was a brief silence down the line. 'But, are you willing to take the risk? In your shoes, Mr. Tolly, I wouldn't be too hasty, at least not without informing Sir Spencer Hall I have a serious proposition for him. I have a feeling it would be a very brave decision on your part not to do so.' He waited for a response, but waited in vain, so continued, 'We both know your boss has, how shall I say, very *personal* reasons for wanting to catch up with Schneider. Besides, Mr. Tolly, time isn't on our side; the *Mendoza* docks in twelve hours. We could meet up at the Anaxos Club again.'

Carter silently swore under his breath, but, under the circumstances, realised he had little alternative, other than comply with Frenzel's demands. 'Give me half an hour. Where can I contact you?'

'I'll call you back on this number.'

'Where are you?'

Frenzel chuckled slightly. 'I'm sure if you ask your surveillance team, they'll let you know. In fact, I can see one of them sitting at the bar, looking at me, right now.' Frenzel set the receiver down, and briefly closed his eyes. He was taking one hell of a chance, and with luck, he might just come out of it alive.

**

Spencer picked up the phone, and blew cigarette smoke slowly through his lips. 'Yes,' he answered, his thoughts elsewhere.

Carter's voice came on the line. 'Our man has just called in.'

He shot back his shirt cuff and glanced down at his wristwatch. It was getting late, 10.30pm, and he'd only just returned from the Naval and Military Club. 'Good or bad?'

'We might have a bite.'

'I'm only interested in a *bite*!' came the acerbic reply.

'He wants to meet.'

'Does he,' Spencer said curiously.

'He suggested the Anaxos Club.'

'Forget it, Carter. It's my way or no way.'

'Yes, sir.'

'Do you know the safe house in Perrymead Street?'

It was a new one on Carter. 'I can't say that I do, sir.'

'Then get Jim Jarvis to drive you over there. Where did he call you from?'

'The surveillance team followed him to the Hen and Chicken Pub near South Kensington Underground Station. Apparently, he seemed quite friendly with the landlord, and used the phone behind the bar.'

'Is he still there?'

'Yes, he's sitting tight.'

'When are you expecting to hear back from him?'

Carter glanced at the hall clock. 'In about twenty minutes.'

'Good. After he calls, I want you to go with Jarvis to the pub and pick him up. I'll meet up with you at Perrymead Street.'

'And if he doesn't buy it?'

'Then tell Herr Frenzel the deal's off!'

Chapter 16
Perrymead Street, Fulham

To all intents and purposes, it was a rather pleasant living room. Elegant furniture, pale blue, silk curtains, and an array of paintings adorned the walls. As Jarvis closed the door behind him, Frenzel knew there had to be one or two hidden microphones. It was no more than he expected. Besides, the ever cautious Sir Spencer Hall would never have countenanced such a meeting without recording their conversation.

If the Director General of MI5 was to be won over by his proposition, Frenzel needed to be at the top of his game. It was a gamble, but one he had to take. There was always a chance he might have miscalculated, but there was no going back. It was literally make or break.

Frenzel mentally started to brace himself for the onslaught. He nervously puffed out his cheeks, breathed deeply, and begun to pace the room. Under his arm, he carried a thin leather folder, which he occasionally tapped almost to reassure himself it was still there. He was acutely aware Spencer was a past master at counterintelligence; it was all about psychological tactics, mind games, and retaining the upper hand.

Although Jarvis had assured him Spencer was on his way to the safe house, he was left, he felt, quite deliberately on his own for over half an hour. In Frenzel's limited experience, Spencer was a closed book. In security circles, he had a reputation for being both ruthless and aggressive, but with an astute head on his shoulders. Whenever he engaged someone in conversation, he always gave the impression of storing up mental notes on them.

Frenzel heard the door click open. He swung around, bracing himself; this was it, and he needed to keep his nerve. Spencer entered the room, and quietly closed the door. Frenzel found himself anxiously adjusting his tie; it didn't go unnoticed.

Spencer gestured toward the sofa. 'Please take a seat, Josef.'

He glanced around and sat down while Spencer eased himself into the high back chair opposite. Frenzel waited anxiously, as Spencer took his time reaching into his jacket pocket to retrieve a slender silver cigarette box. His expression was impassive. 'This better be good. What do you have for me?'

Frenzel passed him a rather awkward smile. 'I have a proposition for you.'

'So I understand,' he said, opening the box.

'I contacted General Aurberg after our meeting.'

Spencer calmly slipped a cigarette between his lips. 'What did the worthy General have to say for himself?'

'I told him everything.'

'Did he believe you?'

'What do you think?'

Spencer clicked on his lighter and took a couple of puffs to light the cigarette fully. 'If I were of a betting persuasion, which I'm not, I'd say he probably didn't believe a word you told him about Schneider working for the Soviets.'

'In General Aurberg's shoes, would you take the word of the Head of MI5?'

Spencer smiled tautly. 'My dear chap, there are times I don't even believe myself.'

Frenzel's expression appeared remote and withdrawn. The conversation lulled, as he desperately tried to keep a grip on his nerves. 'You have to see, without any tangible evidence against Schneider, Aurberg won't budge an inch. Can you give me something? It doesn't have to be that much.'

Spencer leaned forward to the coffee table, and moved the ashtray within easy reach. 'I'm afraid it's a little late in the day to be supplying the *Schamhorst* with evidence. To be perfectly honest with you, had I known that Schneider was heading to Britain, I'd have saved myself a great deal of trouble by leaking our intelligence to General Aurberg and letting the *Schamhorst* do the dirty work for me.'

Frenzel eyed him speculatively. 'So, what's stopped you? It isn't as if you haven't had the time.'

'An old friend asked me for a favour.'

'What kind of favour?'

'To hold back, until we had another fish on our hook.'

'Another fish?' he queried warily. 'You mean *me*?'

'Good lord, *no*; you were just a means to an end. No, this was a much bigger catch.'

He looked at him nervously, not quite sure where he was heading. 'Who are you talking about?'

'Come on, Josef, think!'

'You mean, Professor Zimmerman?' he asked tentatively.

Spencer smiled and nodded slightly. 'I suppose we were always going to catch up with him. It was only a matter of time before Zimmerman finally overstepped the mark.'

'He was forced into it.'

'Forced or not, Schneider's arrival in London has had something of a domino effect on those around him.'

Frenzel could not disagree. He sat quite still. His eyes possessed a faraway look, before coming back to rest on Spencer. 'I think you ought to know, prior to coming here I called Professor Zimmerman.' He waited to see if he'd get a response, but none was forthcoming, so he carried on. 'I assume your people have bugged his phone?'

Spencer's expression said it all. 'Why did you call him?'

'You probably won't understand, but I feel responsible,' Frenzel confessed. 'Perhaps if I hadn't become so heavily involved with Joyce, you might never have managed to link Bernard to the cash drop for Captain Calero.'

'If I were you, Josef, I'd stop beating myself up. Zimmerman knew perfectly well what he was getting himself into. It's not as if he hasn't already got form with the *Schamhorst*. Don't get me wrong, he's been clever and managed to slip under the radar for a very long time.'

'That may be so, but I swear to God, Bernard never wanted to get in this deep, but…'

Spencer cut him off. 'But, refusing the *Schamhorst* isn't exactly an option.'

Frenzel took a sharp intake of breath. 'No, no, it isn't.'

'Did they blackmail him?'

'I really can't say for certain; he never said anything to me. If he'd refused to come up with the money, I guess General Aurberg wouldn't have wasted his time with blackmailing him. Far easier, and quicker, to dispatch an assassin. You know the type of thing, tampered brakes, an unexplained fire, or whatever took their fancy at the time.'

'It's not just Zimmerman, though, is it? You must be concerned about your own safety?'

'Well, Sir Spencer, that all rather depends on your skill at extricating me from this unholy mess.'

'We'll take good care of you,' he assured him.

'Thank you,' he said, with reservation. 'So what's going to happen to Bernard?'

'Do you know Jack Stein?'

'I've met him, but I wouldn't say I know him. CIA, isn't he?'

Spencer nodded. 'Well,' he continued, inhaling on his cigarette, 'I, or should I say, we wanted to keep things under wraps until we had all our ducks in a row. As much as I wanted to screw Schneider, there are certain niceties to observe. Until Washington decided Professor Zimmerman's fate, my hands were somewhat tied. I won't deny it was a lost opportunity.' Spencer casually flicked ash off the tip of his cigarette into the ashtray. 'But, that's not why we're here, is it. It's getting late, and I'm getting tired. You mentioned some kind of proposition?'

Seeing Frenzel shifting uneasily on the sofa, Spencer inclined his head toward the silver box. 'Take one,' he said.

Frenzel reached forward; his hands were shaking.

'Use my lighter,' Spencer offered, pushing it across the coffee table.

In the past, Frenzel had always struck him as being a pretty calm and self-assured character. Admittedly, the photos and transcripts of his affair with Joyce Leader were pretty damning; he had still expected him to bluff his way through the meeting.

Frenzel thanked him with genuine gratitude in his eyes for the cigarette. 'You see, unlike General Aurberg, I don't need convincing about Schneider being a Soviet spy. They're old friends, old comrades in arms. As an officer in the

Abwehr, well, how shall I say, we viewed things rather differently.'

Spencer stared at him quizzically. 'You surprise me.'

'Why?'

'Well, for a start, you know I'd move heaven and earth to avenge my brother's murder. Lie, cheat, blackmail … you name it! So what makes you think I'm not making up the entire story?'

Frenzel shrugged. 'Are you *lying*?'

'No, as a matter of fact, I'm not.'

'Then, we can do business.'

Spencer was curious; this was more like the Frenzel of old, the one he had read about in the intelligence reports. If it had not been for the booze and women, he could have possibly made it to the top of West Germany's post-war intelligence service. However, there had always been a question mark about his reliability. Yet, there was no denying, at his best, Frenzel was a shrewd operator.

'Okay, I'll hear you out, but I can't make any promises.'

'I never thought you would.' Frenzel paused, and sucked slowly on his cigarette. The sudden intake of nicotine was having a calming influence on his nerves. 'Tell me, if I were to give you Schneider, then what kind of deal could I expect from you?'

Spencer eased back in the armchair. 'That all depends on the offer,' he replied cautiously.

'Would you allow me to walk free?'

'With no strings attached, is that what you mean?'

'I'm entirely in your hands. The photos are one thing, but if the Ambassador knew of my links to the *Schamhorst*, well, my reputation would be in tatters. I can almost visualise the headlines: "High-ranking Embassy official sent home in disgrace." You know how the Press will crucify me, but it wouldn't stop there; it never does. They'd keep digging and digging for something else.'

Spencer agreed with him.

'Whatever you may or may not think of me, I've no desire to embarrass either the Ambassador or my family.' As he finished speaking, a slow, ironic smile suddenly crossed his face. 'And, if truth be told, Sir Spencer, I've really no desire to find *myself* on a KGB hit list because of Helmut Schneider!'

He returned his smile.

'Do we have a deal?'

Spencer pulled a face. 'Maybe. So where is he?'

Frenzel raised his hand. 'What do I get in exchange?'

Spencer took his time answering. They were rapidly running out of time, and the last thing he wanted was for Schneider to reach Surrey Docks. It was a vast area, and even with extra help from Special Branch and the Customs Authority is conducting a bow to stern search of the *Mendoza*, there was still always a very real possibility Schneider might somehow slip through the net.

'Perhaps, at your age, Josef, you really ought to start considering taking early retirement,' he said at length.

'I could be persuaded.'

'Here's the deal then. Give me Schneider, and I'll drop everything, including your involvement with the *Schamhorst*.'

It almost seemed too good to be true. Frenzel had expected an offer, but certainly not to walk away scot-free. Retirement, a full pension, his reputation intact, it was more than he could ever have hoped for. He assumed Spencer's generosity was down to one thing his chance to finally avenge his brother's murder. Whatever it was, Frenzel still couldn't quite believe his luck, and found himself readily agreeing.

'You'll have to stay here, of course, until we bag him.'

'Yes, yes, I understand,' he blustered.

Spencer glanced at the leather folder Frenzel had placed so carefully beside him on the sofa. 'Is that for me?'

Frenzel glanced down, and handed it across the table. 'The address, everything you need, is in there.'

'Who's guarding him?'

'Erhard Lange.'

Spencer pulled a face. 'All brawn and no brain, is that the fella?'

Frenzel couldn't help himself and let out a throaty chuckle. 'Yes, that's him, but he's reliable and pretty handy with a gun.'

'Is he alone?'

'Yes, I needed to keep things tight; I didn't want to risk involving anyone else. Erhard might not be the brightest, but he's totally loyal.'

'Yes,' Spencer said thoughtfully, taking a long draw on his cigarette. 'Wasn't his father a colonel in the Waffen SS?'

'You really have done your homework, Sir Spencer.'

'Let's just say, I make it my business to keep a watchful eye on certain Embassy staff in London, including, like yourself, those employed by our Allies.'

Frenzel gave a rather awkward smile. 'I can see that might come in useful.'

'Is there any way you can call Lange off the job?'

'I could, but not without letting the cat out of the bag. You see, Lange Snr, Martin, is a close friend of General Aurberg. His assignment to watch over their old friend Helmut Schneider was something of a certainty. If you must know, I had very little say in the matter. Erhard was their choice, not mine. At that stage, I couldn't very well refuse him.'

'Would I be correct in saying young Erhard's first loyalty is to the *Schamhorst*?'

'Well, it's certainly not to me, *that* I do know!'

Spencer held his gaze. 'Is there anything else I should know?'

'Yes, there is.'

'What is it?' Frenzel was on tenterhooks, and didn't quite know to broach the matter. Spencer made a show of checking his watch. 'Look, I need to get moving with this stuff,' he said, patting the folder.

'It's about Joyce Leader,' he blurted out.

Spencer covered it well, but his heart skipped a beat. 'What about her?' he said coolly.

'Was she a plant?'

Spencer continued to deny it. Frenzel hesitated, still not quite sure whether to believe him. 'General Aurberg didn't want to risk having a body on our hands, at least not until Schneider was on his way to South America.'

It was the first confirmation in days she was still alive. 'Why are you so interested in Joyce Leader?' Spencer managed to ask casually.

'I made a cardinal sin; I fell in love with my mistress.'

There was still, or at least he hoped, no outward flicker of emotion. It was the last thing he had expected, but it was certainly an unanticipated bonus. 'So what do you want from *me*?'

'Lange has orders to kill her.'

'I'm sure he has.'

'Just one last favour, that's all I ask?'

'You mean, to save her?'

Frenzel closed his eyes momentarily. When he opened them again, Spencer was surprised to see them filled with tears. 'You're very good, *very good*, at hiding your tracks, and at what you do, but, please let's not continue playing games with one another. You can try denying it all you like, but I admire your choice. Joyce was the perfect plant. She managed to survive the war in a unique position, trusted by both the Allies and the Nazi old guard. Who better to drag out of retirement to infiltrate a ratline, and, more importantly, to get a handle on Schneider? It was a masterstroke.'

Spencer decided there was probably little point in continuing to refute the truth any longer. There was nothing left to lose. 'You were an easy target, Josef, the weak link in the chain; you've always had a softness for women and booze.'

'There's no denying it. I've had many women in my time.'

'Why didn't you learn from your mistakes?'

'Joyce was, I mean, is different. It's foolish of me, I know. Weakness or not, someone of my experience should have smelt a rat.' He smiled lamely. 'Why else would a woman as stunning as Joyce Leader be attracted to an old fool like me?'

Spencer almost began to feel sorry for him, but it was only a passing thought. 'Where is she?'

'At the same address as Schneider,' he said. 'It's all in the folder there.' Frenzel pensively bit his lower lip in before saying, 'The *Schamhorst* have several highly placed contacts in the West German Intelligence Service. If they ever get wind of all this, my life expectancy will be somewhat limited.'

Spencer thought it was probably an understatement. Frenzel would be lucky to see the rest of the week out. 'Don't worry,' he assured him. 'It'll be on a need-to-know basis.'

'But, who'll need to know?'

'It'll be between the Ambassador and us. I think we're both in agreement Hans von Bitten can be trusted.'

Frenzel conceded.

'I'll ask him to set the ball in motion for your retirement, but we'll obviously give it a month or two until the fuss dies down.' Spencer looked across the table at him and asked, 'Is there anything else you wish to discuss?'

'Nothing that can't wait.'

Spencer stubbed his cigarette out in the ashtray and headed for the door. 'Good. I'll be in touch.'

'Don't let anything happen to her,' Frenzel called after him.

Spencer reached for the brass handle, and said, over his shoulder. 'I think that all rather depends on your man, Lange, don't you?'

Spencer headed upstairs to the room above. He found Jarvis crouched over a tape recorder, a set of earphones draped around his neck. He was chatting to Carter. As he entered, they both stopped what they were doing and looked up at him.

'Did you get everything on tape?'

'Yes, sir, we did,' Jarvis answered.

'Good,' Spencer said, unzipping the leather folder Frenzel had handed him. He removed the papers, and quickly begun to thumb through them. 'Right, we need to go through this lot. We keep Frenzel here until we've bagged Schneider. Who's on duty tonight?'

'Steve Lancaster,' Jarvis said, carefully removing the tape from the recorder.

'He'll need a backup. Get on to the Office, and while you're at it,' he said, addressing Jarvis, 'call Jack Stein. He'll need to know Frenzel has blabbed to Zimmerman that we've linked him to the bag drop for Captain Calero.'

Chapter 17
St. Philips Hotel, Westminster

Jack Stein stepped out of the lift and headed down the corridor to Room 201. The entire second floor had been taken over by the American delegation for the duration of the Millbank Conference. It was guarded by a mix of CIA agents and Garvan's Special Branch Officers. Entry to the floor was restricted, and could only be accessed by showing an identity pass. Anyone who accidently strayed off-limits was politely, but firmly, asked to leave. Stein was on nodding terms with most of Garvan's officers and raised his hand in acknowledgement to the large, muscle-bound detective who was patrolling the floor.

'Hello, sir.'

'I just want to have a word with Chuck Meyer,' he said, gesturing toward one of his agents guarding the rear staircase.

The detective stood aside for him to pass.

'When does your shift end?' Stein asked, making polite conversation.

'We both get off duty at 0300hrs.'

'Has it been a quiet night?'

'So far. We've had a stray drunk getting off on the wrong floor, but that's about all. He had a key in his hand for Room 1014, so Chuck helped me pour him back in the lift, and press the button to the tenth floor. We haven't seen him since, so presumably he got out in one piece.'

Stein returned his smile, and continued down the corridor toward Meyer. Up until five minutes ago, Stein had been happily nursing a large glass of neat Bourbon and a Marlboro in the hotel bar, when a call came through from Spencer. He suggested Stein might want to check on Zimmerman, as Frenzel had let the cat out of the bag.

"You mean, that we're on to him?"

"I'm afraid so."

Stein had cursed down the phone. "Jesus wept, Spence, I really didn't want to mention anything to Zimmerman until we were on our way back to the States!"

“Exactly, so I figured you might want to check to see if he’s okay.”

Up until now, everything had seemed pretty watertight; forewarning Zimmerman would only complicate matters further. Far better to wait until he was safely on the first flight out of Heathrow on Saturday morning, before dropping the bombshell. Earlier in the day, Zimmerman had been out in the West End, happily buying presents for his wife and children. By chance, Stein had bumped into him in the hotel foyer; he had seemed in a pretty good mood and looking forward to getting home. Bond Street jewellery for his wife, and a trip to Selfridges had sorted out his children. But, after the call from Frenzel, he must have realised the game was up.

Stein decided to play it carefully with Meyer. ‘I didn’t see Professor Zimmerman earlier at dinner.’

‘No, sir. He called room service.’

‘I heard he wasn’t feeling too well,’ Stein lied. ‘Would you mind checking on him?’

Stein stood back a little as Meyer approached Room 201, and knocked on the door. He waited. There was no answer, so he knocked again. Much to Stein’s relief, Zimmerman opened the door dressed only in his underpants. The radio was playing Jazz music quietly in the background.

He spoke in not much more than a whisper. ‘Agent Meyer, it’s getting late. Is anything wrong?’

Before Meyer had time to answer, Stein cut in. Zimmerman concealed his surprise. ‘I’m sorry, Professor, it’s my fault entirely. It’s just I didn’t see you at dinner, and I wondered if everything was okay? The Brit guys were throwing a get-together for us. They seemed pretty disappointed you weren’t able to make it.’

Zimmerman met his gaze. ‘I needed an early night, Mr. Stein. I have another lecture in the morning, and I wanted to make a start on my packing. If I’ve caused any offence, then I’ll apologise for my absence at the Conference cocktail party tomorrow evening.’ They were both playing cat and mouse; each knew the other wasn’t telling the truth.

‘I’m sure there’s no need to apologise,’ Stein assured him.

'Maybe not, but everyone has been so kind and generous to me. I feel I really ought to say something.'

'Yeah, I guess so,' he conceded.

'It's really very kind of you to drop by, Mr. Stein. But, as you can see, I am perfectly fine. So, gentlemen, if you don't mind, I'll wish you both a good night,' he said, closing the door on them.

**

Freddy Evans glanced in the rear view mirror. 'We're being followed, sir.'

Spencer glanced over his shoulder, and saw a set of headlights on their tail. 'When did they pick us up?'

'Near Sloane Street.'

'You didn't get a sniff earlier?'

'No, sir. I could try shaking them off, but so far, they've stuck to me like glue.'

'Are they professional?'

'They're kind of slick.'

'Then, I imagine, Freddy, whoever it is wants to be seen.'

'What do you want me to do, sir?'

'Keep circling until we can get a fix on the car. Have you managed to check out the number plate?'

'Y-es,' he answered hesitantly.

'Are you sure?'

Evans nodded. 'Shall I call the Office?'

'I'll do it. You just keep an eye on what they're up to.' Spencer reached forward between the front seats. Lifted the receiver from under the dashboard, pressed a red button. The line was a direct link to MI5. The duty officer answered. 'We have a tail,' Spencer said. 'Do a check for me, will you?'

'Yes, sir.'

Evans had carefully memorized the number plate, and had been quietly going over it in his mind. On Spencer's say so, he repeated it out loud. Spencer then relayed the details down the line and waited. 'Are they still with us?' he asked Evans.

'They're not even trying to avoid being seen. I wonder what their bloody game is?'

The Duty Officer eventually came back on the line. 'The vehicle is a black Ford Zodiac.'

'Okay, we already know that much, Brierley. Just get on with it.'

'I'm not sure what's going on, sir, but it's registered to the Soviet Embassy.'

'Really,' he said thoughtfully. 'Thank you.' He slowly replaced the receiver.

'Anyone we know?' Evans asked.

Spencer sat back and smiled. 'In a manner of speaking, yes. We're being tailed by our friends from the KGB.'

'Jesus Christ, sir, what do you want me to do now?'

'There's no point pissing around. Just carry on back to my place.'

Evans hesitated. 'Is that wise, sir? I mean we don't know.'

'Just do it, Freddy,' he snapped. 'Besides, it's not as if our Soviet comrades don't already know where I live. In fact, I'd be rather disappointed if they didn't.'

Evans anxiously checked out the rear view mirror again. 'But, we don't know what they're up to. Shall I call for back-up?'

'Relax, Freddy. They could have blasted us to kingdom come by now, if they'd wanted to.'

Evans let it rest, but thought the boss was taking one hell of a risk. After a couple of minutes, they took a sharp right onto Chelsea Embankment, headed toward Cheyne Walk, and pulled up outside Spencer's official London residence.

'Where are they?' he asked.

'Parked three cars behind.' Evans switched off the engine, and instinctively removed a pistol from a suede holster beneath his jacket and slipped it into his pocket. 'Wait where you are, sir,' Evans said. He jumped out to open the rear door, and immediately recognised the slim, distinguished looking figure walking toward them. He had a silk scarf draped around his neck and a jauntily angled trilby. Demetri Smolin's official Embassy title was Cultural Secretary. In reality, he was the KGB's top man in Britain.

Spencer emerged from the car, stretched himself to his full height, and followed Evans' gaze. 'My dear Demetri, aren't you taking your life in your hands.'

Smolin smiled in greeting. 'Your bodyguard is far too experienced to become, what is the saying, trigger happy? Is that correct, Mr. Evans?'

'I have my off days, sir,' Evans smirked.

'Then, I'm glad you weren't having one today.'

Spencer turned and reached on the backseat to retrieve his briefcase. 'So, what brings you out at this time of night, Demetri?'

'We have a mutual business interest.'

'Do we?'

'Yes, Helmut Schneider.'

'So far, he seems to have given your people the slip.'

'Then, that's something else we appear to have in common, Sir Spencer.'

'Touché, Demetri.' He smiled and glanced toward the Russian's car parked four doors down. 'Well, we can't stand out here talking all bloody night. Would it perhaps be inappropriate to offer the KGB's Head of Station a large vodka?' Spencer had a feeling the chance of a drink or two might well sway him round.

'You mean, to enter the *lion's den*?' he quizzed good-humouredly.

'I can see it might not go down too well with our political masters,' Spencer agreed, 'but they're not here, are they?'

'The one thing I've learnt since my arrival as Cultural Secretary is an appreciation of malt whisky.'

'You may have whatever you wish to drink.' Spencer inclined his head toward the black Ford Zodiac. 'However, I have a feeling you'd better have a word with your bodyguards first.'

Smolin raised his hand to them. 'They'll be all right,' he assured him, and followed Spencer up the steps to the front door. Once inside, he removed his scarf and hat and left them on the hall table. Smolin felt on edge. The Head of MI5 was not usually given to rash off the cuff decisions. Everything was calculated to the nth degree. They were both taking a high-risk gamble; perhaps Smolin's decision to reach out had been enough to convince Spencer of his sincerity. But, he had to wait and see.

Spencer ushered him into the library, and promptly opened a faux bookcase containing a very well stocked drinks cabinet. 'Would you care for a Glenfiddich?'

'That would be very kind, thank you.'

'I presume a large one, of course.'

'I'm Russian,' he shrugged. 'I can't see the point of small measures.' As Spencer sorted through the bottles, Smolin's eyes travelled thoughtfully around the library. 'You have a nice place here.'

Spencer turned to face him, a decanter in his right hand. 'It comes with the job, Demetri, much like your Dacha on the Black Sea.'

Smolin allowed a brief smile to cross his face.

'Please take a seat,' Spencer said, pouring two large glasses.

He chose a green leather armchair beside an open fireplace and made a point of admiring the artwork adorning the walls. Spencer shrugged dismissively, and said it had nothing to do with him; the house and the contents were a perk of the job.

He smiled half in bemusement and half in sympathy. His own London apartment was luxurious by Soviet standards, but had been thrust upon him. 'Your people will kick up a stink, if they find out about this,' Smolin suggested.

Spencer handed him a neat Glenfiddich. 'As will your people,' he answered. 'Who knows? It may well come back to haunt us.'

'Yes, maybe it will.'

Spencer eased himself into a small, two-seater sofa opposite Smolin, and wearily stretched his legs out on a low coffee table. 'Now, Demetri, what's all this about Schneider? It must be important to bring you out in the middle of the night.'

'I've heard a whisper you've successfully snared Herr Frenzel in a honey trap.'

'Good try, Demetri, but everything else is off limits. I thought we were here to discuss Schneider.'

Demetri took a sip of his whisky, and thoughtfully begun to swirl the amber liquid in the glass. 'I think it's fair to say the one thing we're both agreed on is we can't allow Schneider to board the *Mendoza*.'

'Yes, we are.'

'Tell me something. Do your people intend arresting him for war crimes?'

'I can't vouch for the police, but I intend to *kill* him!'

The Russian's pale grey eyes held his own. 'Ah, you are a man after my own heart.'

'Perhaps,' Spencer mused cautiously. 'But, I think we can both safely assume, we want the same result.'

'Then, I have something for you.'

'What are you offering?'

'If you can guarantee me Schneider will not reach the *Mendoza* alive, I'm prepared to stand down my operation.'

Spencer looked at him searchingly. 'Now, why on Earth would you do such a thing for me, Demetri?'

'What is the English saying?' There was a brief silence as he tried to remember it. 'Yes, do you not say "too many cooks spoil the broth"? We could end up getting in each other's way, and letting the bastard slip off the hook. Schneider has become a liability, and, in my humble opinion, should never have been lifted out of Jamiltz Internment Camp. Personally, I'd have left him there to rot!'

Spencer rolled the glass tumbler slowly between his hands. 'Have you cleared it with Moscow?'

'My decision, my call,' was all he said.

'So what you're saying is you haven't run it by them?'

Demetri shook his head and laughed. 'With due respect, that's pretty rich coming from you! You see, we do have a lot in common.'

'I seriously doubt it.'

'Do you always keep your Home Secretary in the loop?'

Spencer smiled in spite of himself. 'You might have a point, Demetri,' he conceded. 'I don't know about you, but I find politicians generally tend to muddy the waters.'

‘A necessary evil.’ He laughed, before draining the Glenfiddich down in one go. ‘So, do we have a deal?’

‘I’m not sure,’ Spencer said, pouring Smolin another drink.

‘You don’t trust me, do you?’

‘Any more than you trust me, no, I don’t.’

‘Come on, Sir Spencer. We both know how the land lays.’

‘Do we?’

‘You must be aware your good friend, John Eldridge, the Foreign Secretary, has already passed a warning shot about the activities of the KGB on British soil.’

‘He’s also had a quiet word with the Israeli chargé d'affaires, but as we both know, the Mossad connection was nothing more than a red herring.’

‘Yes, that was Schneider’s doing. He needed to cover his tracks and hide the truth, so what better way to persuade the *Schamhorst* to fund his passage to South America than by proclaiming he was on an Israeli hit list.’ A silence fell between the two protagonists. The rhythmic ticking of a longcase clock filled the sudden void. It was Smolin who broke the silence. ‘Have you had the pleasure of meeting the new Soviet chargé d'affaires?’

‘You mean, Alexi Androv?’

Smolin nodded.

‘Well, only in passing.’

‘After your Foreign Secretary had a word with him, Alexi tried throwing his weight around the Embassy.’

‘I’m sure you’re more than capable of handling Androv.’

‘Of course, but he’s not the right man for the job. Alexi is lightweight, but he has powerful friends in the Politburo who secured his appointment. It makes things, how shall I say, a little difficult at times.’

‘I’m sure it does, Demetri.’ Spencer took a mouthful of whisky. ‘You’ll have to excuse me, but there’s something I don’t quite understand. Why offer up Schneider now? What’s in it for you? You’ve everything to gain. With Androv kicking up a fuss at the Embassy, if you bag Schneider, you’d gain kudos with Moscow.’

'I'm a realist, Sir Spencer; we're both in competition for the same target. Why continue to muddy the waters? I have a small select team. As you'd expect, they're very good. Schneider's had more than his fair share of luck and with Frenzel's help has managed to stay one step ahead of the game. The arrival of the *Mendoza* is our one real opportunity to hunt him down.'

'Then why would the KGB not want to take all the accolades?'

'Because I'm sure our presence would be something of an unwelcome distraction for your people.'

'I'm not quite sure what you mean?'

'Your people would end up having one eye on us, and one eye on our target. At the end of the day, what does it matter whether it's a Soviet or a British bullet that takes Schneider out!'

Spencer could see the logic behind Smolin's proposition, but still had certain reservations. It simply seemed too good to be true; the wily old bugger must be up to something, but what? Spencer had a feeling while Smolin might well be prepared to call off his hit squad, he wouldn't leave anything to chance. There was simply too much at stake. Schneider was still at large, and he must have found himself under increasing pressure from Moscow to deliver results. In Smolin's shoes, he'd probably place his best man, a sniper, on standby, in case MI5 screwed up.

Smolin detected his reticence. 'I've taken a huge risk by coming here tonight, if my offer wasn't genuine.'

Spencer raised his hand. 'I know, but why leave Schneider to me? Your men have been trailing him for what, well over a month now.'

'We've been close once or twice, but not close enough. Our best chance is Surrey Docks, but security will be tight, and I've no wish for things to get out of hand. If my team pulled it off, they'd then find themselves in the firing line from your people. At the end of the day, Sir Spencer, I know you want the bastard dead even more than I do.'

'How did our friend Schneider fall foul of the KGB?'

'A leopard cannot change its spots. Schneider became careless in America.'

'How careless?'

'He took things too far.'

Spencer took a guess. 'Did he kill someone?'

Smolin allowed himself a slight smile. 'Yes, yes, he did. Deep down, the man is a psychopath; he's dangerous and out of control. But, I'm talking to the converted; you have personal experience of his particular brand of cruelty. He murdered your brother, I believe?' Smolin set his empty glass down on the coffee table. 'So, *do* we have a deal?'

Spencer took his time. 'Very well, Demetri. You can stand down your men.'

'*Udachi*, my friend, good luck.'

Chapter 18
Gliddon Road, Southwark, London

Lange didn't let on Frenzel had contacted the *Schamhorst*, and he believed Schneider had betrayed the brotherhood, and had become a Soviet agent. Initially, General Aurberg had refused point blank to believe the allegations against his former comrade in arms. After much discussion, it was Erhard's father who stated the British story might have a grain of truth to it. For who else did they know of Schneider's stature who had successfully escaped the Jamiltz Camp?

While the General was prepared to give Schneider the benefit of the doubt, it was by no means open-ended. He ordered an immediate investigation into the allegations. Deep down, Aurberg still feared Frenzel had his own agenda; perhaps, more importantly, British Intelligence had possibly duped him. As things stood, there was no concrete evidence linking Schneider to the KGB. Nor could Aurberg bring himself to believe someone as committed as Schneider would ever betray the Nazi cause.

Lange's father contacted his son about the allegations and his concerns for Erhard's safety. But, orders were orders, and Schneider was to be deemed innocent until proved otherwise. He would have to see the assignment through to the bitter end, and that meant Joyce Leader's life would be spared until Schneider was in international waters. The only thing on Erhard's mind was to be rid of Schneider as soon as possible, and to see him safely delivered into the care of Captain Calero. If he were eventually found guilty of spying for the KGB, then the *Schamhorst* would exact retribution in South America.

Lange was only just starting to appreciate why Frenzel had been so wary of being drawn into the plan. For Erhard, it had been an honour to be chosen to look after such an illustrious former member of the Gestapo. Even his own father was slightly in awe of Schneider's reputation. During the war, he had the ear of Reichsführer Heinrich Himmler, and, by all accounts, had been feared and admired by his fellow officers in equal measure. Such was his standing he had frequently been invited by Hitler to stay at the Berghof in

Berchtesgaden. Initially, things had worked out quite well. Like his father, Schneider was old school. A bit abrupt sometimes, arrogant, yes, clever, well, perhaps too clever by half. At times, he had appeared almost contemptuous of his former colleagues and superiors. As a result, Lange found his role increasingly difficult. The sooner he was rid of his charge, the better.

**

Joyce Leader woke up with a start to the sound of raised voices. The bare brick walls of the dark basement dripped with water from a broken pipe. A single, weak light bulb hung from the centre of the ceiling. Her only creature comforts were a rickety old bed and a galvanised bucket, which served as a toilet. A single handcuff attached to a metal chain was on her left wrist secured by a leash to the bed. Twice a day, Lange would deliver food and water. The routine never varied. Joyce was allowed a little privacy to wash, but her clothes were now beginning to smell. She was allowed off the leash every morning to empty the bucket in the outside toilet situated in the small backyard.

Joyce heard more shouting, and sat bolt upright, leaning her head to one side, and trying to listen to what was being said. It sounded like Schneider's voice interspersed by Lange, but she only managed to catch the occasional word. She knew from bitter experience the leash was way too short to reach the door. As quietly as she could, Joyce dragged the bed away from the wall and across the uneven stone floor. A couple of feet was all it would take. When she was satisfied, Joyce tested the length of the metal chain. It was still a stretch, but she just managed to press her ear against the heavy wooden door.

'I'm not disobeying orders!' she heard Lange shout angrily.

'Then you're a bigger bloody fool than I thought you were,' Schneider snorted dismissively.

She could not quite make out what was said next, but it sounded like someone stumbled on the stairs and thudded into the wall.

**

Schneider took a swing at the younger man and narrowly missed connecting a punch. Lange saw it coming, ducked out of the way, and crashed heavily into the wall. He grimaced in pain, and felt his shoulder before angrily turning around on the staircase to confront him.

'Do that again,' Lange swore, 'and so help me, I'll kill you *myself*!'

Schneider hesitated; Lange had a pistol in his hand. 'It's one thing to point a gun, but it's quite another to take a man's life in cold blood,' he suggested.

There was a sarcastic edge to Lange's voice. 'Well, Herr Schneider, of course, you'd know all about that, *wouldn't you*?' All it would take was one quick squeeze of the trigger to wipe that smug expression off his face. Lange silently cursed beneath his breath. However much he might want to take matters into his own hands, he thought better of it. Reluctantly, he slipped the pistol back into its shoulder holster and continued down the stairs.

Schneider still wasn't quite done with him. 'We don't have time for messing around,' he persisted. 'Think about it, Erhard; we can't afford excess baggage. So, why wait?'

Lange carried on down the basement stairs. 'Because, sir, I'm following the General's orders, that's why!' He reached into his trouser pocket for a set of keys. Joyce automatically flinched away from the door. By now, they were directly outside, so she hurried back to the bed. She guessed there was no point in moving it back to the wall.

Schneider was not prepared to give and persisted, 'But, can't you see, we're taking too much of a risk keeping Frenzel's whore alive. Why not just kill her now, and get it over and done with? What's the point of waiting until I board the *Mendoza*?'

Lange placed the key in the lock, and once again tried to keep his temper in check. He took a sharp intake of breath, and turned to face him. 'As I've already explained, sir, General Aurberg's orders are quite clear; we keep Leader alive until the *Mendoza* leaves British waters, and you're safely on your way back to South America. There's really no room for negotiation. I cannot, and will not, disobey orders.'

Before Schneider had a chance to respond, Lange opened the door. Joyce was standing beside the bed. There was no way to disguise the fact she'd moved the bed several feet away from the wall. Lange hesitated. Her eyes held no expression other than a piercing hardness. Schneider hadn't seen Joyce since her arrival in Gliddon Road. He paused behind the younger man, appraising the tall, attractive figure before him. She was unkempt, without a scrap of make-up. So how was it she still looked stunning? Even Schneider admitted to himself he could quite understand how Frenzel had fallen for her hook, line, and sinker. The bloody woman was lethal. Although it was evident she'd overheard them discussing her imminent death, she still returned their gaze with surprising defiance.

'We need to leave right away,' Lange announced.

'What's the point?' she shot back at him. 'I'd as soon as die in this godforsaken dump than as anywhere else. Just make it quick, and make it clean.'

Schneider could not help admiring her style.

'Are you going to make this difficult?' Lange said, with a hint of resignation.

'Why should I make it any easier than it already is?' She held her right hand aloft and flicked her wrist, so the heavy link chain rattled across the stone floor. 'I never thought I'd live to see the day when I agreed with Helmut,' she said, shooting him a hint of a smile. 'But, think about it, Erhard. Why bother moving me out of the house? Being chained up to the bed, like some poor defenceless animal, surely makes your life pretty easy, doesn't it? Why risk moving me?'

What the hell was the woman up to, Schneider wondered. Most people in her situation would have been pleading for their life. It was a high-risk gamble; Lange's nerves were obviously already on edge. Joyce was acutely aware she was playing with fire, but she wanted to test Lange, to look him in the eye and see whether he possessed the steel to take her out there and then. Judging by his expression, she figured Schneider was probably more in danger of being killed by his bodyguard than she was.

Lange took his time to answer. Slowly, he began to search through the bunch of keys and picked one out between his thumb and forefinger. 'Hold your hand out,' he said gruffly. She held out her right hand for him to unlock the cuff. Without looking at her, Lange murmured, 'You're my insurance policy.'

'Insurance policy?' she repeated.

'If you are a British spy, Miss Leader, you're certainly worth far more to me alive than dead. A bargaining chip, if you like.'

Joyce began to wonder whether she had been too quick in underestimating him. Joyce recalled meeting Erhard's father during the War. But, Waffen SS Colonel Martin Lange was an entirely difficult kettle of fish to his son. While it was true they might share the same blond good looks and the same ruthlessness, it was apparent, or so she had thought, Erhard wasn't blessed with his father's razor sharp intellect. Right now, she wasn't quite so sure.

'General Aurberg and the *Schamhorst* have their own priorities. I owe my father a debt of honour. While I have every intention of fulfilling my obligations, there might still be a way for both of us to come out of this mess alive.'

Her eyes met his. She was curious, not quite sure what he was playing at, and judging by the thunderous expression on Schneider's face, nor did he.

Lange shrugged slightly. 'I could, of course, shoot you dead here. But, I have a feeling your British Intelligence friends wouldn't hesitate to avenge your murder.'

Schneider shook his head in despair. 'My God, so, she's got to you as well! What's up with you all?'

Lange rounded on him. 'Well, we all have our secrets, sir, don't *we*?' He spoke with such venom even Schneider was taken aback.

'What the hell's that supposed to mean?' he demanded.

'That things aren't quite always as they seem.'

'Meaning?'

'We really don't have time for this!' Lange said irritably. 'We need to leave, and leave now!'

Lange slipped the keys back in his hip pocket, and when he looked at Joyce, there was something about his expression. From the depths of despair, she began to sense a small glimmer of hope. Something drastic had happened to change the ultra-loyal Lange's blind obedience.

Schneider caught the exchange between them; he'd been on the point of coming back to him but decided against it. However much he might want to take Lange down a peg or two, the fact remained, without his help, he'd never make it safely to the *Mendoza.* Schneider was accustomed to getting his own way, and it rankled him how he'd ended up taking orders from some whippersnapper young enough to be his son. It also had crossed his mind whether Lange was on to him; in the last twenty-four hours, his attitude had changed.

The original plan was to sit tight in Gliddon Road until Captain Calero gave the all clear to move. Lange brushed off Schneider's inquiries by saying he was merely obeying orders, and it wasn't his place to question General Aurberg's change of plan. Whether Schneider believed him, or not, was neither here, nor there. Lange was rapidly running out of options. Having been unable to contact Frenzel, he feared their position had possibly already been compromised. Perhaps Frenzel had bailed out or been arrested by the authorities. Either way, he wasn't going to risk hanging around.

Chapter 19
Bishop's Place, Southwark, South London

Its name suggested an element of grandeur, but Bishop's Place was a rather rundown, narrow cul-de-sac, a short walk from their hideout in Gliddon Road. The name was a throwback to some medieval Bishop's residence, which had once proudly overlooked the sprawling River Thames. Those days were long-lost in the mists of time, and all that remained was its grandiose name. Bishop's Place now housed a series of cheap to rent businesses, nestled under the railway arches.

Joyce and Schneider followed Lange along the cobbled road; it was still dark, and the fresh early morning breeze was a welcome change to the stale, damp cellar. Lange had done his homework, and knew every conceivable route to Surrey Docks like the back of his hand. Nothing had been left to chance. To their left stood a row of derelict shops awaiting demolition, and built into the Victorian railway arches on the opposite side of the road was a collection of warehouses, workshops, and garages, all supporting a variety of local businesses. Lange opened up the third one down, and nudged back the large, black painted wooden doors, flicked on the light, and stood back for Joyce and Schneider to enter.

'Hurry up,' he said, beckoning them forward.

They found themselves in a surprisingly large cavernous space housing a disused mechanical workshop, with a couple of abandoned trucks in various states of disrepair. Centre stage stood an ambulance. The lighting was poor, with deep shadows lurking in the dark recesses.

Schneider thrust his hands into his pockets, and took himself off to take a closer look at the ambulance. As he opened the driver's door, the whole workshop began to rumble as a train passed noisily overhead. Joyce instinctively glanced up toward the arched bricked ceiling. The lights started to rattle, and dust floated down over their heads. Lange checked his watch. The sound was deafening, and they could hardly hear him speak. 'It's the first train out of London Bridge,' he explained.

As the noise started to subside, Joyce asked, 'Whose idea was the ambulance?'

'Frenzel will no doubt tell you it was his brainwave, but it was mine actually,' Lange said. 'Do you approve?'

They exchanged smiles. He knew she did. 'Who questions an ambulance?' She shrugged.

Schneider completed a full circuit of the vehicle. It was evident he was still unhappy about the last minute change in plan. 'So what happens now? The *Mendoza* isn't due to dock until an hour from now. By the time Customs have given the all clear to unload the cargo, we're talking about what, at least another couple of hours. The whole idea of waiting until the ship was ready to turnaround was I could quietly slip on-board, and wouldn't be left kicking my heels waiting for the *Mendoza* to sail. It's less risky to be in and out of the docks, as quickly as possible.'

'I'm well aware of that, sir,' he answered, and placed an attaché case containing Captain Calero's payment in the well of the passenger seat.

'Then, I just don't see the point of breaking cover until we have to.'

Lange answered evenly enough. 'Because it's far safer to be on the road. No-one is going to be looking for us in an ambulance, and even if they were, it'd be like looking for a needle in a haystack.'

Schneider still wouldn't buy it. 'We've never exactly seen eye to eye, Erhard, but I do know when someone is holding out on me. If you remember, our original plan was to remain at the safe house until Captain Calero gave us the okay to move. What's changed?'

Lange coolly held the older man's gaze and lied, 'It's not my place to question General Aurberg's orders.'

Schneider shook his head. 'No, this isn't down to the *Schamhorst*. I can see what's happened here.'

'Can you?' Lange answered flatly.

Schneider gestured toward Joyce. 'Cosying up to the whore is one thing, but last minute changes to the planning smacks of panic. I've always had my doubts about you.'

Lange cut him off. 'You can think whatever you like, sir, but I'm just doing my best to keep you alive long enough to board the *Mendoza* in one piece!' They were wasting valuable time. Lange re-checked his watch. 'All right, both of you get in the back of the ambulance.'

'I'm not sitting in there with *her*!' Schneider protested. 'I'll sit in the front with you.'

'You have a choice, sir. Either do as I say, or God help me, I'll drop you where you stand.'

While Schneider's expression remained impassive, he began to comprehend Lange was deadly serious. But, Schneider still wouldn't budge, and defiantly standing his ground. He, too, was armed, and it ran through his mind he could probably make it to the docks on his own. It wasn't that far. More to the point, he simply didn't trust Lange not to put a bullet in the back of his head. No, he'd much rather take a chance than play second fiddle to someone he would once have squashed without even drawing breath. Besides, it really wouldn't take too much of an effort to kill both of them.

As Joyce stared across the garage at Schneider, she could feel her pulse start to quicken. She could almost read his mind; something was going to kick off. There was no way he'd back down and allow Lange to gain the upper hand. She remembered Frenzel describing him as a psychologically flawed maverick, who was both feared and admired in equal measure. Lange also knew they'd reached the end of the line, and instinctively reached for his gun, but Schneider proved too fast. The crack of the shot echoed around the workshop, and the bullet slammed into Lange's chest. A hideous crimson stain spread across his once crisp white shirt. A look of disbelief crossed his face. Lange clutched his chest and slumped to his knees. His face contorted in pain.

A well of sickness rose from Joyce's stomach into her throat; she feared if she didn't act fast, she'd soon find herself lying dead beside Lange. Schneider looked down at him with something approaching smug satisfaction at his bloody handiwork. He calmly removed the Luger from Lange's grasp, and searched through his pockets for ammunition clips and keys, and then stuffed them into his jacket.

Joyce saw her chance, and picked up a wrench off the stone floor and swung it at him. Out of the corner of his eye, he saw what she was doing, and half turned to defend himself, the main force of the blow thudded into his upraised arms. He reeled back. By now, Joyce was swinging the wrench like a baseball bat and slammed it into his shoulder. The blow spun him into the side of the ambulance. Instead of backing away and fleeing for her life, she was still coming at him like a woman possessed. He felt another bone-crunching crack and stumbled to the ground. He raised his hands again in self-defence. The blows were raining down on him and hurt like hell.

He watched helplessly as his pistol spun out of his grasp across the oil-stained, stone floor. He made a desperate lunge, grabbed the gun, staggered to his feet, and managed to fire off another shot. Although it winged past her head, Joyce didn't flinch, and brought the heavy wrench crashing down on his left hand. Schneider yelled out in pain; he heard it snap. She'd broken his wrist. The pistol again slipped out of his grasp and slithered across the floor. Joyce took another swing, missed, and smashed the wrench into one of the ambulance's headlights. The glass shattered into a myriad of pieces.

Fearing for his life, Schneider fumbled frantically in his jacket pocket with his right hand for Lange's Luger, but he tripped. He desperately reached out to steady himself against the side of the ambulance, only to end up stumbling again, falling heavily to the ground. By now, Joyce was standing over him. She couldn't afford to let up. Cowering or not, he was still a dangerous killer. If he survived, how many more lives would be taken? How many others would be ruined?

Schneider looked up at her, and for once, his eyes were filled with terror. She was about to thwack the wrench down again on him with a sickening thud, and he was almost on the point of begging for his life, but somehow managed to get a grip on Lange's handgun and fired off several shots. Joyce froze, and instinctively closed her eyes, waiting for the inevitable thud and pain. At this distance, he couldn't miss. *Please God, make it quick, please*, she said to herself. But, each of the three shots narrowly winged past her head.

'The next one,' Schneider said through gritted teeth, 'won't miss!'

Joyce re-opened her eyes. Why had he spared her?

'Put the wrench down!' he commanded and eased himself back to his feet.

She hesitated, swiftly weighing up her options. No matter how bloodied and bruised Schneider was, adrenaline had kicked in, and he was more than capable of finishing her off. Joyce glanced at the Luger's barrel; it was aimed straight at her head. Reluctantly, she decided to release the wrench from her grasp, allowing it to clatter to the floor.

'Can you drive?' he demanded.

'Yes, I can.'

He gestured toward the ambulance with the pistol. 'Get in!'

Joyce looked at him carefully, with a wary curiosity, and silently complied. She climbed in the driver's side and sat tight, as he joined her in the passenger seat. He reached for the keys in his jacket and handed them across to her. Schneider was in a God awful state, but he still had the Luger firmly trained on her.

Joyce turned on the engine, leaving it idling. 'Why didn't you kill me?' she asked.

He held up his left hand; the wrist was crooked and bent. It was answer enough; he was unable to drive. Joyce thrust the gear lever into first, and crashed the accelerator to the floor.

Chapter 20
Bishop's Place, Southwark, South London

Spencer's presence had caused quite a stir amongst the backup team. Until then, it had been just another routine assignment. They were well aware of Schneider's background, but not of his involvement with his brother's brutal murder. By the time they arrived in Bishop's Place, the garage doors were still wide open. The team was heavily armed, and, as planned, it was decided Carter would be the first to go in, with Jim Jarvis as his immediate backup.

They slowly edged their way along the outside of the garage toward the doorway. Carter paused, and gave the thumbs up to Jarvis, indicating he was ready. He briefly peered inside; Lange's lifeless body was sprawled out on the cold concrete floor. While the garage might look empty, there was no point leaving anything to chance. He and Jarvis steadily edged their way inside to check it out.

There was an anxious wait until Carter re-appeared in the doorway. 'It's okay; we can stand down,' he announced, and made a throw-away gesture with his right hand for the team to stay where they were.

Spencer was by now at Carter's side and swiftly took in the scene. Finding the garage empty didn't lighten his mood any; Schneider was still one step ahead of them. After discovering Gliddon Street abandoned and signs Joyce had been kept chained up in the cellar, Spencer had convinced himself they were already too late to save her. He crouched down beside Lange's body; it was still warm.

'Take a look at this,' Carter said, pointing toward the heavy metal wrench Joyce used on Schneider. Spencer joined him. 'What do you reckon? Is it blood on the end?'

'I'd say so,' he said.

'She might still be alive,' Jarvis suggested, more in hope than expectation.

It was probable, but Spencer felt it unlikely. His gaze roamed slowly around the garage before coming back to rest on Lange's body. He'd hoped to snare Schneider, but Luke Garvan was now in charge of their last line of defence at Surrey Docks.

'Come on,' he said sharply. 'There's no point in us hanging around here. Ask one of Garvan's guys to contact the local nick and secure the area, will you?'

'Yes, sir,' Jarvis said, heading out of the garage.

Garvan was waiting on standby in the customs office at Surrey Docks when the call finally came through from Spencer. In the distance loomed the *Mendoza*, surrounded by large cranes and still fully laden with prime Argentinian beef. On Garvan's instructions, the local customs officers had placed a temporary embargo on the shipment. Whereas, by now, the *Mendoza* would otherwise have been a hive of activity, with Dockers unloading the cargo and a line of trucks waiting to be loaded, a strict perimeter was enforced around the vessel. Garvan had gone over the plan with a fine toothcomb before finally submitting it to Spencer, who not only trusted his judgment, but was more than happy to allow him to take the lead. It was 0845hrs when the call came through to his command post. Johnny Mortimer, the head of the customs operation, picked up the phone.

'Is Assistant Commissioner Garvan with you?' Spencer asked.

'Yes, he is. Who shall I say is calling?'

'Sir Spencer Hall. Tell him it's urgent.'

The name didn't ring any particular bells to the Customs Officer. He cupped his hand over the receiver. 'There's a Sir Spencer Hall on the line for you; he says it's urgent.'

Garvan nodded, and held out his hand for the phone. 'Garvan here.'

'You're on, Luke.'

'What's happened?'

'Lange's dead. We found his body in the garage.'

'What happened to him?'

'It was a nice piece of handiwork, professional, one shot between the eyes.'

There was a long pause before Garvan answered. His voice was sharp with anxiety. He choked back a well of emotion before managing to ask. 'Have you managed to find Joyce? Is she all right?

'No, we haven't.'

'What about Gliddon Road?'

'They'd obviously kept her holed up in the basement.'

'And?'

'I'm sorry, Luke, there's no sign of her. I wish only to God I knew what's happened, but I don't!'

Garvan detected the tension in Spencer's voice; it was unusual. 'Are you holding out on me?'

'No, why should I?'

'It wouldn't be the first time.'

Spencer pulled a face. Garvan knew him too well. He'd already decided to err on the side of caution and not mention the blood they'd found on the wrench. He figured it would only complicate matters. 'Listen, Luke, there's not much more to tell you. Lange's body was still warm, so we only just missed Schneider. By the time we arrived at the garage, the ambulance had already left. I'm not quite sure why they didn't stick to the original plan and sit tight until Calero gave them the okay.'

'Where are you now?'

Spencer glanced at his watch. 'We're on our way to the Docks. We should be with you in, say, about five-ten minutes. Schneider's got a good head start on us, so I image he'll be with you any minute.'

On hearing the line click dead, Garvan's knuckles turned white, as he gripped the phone and cursed uselessly into the mouthpiece.

Mortimer asked anxiously, 'Is there a problem, sir?'

Garvan regained his composure, set the receiver into the cradle, and met the man's uneasy gaze. 'Our target's on his way to the docks, Johnny.' With that, he left the office, leaving Mortimer wondering who the hell was Sir Spencer Hall.

**

The *Mendoza* was still fully laden with its cargo. Garvan had deliberately retained a low-key security presence. He certainly didn't want to arouse any undue interest or suspicion. Shortly after its arrival, an exclusion zone had been thrown around the vessel, both the drivers and Dockers were placed on standby, and, by all accounts, were enjoying a welcome extended breakfast at the surrounding local greasy spoon cafes.

Although the *Mendoza's* cargo contained prime beef, the fact Customs had placed a temporary embargo on the shipment wasn't particularly unexpected, given there had recently been a widely reported health scare involving contaminated cans of Argentinian corned beef. Fortunately, the delay in off-loading the cargo had been accepted by everyone, including the *Mendoza's* crew, as a routine precaution.

Even Captain Calero hadn't appeared to be unduly alarmed by the presence of both customs officers and representatives from the Ministry of Health. As far as he was concerned, they were merely doing their duty to check not only the beef but also the ship's hygiene standards. He wasn't to know the Ministry officials were actually, undercover Special Branch officers.

Freddy Evans opened the rear door of the green Rover, and waited for Spencer to alight. As he drew himself up to his full height, Spencer's gaze travelled toward the white hulled *Mendoza*. He was no expert on ships, but the vessel was larger than he'd expected. Two gangplanks were leading from the ship; one in the centre and the second toward the rear. Parked up on the dockside, stood the neat serried row of trucks, waiting to collect the cargo of prime beef. The remainder of the consignment was to be stored in one of the nearby refrigeration units.

Garvan was there to meet them.

Spencer looked surprised. 'Still no sign of Schneider?'

'Not yet.'

'He should have been here by now.'

'How sure are you about this ambulance?'

'Frenzel was quite specific about it. Besides, it's actually quite a good idea.'

Garvan found himself agreeing.

'How's Calero taking the delay?'

‘Surprisingly well. If he does suspect something’s wrong, he’s certainly not giving anything away.’

Spencer turned to Evans. ‘You’d better park up out of sight.’

‘Yes, sir.’

‘Where’s the rest of your team?’

‘They’re behind the customs office; I take it that’s okay by you?’

Garvan nodded. The office provided a bird’s eye view of the *Mendoza*. ‘If the call comes through, we’ll be the first to know.’

Chapter 21
Surrey Commercial Docks

Since leaving Gliddon Road, things hadn't quite gone according to plan. Schneider's confidence in navigating their way to the docks far exceeded his ability, and, at best, it was sketchy. Having taken several wrong turnings, they ended up doubling back on themselves. Lange had reckoned it was no more than a ten-minute drive from the lock-up, but they'd already been on the road for a good twenty minutes. Maybe he should have played it differently and kept Lange alive long enough to reach the *Mendoza*? But, Schneider let the thought go. Lange had proved untrustworthy and deserved to die.

They stopped at a junction 'Where now?' Joyce demanded.

'Take a right!'

She shot him an irritated glance. 'Are you sure?'

He pointed to the signage across the road. It was more by luck than judgement they'd managed to navigate their way to almost within spitting distance of the docks. Joyce turned right, and joined the increasingly heavy traffic. They were now travelling at a snail's pace, stopping and starting. Schneider's growing frustration wasn't helped any when she stalled the ambulance at a set of traffic lights. He leaned toward her, the Luger pointed to her face.

'Do that again, and so help me.'

Joyce re-started the engine, and rammed the gear stick into first. 'Or what?' she countered angrily. 'You'll shoot me?'

Schneider held back. As much he'd have loved to squeeze the trigger, he was in no fit state to drive, and the bitch knew that. Schneider saw the murderous expression on her face. She was more than a match for him, and however much he believed he had the upper hand, Joyce was not only ruthless but had already proved a deadly opponent. *How much did she know about the escape plan? Had she informed MI5?* He had no way of knowing, but right now, he needed her help.

Joyce followed the signs to the docks, but was acutely aware once she'd outlived her usefulness, Schneider wouldn't hesitate to kill her. She prayed to God Spencer had the *Mendoza* covered. It was her only hope. Schneider tentatively tried to flex his left hand, and carefully kneaded it with his right. Joyce noted the movement; he was obviously in a good deal of pain.

As they approached the main entrance, Schneider flicked on the emergency bell. They were waved through, but Joyce had no idea where the *Mendoza* was moored.

'Put your foot down, and follow the signs to Baynes Dock!' he commanded.

In the distance, the *Mendoza* loomed large against a backdrop of cranes. Squinting with exhausted eyes, Joyce knew this was it. She was rapidly running out of options. Once they reached the ship, Schneider wouldn't hesitate in squeezing the trigger. *Where the hell were they? Where was Spencer?* He'd promised to be there for her, to watch her back. Schneider certainly wasn't worth dying for.

'Over there!' he yelled, pointing through the windscreen. 'Drive over to the trucks. Park up behind them.'

Joyce briefly followed his gaze, but was distracted when something caught her eye. A car shot out from behind one of the buildings to her right, and was speeding toward the ambulance. God, she didn't know what to do. Schneider was still barking out orders. Joyce knew she needed to make a snap decision. There was nothing for it. She braced herself, before deliberately oversteering to avoid the oncoming car and slammed on the brakes. There was a sound of crunching metal, as the ambulance clipped the rear wing of a truck. Joyce caught her breath, as she smashed her chest against the steering wheel. The momentum sent Schneider crashing into the dashboard, his face contorted in pain. This was her chance; she opened the driver's door and practically fell out of the ambulance, then ran for her life toward the trucks.

A shot rang out and smashed through the windscreen, sending small fragments of glass into the ambulance. Schneider had already dived for cover, but knew he was a sitting duck where he was. He needed to get out of the ambulance. Schneider opened the passenger door, and blindly fired off a volley of shots through the broken windscreen, before taking his chances and scurrying for cover between the trucks. A shot winged past his head, and Schneider only just managed to make it. He stumbled, but managed to keep upright, and stood for a moment nursing his badly distorted, broken wrist. Another car drew up, and he could hear low, urgent voices. The *Mendoza* was tantalisingly close, almost within touching distance. Schneider began snaking his way between the trucks. Another shot rang out; he flinched, paused, held his breath, and returned fire.

He struck lucky; a bullet ripped into Jarvis's side, and the blow spun him into the side of a truck. Carter called out and asked if he was okay. At first, Jarvis scarcely felt any pain, but as he begun to edge forward, the searing pain suddenly hit him. Carter couldn't see him, but called out again to him. Jarvis didn't answer immediately, but by the sound of it, he was in a good deal of pain. Eventually, Jarvis managed to reassure Carter he'd be okay, but as he made to move again, his legs gave way, and he collapsed by the truck.

Carter began to retrace his steps back toward Jarvis; he was obviously in a bad way. As he knelt down beside his fallen colleague, he heard Joyce call to him. He spun around to see her crawling out from beneath another of the trucks.

'Until we saw you at the wheel of the ambulance, we thought you...' His words trailed off.

'Were dead?' she offered, and knelt down beside him to tend Jarvis, who was groaning and drifting in an out of consciousness. 'I'll stay here with Jarvis.' Her eyes held his for a fraction of a second. 'Be careful, Jed.'

'I don't like leaving you here.'

She noticed Jarvis's pistol lying on the ground. Carter followed her gaze and reluctantly stood up. By now, Garvan had joined them.

'Look after him,' Carter said, barely above a whisper, and headed back between the vehicles.

As he ducked another volley of shots, Schneider knew the game was up. The bastards had pinned him down. He peered tentatively toward the ship, only to see undercover officers removing the aft gangway. Schneider figured he had two choices, to wait for the inevitable or go down fighting. He checked his pockets for ammunition. Even though he had betrayed the Fatherland by spying for the Soviets, at heart, he still had only one allegiance; to the SS and Adolf Hitler. Obedience unto death.

A shot cracked past Schneider's face, and ricocheted off the side of a truck; he flinched, and then heard a calm voice say in perfect German, 'I believe this is yours.' Spencer tossed the attaché case containing Captain Calero's payment toward him. The clasp broke open, and the neatly bundled piles of banknotes cascaded onto the ground.

Schneider took aim, but heard another voice, again who spoke in German. 'I wouldn't, if I were you.' Carter was no more than ten feet away from him, and had a PPK aimed at him. 'Drop it!'

Schneider considered his options; he wasn't quite finished, but lowered the Luger and placed it on the ground.

Spencer had been after Schneider for years. Perhaps, at last, the payoff had finally come, but he needed to divorce his feelings and concentrate. He needed to rid himself of the eyewitness accounts of how his brother had been forced to strip naked by Schneider before he shot him in the back of the head.

'You have a lot of explaining to do.'

Schneider's tense, pale face was beaded with the sweat of anxiety. He looked candidly into the eyes of this Englishmen, who spoke German like a native. He then glanced toward Carter. He hadn't moved a muscle, and still had the PPK aimed at his head. Other members of their team were closing in fast, but kept a respectful distance.

'What kind of explaining?' he said to Spencer.

'Does the name Demetri Smolin mean anything to you?'

Schneider's eyes narrowed speculatively. 'It might.'

'I understand since your release from Jamiltz, you've been working for the KGB, is that correct?' Spencer flashed him a slight, fixed smile.

'Did Smolin tell you this?'

'What do you think?'

It was answer enough. Schneider's face creased up; he wanted to explain. 'My sister, did he tell you about Anna?'

'It doesn't matter what I believe, but General Aurberg and the *Schamhorst* now have proof of your involvement with the Soviets.'

Schneider's heart jumped into his throat. 'Proof!' he barked. 'What kind of proof?'

'I leaked it to them, how else?'

'Who are *you*?'

'Spencer Hall.'

His face registered surprise, and he said sarcastically, 'What an honour. Am I really that important for the Director of General of MI5 to come here in person?'

'Let's just say, my interest is personal.'

Schneider considered his response carefully. 'I'm not quite sure what you mean by personal?'

He told him about Jamie, about the accounts of how his brother and his SAS colleagues had died. Schneider expressed it was no more than his duty. There was no repentance for the past, only he'd do it all over again. Spencer's grip tightened around the PPK; it crossed his mind rather than face justice, he'd actually be doing Schneider a favour by killing him. It was the first time in his life he'd hesitated, but that flicker of uncertainty was just enough for Schneider to see an opportunity. If he was to die, then why not make it worthwhile. He went to reach for the Luger, but two shots rang out in rapid succession; it was a classic double tap. Schneider died instantly.

Spencer and Carter spun around; Joyce Leader was standing behind them, with Jarvis's pistol still gripped firmly in her hands. All her rage and training had kicked in. She'd focussed on Schneider, aimed and fired, shooting him once in the shoulder and once in the head. Her thought was she'd finally killed the bastard. There were no regrets, only an overwhelming sense she'd survived.

Garvan came up behind her. 'Joyce,' he said gently, 'why not hand me the gun.'

She was rooted to the spot; she refused to hand it over.

'How's Jarvis?' Spencer asked of Garvan.

He shook his head. 'We tried. I'm sorry, he didn't make it.'

Carter turned away; he'd had his differences with Jarvis, but he certainly didn't deserve this, nor did Dawn Abrams. Someone would have to tell her Jim was dead, and he knew it was down to him.

Spencer took a sharp intake of breath, and walked over to Joyce. 'Are you all right?' He reached out to her, but she angrily shrugged away from him.

Her expression spoke volumes; there was still a deadly glint in her eyes which made him hold his tongue. Joyce inclined her head toward Schneider. 'Lange was his handiwork.'

'Why did he kill him?'

'They got into an argument. But, it was never going to take much to send Schneider over the edge.' As if by rote, she began to tell them how, after Lange had been killed, she'd looked around desperately searching for something she could fight back with to defend herself. If she hadn't picked up the wrench, and hit Schneider with such force, she'd have ended up lying dead beside Lange.

Spencer's eyes strayed back toward Schneider; it wasn't just his wrist she'd broken. He had a huge welt on the side of his face, where she'd obviously pummelled him with the wrench. Spencer didn't allow his feelings to show, but, like Carter, he'd feared the worse. It never paid to underestimate Joyce. As she continued to keep a tight grip on Jarvis's pistol, it was evident to him she was still high on adrenaline, but slowly it tapered off into anger.

Joyce went up to him and hissed angrily in his face. 'That's it, Spence. We're even *now*!'

He couldn't deny it.

Joyce thrust the PPK into his hands. 'If you have another assignment, you can shove it right up...'

'I can well imagine where you might well want to shove it,' he said evenly.

Joyce swept past him before rounding on him again. 'And another thing, don't *ever* call me again!' Without looking back, she made a rude finger gesture, as she disappeared between the trucks.

A slow, admiring smile began to cross Spencer's face. 'Carter, you'd better get after her, and give her a lift.'

'Where to?'

He pulled a face. 'Wherever she wants.'

Perhaps Carter ought never to have doubted Joyce was still very much at the top of her game. He hesitated, but needed to say what was on his mind. 'If she's this good now, what the hell was she like during the War?'

'The best of the best!' Spencer replied thoughtfully. 'But, she's right about one thing; this makes us more than even.'

Garvan stayed put. He still had to wind up the operation and arrange for Schneider's body to be removed from the docks. Spencer noted he looked shaken. While desperately trying to help Joyce save Jarvis's life, he'd seen him slip away in front of their eyes. He kept wondering if he hadn't done quite enough.

'Are you okay?' Spencer asked him.

'I'll be all right,' he said flatly. 'Are you going to tell Dawn?'

'Yes, that's my job. I couldn't possibly leave it to anyone else to do. But, no-one is to make a direct report to my office about Jarvis, until I've spoken to Dawn. Is that understood?

'I'll pass the word around.'

Spencer took one last lingering look at Schneider's body, almost as if to reassure him his arch nemesis was dead. After all these years of searching and trying to track Schneider down, his brother's brutal torture and murder had finally been avenged. 'Give me a call, if you need anything,' was all he could think of saying.

Spencer placed his revolver back in its holster, and headed toward his car. He had it in mind he would call Garvan again this evening to see how things were; it was the least he could do. It might also go some way in helping to salvage his conscience. Once Garvan had finished work, he'd no doubt touch base with Joyce. He presumed she'd want to return to the Savoy, but he could check that out with Carter. Perhaps, more importantly, although she was battered and bruised, Joyce had at least walked away from the assignment alive. Twenty-four hours earlier, Spencer had been resigned to the fact they'd almost certainly lost her altogether. He'd even found himself going over in his mind how to break the news of her death to Garvan. It wouldn't only have tested their friendship, but probably have broken it irrevocably.

As things stood, Spencer decided the wisest course of action was to give her a wide berth for a while. Even at the best of times, she'd always been mercurial, with a volatile temperament. However, he'd known her long enough to realise once Joyce had finally worked through her demons, she'd eventually welcome him back into her close-knit circle of trusted friends. At heart, he deeply valued her friendship, almost as much as he did Garvan's. It was a close bond, born out of their time spent at the epicentre of the ultra-secret Double Cross System, supervising a small team of highly skilled, double agents controlled by British Intelligence.

**

Freddy Evans was waiting for Spencer outside MI5. As he headed down the steps toward the car, the boss had a face like granite. Evans sucked in his lower lip, and opened the rear door. 'Everything all right, sir?'

'I've had easier days,' he said, with characteristic understatement.

'How's Dawn?'

Spencer paused outside the car. 'I've asked one of the girls to take her home.'

'Poor luv. She was besotted by young Jarvis.'

'Yes, I know,' Spencer said distractedly. 'Come on, Freddy. Let's get this over and down with!'

Evans drove him to Perrymead Street. Right now, there was only one other thing left to do; to let Josef Frenzel know Schneider was dead.

Frenzel was pale and intense, as he listened to the story unfold. He appeared suitably upset about Erhard Lange, but Spencer had a hunch his reaction was probably more for show than genuine. On the other hand, Frenzel's response to the news of Schneider's death was little short of heartfelt relief. Albeit, when he discovered Joyce was responsible for killing Schneider, he was stunned into silence, and probably considered himself lucky to have escaped with his own life.

After Spencer had left the safe house, Frenzel still couldn't quite bring himself to believe the elegant blonde he'd come to love was capable of getting the better of Schneider, and killing him in cold blood. He reached for the soda syphon to top up his freshly poured whisky, and stared unseeingly out of the window to the street below. He still didn't regret his decision to betray Schneider; he was, after all, a Soviet agent. In time, General Aurberg and his *Schamhorst* colleagues would learn the truth about Schneider's self-serving deceit. Spencer had already started to drip feed information to them. By the time they discovered the full extent of his treachery, Frenzel would be safely back at the family home in Osnabrück.

Perhaps he might even be fortunate enough to live out his retirement into old age, but there was a blight on the horizon, for the *Schamhorst* was totally unforgiving. If they were ever to discover he had betrayed Schneider to British Intelligence, there would be a heavy price to pay. Retribution against former Nazi colleagues who transgressed was to be kept in-house, not palmed off to enemy intelligence agencies. In time, the *Schamhorst* would have caught up with Schneider, but Frenzel had already run out of time. God willing, Spencer would honour his promise to him, but only time would tell.

He drained his glass and promptly refilled it. Perhaps the saying "there's no fool like an old fool," was true. She probably viewed him as nothing more than business, just another notch on her bedpost to discard and forget, but, try as he might; he still had strong feelings for Joyce. Since their first delicious night of lovemaking, he'd been nothing more than putty in her hands. But, even General Aurberg had spoken admiringly of her work. There was no reason to suspect her of spying for British Intelligence; that is, until Schneider planted a seed of doubt, not only in his own mind, but more importantly, in the General's. At first, Frenzel hadn't known quite which way to turn, but there was no question of disobeying orders.

Shortly afterwards, a message arrived by courier from Aurberg, short and to the point. Joyce was to be eliminated, but kept alive until Schneider was en-route to South America. He'd followed orders, and reluctantly played along with their plans by spiking her drink. But, long before his meeting with Sir Spencer Hall at the Anaxos Club, Frenzel had always harboured niggling doubts about Schneider.

At first, he'd just put it down to old enmities and the mutual distrust between the Gestapo and German Intelligence. Allegiance was one thing, but in the cold light of day, there was something about him that had started to make Frenzel feel distinctly uncomfortable. The atrocities he committed in the name of the Third Reich were well documented; he was a war criminal on the run. The long reach of the *Schamhorst* had called in old favours, old allegiances; failure to comply would have resulted in almost certain death. For good, or bad, fear had guided all of Frenzel's subsequent decisions.

He glanced down at his glass; it was empty. Drink helped mask his feelings, so he poured another, only larger this time. As much as Frenzel tried to divorce his feelings and concentrate on the future, his thoughts kept returning to Joyce. No, he didn't regret trying to save her life. For all her duplicity, he still wished to God there was some way of turning back the clock, and there was some way of seeing her again.

Chapter 22
St. Philips Hotel, Westminster

As Jack Stein stared down at the blood-filled bath, he silently cursed under his breath. Zimmerman had slashed straight up from the inside of his wrists to the crook of his elbows. A discarded razor blade lay on the bathmat. There were no half measures; the eminent scientist knew precisely what he had been doing. Perhaps things might have turned out differently, if he'd gone over things with Zimmerman earlier.

Once back in the States, Zimmerman would have been discreetly side-lined; there were any number of projects or lecturing tours to which he could have been assigned. The White House couldn't afford a public scandal. He would have been allowed more time with his family, accompanied by one or two well-placed editorials suggesting Zimmerman had stepped back from NASA because of failing ill-health. Handled correctly, no-one would have questioned it. As things stood, the real victims in all this unholy mess were his family.

There was nothing Stein could do, so he headed back into the bedroom, when something caught his eye in the bathroom. There was an envelope addressed to Zimmerman's wife wedged under the mirror. He recognised the Professor's untidy, spidery writing. He ripped the envelope open and unfolded the note. The suicide note was written on the hotel's headed paper. All in all, Stein had seen quite a few in his time. One or two words were difficult to read, but there was nothing out of the ordinary. Zimmerman had penned what amounted to be an apology to his wife and children. There was a brief explanation, warts and all, of why he had chosen to end his life.

Stein refolded the note and slipped it into his jacket pocket. One thing was sure, Zimmerman's wife would never be allowed to receive it. He took a sharp intake of breath, moved back to the bedroom, picked up the phone, and called MI5. A red light blinked on Dawn Abrams stand-in's intercom; it was Spencer's private line. She picked up a grey phone from a bank of four.

'Stein here. Is your boss there?'

The girl hesitated. She didn't recognise the laid back American drawl, and queried his identity.

'I'm an old CIA buddy,' he explained.

'Yes, sir. I'll put you through.' She pressed the hold button and waited for Spencer to answer. 'I have Mr. Stein on the line for you.'

Spencer cupped the receiver over his ear as he continued writing. 'Okay, put him on.' She clicked the call through. 'What can I do for you, Jack?'

There was a slight pause before he answered, 'I have a removal job,'

Spencer closed his eyes, and threw his pen down on the desk in exasperation. His old friend had a body for disposal. 'For Christ's sake, Jack. You're meant to be on a flight back to the States in four hours' time.'

'Yeah, well, I might just have to cancel my ticket.'

'So, where the hell are you?'

'I'm still at the hotel.'

Spencer checked his watch. Being a Saturday morning, the traffic would be lighter, but he'd have expected them to be on the road by now. 'So, you haven't even left for the airport?'

'I've not even settled the goddamn bill!'

Spencer glanced at the mound of paperwork in his in-tray, piled high with the usual cipher stuff and reports. He'd been hoping for a couple of hours' peace and quiet to catch up with the huge backlog. 'Go on, who is it?'

'Professor Zimmerman.'

Spencer's mind went into overdrive. Just when he thought everything had been neatly sewn up, Jack went and dropped this on him. He was almost afraid to ask. 'Was it your handy work?'

'Nah,' Jack said, glancing toward the bathroom. 'He made a pretty damn good job of it by himself.'

'Is Garvan still at the hotel?'

'I'm really not sure. We had breakfast earlier. His guys are here, of course. He might be downstairs somewhere.'

'If he is, you'll need him to secure the area. I'll meet you at the hotel.'

Stein put the phone down, and headed for the corridor, speaking to one of his agents who was waiting outside Zimmerman's room. 'Go check if Assistant Commissioner Garvan is still here, will you?'

Jo Myers snapped to attention. 'Yes, sir.'

Stein guessed Myers was probably not too long out of the Marines. He was all muscle, a real thick chest and wide shoulders bulging under his suit. 'If he is, tell him it's urgent, and I need to see him right away.'

Stein closed the door and waited by the window, arms folded as he stared unseeingly across the skyline toward the treetops of St. James's Park. He'd have to call the Ambassador and the CIA's top guy at the Embassy. Between them, they'd spread the news of Zimmerman's suicide stateside. In the meantime, he'd have to stay in London to help ensure the sordid details surrounding Zimmerman's death didn't leak out. If the Press got wind of his suicide, they'd start snooping around and digging again into his personal and professional life. God forbid, but if they managed to find a link to the ultra-hardline Nazi *Schamhorst*, the political fallout would be nothing short of catastrophic.

But, Stein knew it wouldn't just end with Zimmerman. Smelling blood, the newspapers, with their bold front-page headlines, would undoubtedly turn their attention to his fellow German rocket scientists, led by the brilliant Wernher von Braun. Difficult questions would be asked of NASA. The White House would be forced to defend their leading role on the Saturn rocket programme. They'd be placed increasingly under the spotlight. The old stories, the ghosts of the past, would once again be raked up again for public consumption. The ripple effect of Zimmerman's connections to the *Schamhors*t would put the spotlight on his colleagues. Since the successful launch of Russia's Sputnik back in 1957, the nagging question was whether their German scientists had the edge over the American's German scientists. The pressure was on, and Zimmerman and his brilliant colleagues had been pivotal in the West's fight to regain the upper hand.

There was a knock on the door. Stein turned from the window. 'Who is it?'

'It's Myers, sir.'

'Okay, come in.'

Myers opened the door. Garvan was at his side, thanked him, and breezed into the suite. Stein raised the flat of his hand and told Myers to stand down.

Garvan waited until the door closed behind them. 'Your guy said it was urgent?'

Stein inclined his head toward the bathroom. 'Yeah, you'd better take a look.'

Garvan followed his gaze across the room; even from where they were standing, Zimmerman's body was clearly visible in the bath tub. 'You're a bloody walking disaster zone, Jack! Every time we meet, someone's either living on borrowed time or they're already dead.'

Stein shrugged indifferently; he couldn't exactly deny it.

'How long ago did you find him?'

'Just now. As we had an early start this morning, we loaded up most of the delegates' luggage last night. When Zimmerman didn't surface from his room, Myer's raised the alert.'

Stein followed him into the bathroom. He knew Garvan had earned his spurs at Scotland Yard on the murder squad. So, he stood back a little to give him some space. He swiftly appraised Zimmerman's body; his head was lolled back against the head of the wrought iron bath.

A strait-razor blade lay on the bathmat. Even though the water was discoloured, he could still just make out that Zimmerman had placed the tip of the razor on the radial artery then cut straight down toward each of his left wrists.

'Was he right-or left-handed?'

'Right-handed.'

'He'd have cut the left first,' he explained, matter-of-factly. 'The pain would have been excruciating, so he must have quickly repeated the same action on his right arm.'

Garvan glanced around at Stein. 'He certainly knew what he was doing.'

'Yeah, he certainly did.' Stein's voice sounded distracted. 'How long do you think he's been dead?'

Garvan stared down at Zimmerman's deathly pallor. 'A good few hours, probably late last night. Did anyone see him?'

'He ordered room service.'

'Did he have a meal?' Garvan asked, returning the bedroom

'Zimmerman wasn't the sociable type. He preferred to keep himself to himself. As far as anyone could tell, he seemed okay, not that he ever gave much away. After Frenzel had tipped him off about Schneider, Spencer called me, and said I might want to check on him.'

'So, how was he?'

Stein pulled a face. 'He'd been out shopping, buying presents for his wife and kids. Everything seemed pretty normal.'

'Interesting. I wonder what finally tipped him over the edge.'

Stein inclined his head toward the dressing table. Garvan followed his gaze. There was an empty bottle of Bourbon. Beside it, was a glass containing the last few dregs he hadn't bothered to finish off. Stein suggested in the cold light of day, Zimmerman might not have taken his life, and it could have been the booze talking.

'Perhaps,' Garvan said methodically. 'Or, maybe, it was just easier tanked on Bourbon. It would certainly have helped to deaden the pain.' Garvan picked up the bottle and smelt the contents.

'What are you doing?'

'Just making sure it's not laced with anything else.'

Stein looked at him questioningly.

'Don't worry, Jack, it smells pretty neat to me, but just to be on the safe side, we'll ask the lab to check it out.' Garvan set the bottle down. 'Was he a heavy drinker?'

'No, not usually. He liked the odd glass, but don't we all. We never detected anything excessive.'

Garvan drew in his lower lip. 'Did you get around to discussing Schneider with him?'

'I didn't intend to until we were on our way back to the States.'

'Even so, he must have known something was not quite right.'

'I figure that's where I screwed up.'

'What do you mean?'

'It was a tough call. Come down hard on him straight away, or lay off for a while.' Stein slipped a Marlboro cigarette between his lips and lit it. 'I didn't want to put too much pressure on him, especially not here in London. I was afraid this might happen, you know, that he'd do something stupid.' A slow ironic smile crossed Stein's face. 'Well, as you can see, things didn't quite go according to plan.'

'Did he leave a suicide note?'

Stein reached into his jacket pocket, and produced the note. 'Yeah, take a look.'

Garvan scanned the untidy scrawl then handed it back to Stein. 'What are you going to do with it?'

He creased up his face. 'That's not my call, but I guess they'll ask me to destroy it.'

It was no more than Garvan expected. 'Okay,' he announced. 'I better get moving on this lot. I'll get my people to deal with the hotel management.'

'Thanks. You do realise it'll have to be a cover up job,' Stein pressed him.

Garvan held his gaze. 'I take it you've already called Spencer about Zimmerman?'

Stein blew out a plume of smoke from his freshly lit cigarette. 'He told me to contact you.'

'I'm sure he did.'

'So, what happens now?'

'Well, for a start, I'll have to call in Dr. Brabant.'

Stein eyed him suspiciously. 'Is this Brabant guy to be trusted? I mean, if Zimmerman's suicide leaks out, it'll be political dynamite!'

'He's a Home Office pathologist,' Garvan explained.

Stein still seemed uneasy. 'I don't give a damn who he is; we really can't afford for some smart arse doctor to go issuing a death certificate.'

Garvan interrupted him. 'Don't go worrying about Brabant. Let's just say, he's worked for British Intelligence on some of their more sensitive cases.'

'So, he can keep his mouth shut?'

'They've never had a problem with him before. Besides, he's an old friend of Spencer's. You've got to remember, Jack, there are certain niceties to observe, if you don't have the official Home Office paperwork. Even if it is a rubber stamp job, without it, you'll end up running into a mound of red tape.'

'How long will it take to push things through?'

'I can't promise anything, but hopefully, by the middle of next week, we should be able to start thinking of flying his body back to the States. Under the circumstances, I'm sure our politicians will be just as eager as your own to keep things under wraps.'

'What are you gonna say to the hotel management?'

Garvan really hadn't thought it through. He shrugged slightly. 'A heart attack, perhaps, something sudden.'

Stein nodded his agreement. 'Who'll do the clean-up job?'

Garvan headed toward the door. 'I think we'll leave that to Spencer's lot.'

Stein gave him a bleak, somewhat forced smile. 'I thought you might say that.' As Garvan opened the door, Stein called after him, 'Is Joyce doing okay?'

'It's good of you to ask.'

'You know we go back a long way.'

'Yes, I do.'

'Joyce was always pretty slick, but this time, well, killing Schneider was something else!'

Garvan's grip tightened around the door handle. 'She's lucky to be alive.'

'We all need a little luck. So, how is she?'

'Still a little shaken up,' he replied evenly.

'Tell Joyce when this all dies down, I'll give her a call.'

Garvan opened the door. 'I should be back before Brabant arrives.' He could see Stein still wasn't happy with the arrangement. 'Don't worry,' he assured him. 'Brabant only lives a couple of miles away. He'll be here within the hour.'

'Spencer's on his way over here.'

'Good.' Garvan smiled. 'As soon as he arrives, he can take charge of the removal job.'

After Garvan had closed the door, Stein reached for the phone. He'd have to start making a few urgent calls, the first being to the American Ambassador. After that, all hell was likely to break loose.

Chapter 23
St. Philips Hotel

The headlines, on the morning after Zimmerman's death, read: "*TOP US SCIENTIST FOUND DEAD IN LONDON HOTEL.*" Stein found himself breathing a huge sigh of relief as he read *The Times* editorial, proclaiming how the renowned scientist had died of a suspected heart attack. Until the papers arrived, he'd spent a pretty sleepless night tossing and turning, wondering if all hell was about to break lose. Although he had complete faith in Garvan and Spencer, there was always an outside chance something might slip through the net and leak to the media. Fortunately, the *Daily Telegraph* and *The Mirror* all carried similar stories. In fact, all the major newspapers had picked up on Scotland Yard's news release about Zimmerman.

A quick phone call to Winthrop Alder, the American Ambassador, confirmed similar reports would be appearing in the New York and Washington papers.

Stein headed out of the St. Philips Hotel, and walked the short distance to MI5 HQ. Spencer was expecting him. Dawn Abrams was unexpectedly waiting to greet Stein in the reception area and booked him in at the security desk.

On seeing her, his expression softened. 'I'm so sorry about Jim.'

'Thank you.'

'But, what the hell are you doing back at work so soon?'

She smiled a sad, vulnerable smile. 'I need to keep myself busy; I couldn't stand being on my own at home.' Dawn's eyes burned with tears. She hurriedly brushed them away with the back of her hand. Stein instinctively placed a comforting arm around her shoulders. Dawn felt the tears welling up again. She squeezed his hand. Not quite trusting her voice, she mouthed her thanks. Although there were still deadlines to meet, Spencer had ensured Dawn was cushioned by willing colleagues, who wanted to take on some of her heavy workload.

They caught the lift to the fifth floor, and headed two doors down the passage to Spencer's office. Together, he and

Stein went over the daily newspapers, and any lingering sense of apprehension on Stein's part was soon forgotten. So far, everything had been sewn up tightly and was going according to plan. The clean-up job of Zimmerman's room and the removal of his body from the hotel had also gone off without a hitch.

However, Stein still harboured serious doubts about Dr. Brabant's involvement, and once again, queried why he and Garvan hadn't bypassed standard procedures. But, Spencer held firm, and wouldn't budge from Garvan's original decision to rubber stamp the medical paperwork. In the future, they might well live to regret the action. If some nosy journalist starts digging around and found inconsistencies surrounding Zimmerman's death, it would open up yet another potential can of worms.

'Don't worry about Brabant. He's ex-army,' Spencer reassured him. 'He knows the score.'

Stein was still uneasy. 'Even if this doc of yours is sound, can you vouch for his staff?'

'It's covered. We had Zimmerman's body moved to the pathology lab at the Royal Army Medical College at Millbank. I understand Brabant's called in a favour from an old friend to act as his assistant at the post-mortem. They studied together at the same medical school.'

'Who is it?'

A slow smile crossed Spencer's face. 'The Director of Army Pathology. I imagine it's a bit of a demotion for the General, but under the circumstances, he's agreed to help out.' Then, he added as an afterthought, "Agree" might not quite be the right word. Friends or not, let's just say he's been ordered to assist Brabant to conduct the post-mortem.'

Stein appeared slightly mollified; it wasn't his show, but an awful lot was riding on the next few days and how Zimmerman's death continued to be handled. Although, so far, things had gone well, it would only take one slip up, and the whole house of cards would come crashing down around their ears.

Dawn knocked on the door and entered carrying a file. Spencer looked at her expectantly. 'Have you finished typing up the draft?'

'Yes, sir. Only, I've highlighted a couple of points I'd like you to confirm for me.'

'Thank you, Dawn,' he said, accepting the buff coloured file.

'The Prime Minister's office has been on the line, asking when they can see the report.'

His pale blue eyes fixed on her. 'Tell them when I'm ready.'

Her face creased into a smile. 'I somehow doubt that'll go down too well with the PM's staff, don't you?'

'No,' he answered softening his tone. 'Probably not. Give me an hour or so.'

'I'll get onto to them straightaway; it's just the Prime Minister is expecting a call from the President on their private line about the Professor.'

'I'd be more surprised if he wasn't,' Spencer replied with quiet authority. 'Tell No 10 they'll have their report in plenty of time.'

Dawn made to leave but hesitated. 'The Home Secretary's people have been badgering on about a meeting with you and Assistant Commissioner Garvan.'

Spencer opened the file and spread it open on the desk. 'No10 takes priority. We can sort something out in due course, but I'd much rather wait until the Prime Minister has read the report about Zimmerman and his involvement with Schneider.' Dawn was about to close the door on them, when Spencer called after her. 'If anyone cuts up rough and starts giving you a hard time, then just put them through to *me*.'

She looked amused. 'With due respect, sir, I have a feeling the prospect of discussing anything with *you* would be enough to put anyone off!'

'Am I that much of an ogre?'

Dawn laughed. A genuine laugh, probably the first since Jarvis's death. 'The offer still stands.' He smiled warmly at her. 'If anyone gives you a hard time, I'll deal with them.'

'Thank you,' she said, returning his smile and closing the door.

When they were alone, Stein asked him, 'So, what's with this report?'

‘I’d like you to read over it.’

Stein shot him a questioning look. ‘Any particular reason why?’

‘I just want to make sure we’re singing off the same hymn sheet. You’ve briefed Winthrop Alder, I take it?’

‘Yeah,’ Stein said, with a flicker of amusement. ‘He looked so goddamn awful when I told him about Zimmerman, I thought he was going to croak on me.’

‘I can see losing the Professor and the American Ambassador on your watch might not look too good for you back in Washington.’

Stein laughed. ‘But, if you’re gonna go down, then why not do it in style.’

Before passing over the file, Spencer quickly checked through Dawn’s highlights. He scored through a couple and annotated an amendment. Spencer handed Stein the file, and sat back, lit a cigarette, and waited until he’d finished reading.

The report was concise, with just the right amount of detail. It was a delicate balancing act between too much and too little intelligence. Spencer had kept it relatively short and straightforward. One rather glaring admission was his secret meeting with Demetri Smolin. He knew the Home Secretary would kick up a god-almighty fuss, and start questioning the propriety of associating with a leading member of the KGB. Parker’s views were rigidly conservative, with a capital C, and Spencer’s occasional maverick approach to his role as Head of MI5 frequently filled him with dread. Although, by his own admission, Parker had no more knowledge of the intelligence world than the man in the moon, however, as Home Secretary, any fallout would end up on his desk, and he’d be expected to take the ensuing flak.

Stein closed the file and looked across the desk.

‘Well?’ Spencer asked expectantly. ‘What do you think?’

‘It’s pretty slick.’

‘But, are we singing off the same hymn sheet? Is there anything in the report your people might have a different take on?’

Stein leaned back in his chair. ‘I wouldn’t have thought so.’ But, he queried whether it was necessary to go into so much detail about Zimmerman's death; the report carried a pretty graphic description of the suicide. Spencer explained he had considered removing it, but on balance decided to keep it in.

It wasn't a deal breaker, so Stein let it rest.

Spencer drew heavily on his cigarette and regarded him searchingly. 'Come on, Jack, there's something else. What is it?'

Stein reached forward and lightly tapped the file. 'I love where you describe Schneider as having died resisting arrest.'

Spencer shrugged slightly and took a long deep breath. 'I guess it's all about interpreting the facts.'

'Well, if you don't mind my saying, that's one hell of an interpretation.'

'It's no more of a lie than Zimmerman dying of a heart attack. Besides, I need to protect her identity.'

Stein narrowed his eyes. He had a gut feeling Spencer was holding out on him. 'Who exactly are you protecting Joyce from?'

Spencer exhaled cigarette smoke slowly through his lips. 'It's a little delicate.'

'Hell, Spence, it's always a little delicate.'

'Joyce belongs to the same Bridge Club as the Prime Minister's wife.'

Stein whistled softly. 'I can see that might make future dinner parties at No10 just a little awkward.'

'You're probably right, but, more importantly, Mrs. Everett loves to gossip.'

'You mean, about her husband?'

'Not just the PM, no. Let's say, it's more of a scatter gun approach. In the early days of his premiership, Carol Everett was heavily criticised for appearing to capitalise on her husband's position.'

'And did she?'

'Well, that's open to debate. Carol has a double first from Oxford, and years before her husband entered Parliament, she was running her own successful cosmetic business. Since her husband became PM, she's had to take something of a backseat to her own ambitions. The papers ran a series of stories about her, but there was really nothing much in them. I think she was a little stung by all the criticism, but it comes with the territory. Joyce feeds me the odd snippet of gossip. It's usually something wildly indiscreet Carol lets drop in conversation. But, we're not here to discuss the PM's wife. If you're content, we'll go ahead with the report as it stands.'

'It's fine by me.'

Spencer reached forward and flicked on the intercom, asking Dawn to collect the report. 'It'll be the usual distribution to the Home and Foreign Offices, and while you're at it, you might as well pass a copy to the War Office, and the American Embassy. As soon as I've signed it off, have a courier deliver them to each of the copy addressees. You'd also better phone No 10 and let them know the report's on its way.'

'And the security caveat?'

'Top Secret UK & US Eyes only.'

Chapter 24
The Home Office, Whitehall

The Home Secretary, Chris Parker, had often been described as a safe pair of hands and not likely to rock the boat. In a political party riven by internal feuds and rivalries, the Prime Minister, Anthony Everett, needed someone he could trust to mind his back, rather than stab him in the back. While Parker's tenure as Home Secretary was viewed as a political necessity, for those under his direct command, his time in Office had been fraught with difficulties and constant indecision. He had also come under increasing attack from the Press, who had branded his performance as at best ineffectual.

Parker possessed an innate mistrust of his senior departmental staff. In the past, he'd witnessed too many of his Cabinet colleagues allow themselves to be manipulated by their civil servants. But, his mistrust went way beyond the confines of the Home Office, and encompassed both British Intelligence and Scotland Yard, all of whom he felt were riddled by self-interest rather than national interest.

During one particularly intense meeting with Parker, Spencer had rounded angrily on him. "With due respect, Home Secretary, I suggest you take a long hard look at yourself in the mirror before accusing others of self-interest!" In short, they'd grown accustomed to despising each other's company.

Even at the best of times, Parker didn't take kindly to criticism. As a consequence, relations between Spencer and his political master had rapidly hit rock bottom. Neither trusted the other, and by mutual consent, kept their business meetings to a bare minimum. During his time at the Home Office, Parker had initially warmed to Garvan; he viewed him as someone he could do business with, but had soon realised it was foolish to underestimate him. Unlike Spencer, Garvan appeared far more relaxed, far less formidable than he really was. Neither man was afraid to hold their ground.

But, ultimately, as Home Secretary, he had the final say. Parker always found himself wondering what lay behind Spencer's cold smiles, the hesitations, and the occasional little nuances. Spencer was a clever bastard, and, in his day, had worked with the best. During the darkest days of the war, he'd met Churchill. Parker feared the Head of MI5 viewed him as a pygmy in comparison to the great man. Parker's ego was notoriously fragile, and as a consequence, he imagined slights where none was intended. While he had made a policy of not passing judgment on his political colleagues, Parker's largesse did not extend to either Garvan, or Spencer.

After reading Spencer's report about Zimmerman's connections to Schneider and the *Schamhorst*, it soon became apparent why things needed to be kept under wraps. But, why, given the high profile and potential risks involved, had they kept him out of the loop until the last possible moment? As Home Secretary, he was responsible for the police, and matters of security. Therefore, both Scotland Yard and MI5 were directly accountable to him, and by rights, he should have been consulted from the outset.

A call from No 10 had gone some way in easing his belief Spencer and Garvan were hell bent on marginalising his authority. The Prime Minister was delighted Bernard Zimmerman's suicide was handled by the security services and Special Branch with professional efficiency. If Zimmerman's association with the *Schamhorst* had become public knowledge, the political fallout would have been nothing short of catastrophic. Throw into the mix Schneider's links to the KGB, then the Press on either side of the Atlantic would have had an absolute field day exposing the whole sordid story.

By the time Parker had arrived at No 10, Anthony Everett was in a particularly buoyant mood. The American Ambassador had already visited and expressed his gratitude, as had the President during a lengthy trans-Atlantic phone call to Downing Street. Everett felt congratulations were in order all round, and amongst the select few, there was a lot of political back slapping.

**

Spencer and Garvan were ushered into Parker's office by an attractive young civil servant carrying an armful of files. 'Please take a seat gentleman.' She smiled sweetly. 'The Home Secretary will be with you shortly.'

They thanked the young girl and settled into two rather uncomfortable chairs without arms in front of a large, mahogany desk.

It fleetingly crossed Spencer's mind, knowing Parker's renowned roving eye, he'd personally chosen the girl to serve in his outer office. His diary secretary, Alice Grey, was equally young, and rumours abounded Whitehall that they were having an affair. But, then again, office affairs were two a penny. Since his appointment as Director General of MI5, the one thing he'd soon come to realise was top politicians often threw caution to the wind in the trouser department. What the Prime Minister would make of his Home Secretary's philandering was quite another matter entirely. But, one thing was sure. Parker would never receive his ultimate accolade, a seat in the House of Lords.

Garvan waited until they were alone before saying, 'Have you noticed how bloody high Parker's chair is?'

Spencer followed his gaze to the large swivel chair behind the desk. It suddenly dawned on him. The setup was a little like being hauled into the headmaster's office. 'I guess looking down on his guests gives the Home Secretary a sense of superiority. What *was* it Eldridge called it?'

Garvan grinned. 'Wasn't it "little man syndrome"?'

'Yes, something like that,' Spencer responded absent-mindedly.

'I wonder what's keeping the old bugger.'

'Who knows? Perhaps he's in the loo, adjusting his toupee.'

'Are you joking?'

'Well it's either that, or his barber ought to be taken out and shot!'

Garvan laughed. There were times when he was never entirely sure whether Spencer was joking or being deadly serious. 'How's Dawn doing? Okay?'

'She's pretty up and down at the moment.'

'Isn't the funeral next week?'

'Friday. I take it you'll be there?'

'Yes, of course, I will.'

Spencer checked his watch, and said almost as a throwaway line, 'Tell me something. Has Joyce forgiven me yet?'

Garvan shrugged indifferently and said casually, 'I suppose she must have.'

'What makes you say that?'

'You've been invited to our wedding.'

It wasn't often Spencer was rendered speechless, but this was one such occasion. 'Married,' he eventually managed to say.

'Don't look so surprised.'

'We've been here before; you called it off last time around.'

'I think you'll find it was Joyce who called it off.'

'Well, anyway, the date's set for the 3rd of September.'

Spencer suddenly threw his head back and laughed. 'Whose idea was the 3rd?'

Garvan looked quizzically at him. 'It was Joyce's idea, why?'

'I thought as much. Don't you get it?'

'No, I can't say as I do.'

'The 3rd is the anniversary of the outbreak of World War II.' He grinned broadly. 'Let's hope it's not an omen of things to come.'

Even Garvan laughed, though he had to confess, until now, the significance of the date hadn't actually occurred to him. 'I'd like you to be my best man.'

Spencer was genuinely touched. 'And is *Joyce* okay with that?'

'We wouldn't be having this conversation, if she wasn't.'

'I'd better clear my diary then.'

'We only want a quiet wedding, just you and Dawn as witnesses, plus my boys from,' he hesitated slightly, 'from my first marriage. Before then, I'll hand in my resignation.'

Spencer shot him a questioning look. 'Resign? Are you joking?'

‘Come on, Spence. You know how things stand. Joyce’s past would only come back to haunt us. You know that’s why she called it off before.’

‘That was then. It’s a different situation now.’

A look of doubt came over Garvan’s face. ‘As soon I announce I’m getting married, my security vetting will be re-assessed. Once they’ve checked out her background, it won’t even get past the Met Commissioner, let alone the Home Secretary. Without the right level of security, I won’t have a choice other than to stand down. I’ve accepted all that!’

A slow smile crossed Spencer’s face. ‘You may or may not know, our work for the Double Cross is still considered to be top secret. The State papers and MI5’s records are not going to be released for at least thirty years or so, and before you ask, that includes the personnel files of our double agents.’ He could see that Garvan still didn’t quite get it. ‘May I make a suggestion?’

‘I’m sure you will. You always do.’

‘The system has a way of protecting its own.’

‘And, sometimes, it hangs them out to dry.’

‘Listen. I’m telling you there’s no reason for you to resign. Just fill out the security papers and add a covering letter.’

‘So, what am I supposed to say, exactly?’

‘That all inquiries concerning your future wife are to be referred marked for the attention of the Director-General of MI5. I think you’ll find that will send your vetting team scurrying for cover.’

‘I can see it would focus their attention a little.’

Spencer shrugged dismissively. ‘They’re not entitled to access the Double Cross records; it’s as simple as that. It’ll be quite straightforward; I’ll sign off the security clearance myself, and write a separate letter to the Commissioner, explain the reasons behind my intervention, without, of course, going into too much detail.’

Garvan smiled genuine gratitude in his eyes. ‘Thank you, Spence.’

‘I owe Joyce a great deal. It’s the very least I could do.’

They stopped talking as the door opened; it was the Home Secretary. 'So sorry I'm running late gentlemen,' he apologised in his customary sepulchral tones. 'I do hope I haven't kept you waiting too long.'

'Not at all, sir,' Garvan said, hoping to override the usual bullshit.

Parker set his briefcase down beside his chair and looked slightly flustered. 'I've just returned from a meeting with the PM.'

Garvan's gaze was pleasant enough but closed. 'About the MI5 report?' he asked politely.

'Yes,' came the clipped response. 'I'm afraid it overran by a good quarter of an hour.' He shot Spencer a knowing look. 'Don't worry. It was on a need to know basis, just those copy addressees on the circulation of your report.

Try as he might, Garvan found himself riveted by Parker's dubious hairline, and whether or not he was, in fact, wearing a toupee.

Parker eased himself down in the large swivel chair and peered over his half-moon glasses at them. 'The Prime Minister is delighted at the way things have turned out.'

'I'm relieved to hear it,' Spencer said, without enthusiasm. No-one within government circles had, as yet, questioned the version of events in Spencer's report how Schneider died while resisting arrest. It was all very plausible, and one Government officials were seemingly only too happy to accept.

'The PM received a call from the President earlier,' Parker continued briskly.

Spencer feigned surprise.

'The President expressed his gratitude at the way Professor Zimmerman's death was handled. I understand the body is to be flown back to the States on Wednesday, is that correct?'

Garvan answered, 'Yes, sir. We're in contact with the American Embassy about releasing the body to them.'

'Good, good,' he said, reaching into his desk drawer. 'I don't mind admitting I'll sleep a lot easier when all this is over and done with!' Parker retrieved a meerschaum pipe and set it down on a large green inkpad. He was trying to give up smoking, but found his cravings were alleviated by going through the motions. 'Of course, things could have turned quite nasty, if this Schneider character had managed to reach the *Mendoza*.'

Garvan agreed with him. 'Yes, we'd have ended up being forced to prevent the *Mendoza* leaving British shores.'

Parker winced at the idea.

'I can well imagine, sir, it might not have gone down too well in Buenos Aires.'

'That's one way of putting it, yes, Garvan. It's just as well you managed to stop him when you did! Can you imagine, on top of everything else, we'd now find ourselves facing a full-blown diplomatic incident with Argentina.' He leaned back in the swivel chair, with his hands clasped behind his head, swaying slowly from side to side. 'There's just one thing I don't quite understand, Sir Spencer. Why on Earth wasn't I made aware of Zimmerman's involvement with this Schneider character earlier?' There was a thin veneer of politeness about his tone, but it did little to disguise his irritation.

Spencer didn't miss a beat and lied smoothly, 'For the simple reason, sir, we didn't know there was a connection until the CIA dropped the bombshell on us.'

Parker went very quiet. It sounded probable, but Spencer always made things sound completely plausible. The trouble was, Parker never quite knew where the truth began, and the lies ended. Spencer's expression, as always, was entirely unreadable. MI5's spymaster was, at heart, a single-minded, ruthless operator, who had honed his skills during the war, and now navigated Whitehall with the same deadly efficient professionalism. Parker had always prided himself on being a good judge of human nature and a ready listener, but he'd never quite managed to get Spencer's measure.

Parker met his steady, watchful gaze. There was a cold, divorced detachment about the eyes that, at times, he found quite unnerving. Although Parker came to the conclusion Spencer was probably holding out on him, he decided to err on the side of caution. It was probably wiser to let the matter drop. Spencer was currently riding high in the Prime Minister's estimation, so there was really no point in creating unnecessary waves. If he wanted to score points, it was all about the timing, and now was not the right time.

'Do you mind if I smoke?' Spencer asked.

'No, not at all.'

He produced a pack of cigarettes and a lighter from his hip pocket.

'Your report mentions an official at the West German Embassy was heavily involved with Schneider and Zimmerman,' Parker continued.

Spencer clicked on the lighter. 'You mean, Josef Frenzel?'

'Yes, where do things stand with him?'

'He won't blab, if that's what you're worried about,' he answered through a swirl of smoke.

'Are you *sure*?'

'Let's just say Frenzel knows which side his bread's buttered.'

'Well, that is all well and good, but we can't allow him to remain in post at the Embassy!'

'With due respect, sir, let's not act too hastily.'

'What are you proposing?'

'That, for the time being, we leave Frenzel where he is.'

Parker leaned forward on the desk and clasped his hands together. 'Really, and why's that?' he asked sceptically.

'If we send him packing on the next available flight back to Germany, we risk giving the game away.'

'What game?'

Spencer's response was clipped. 'If Frenzel hadn't provided us with the information about Schneider's safe house and the lock-up, then it could well have ended in a complete bloodbath at Surrey Docks. And now, rather than congratulating ourselves on a job well done, we'd be facing a potential media frenzy. All it would take is some smart arsed journalist to get a hook linking Schneider to Zimmerman, and we'd all end up being pensioned off.'

Parker agreed it wasn't worth thinking about, and, in hindsight, they'd probably had a pretty lucky escape. He began toying thoughtfully with his empty pipe. He still felt he needed to clear the air, to get things straight, or at least straight in his mind. 'I do hope you're not seriously proposing this Frenzel character stays on here indefinitely, are *you*?'

'No, sir, I'm not. But, I think we do owe him a little leeway.'

'Maybe, but how much leeway are you thinking of giving him?'

'Well, just enough for the dust to settle.'

Parker set the pipe down, opened his spectacles case, and started to clean the lenses. 'So just how much dust are we talking about? I'd like an answer.'

'I didn't mention it in the report, but Frenzel's applied for early retirement from the West German intelligence service.'

Parker snapped the case shut. 'No doubt at your suggestion, was it?'

'It keeps things neat and tidy.'

'Quite.'

'I understand the Ambassador has agreed for him to work his notice out here in London.'

'When can we expect to see the back of him?'

'I'd say three months max.'

Parker settled back in his chair and placed his hands together, as if in prayer. It was apparent to him decisions had already been taken at the very highest level. Even though Parker had occasionally accused Spencer of being a dangerous maverick, he would never have approached the Ambassador without the tacit approval of both the Prime Minister and the Foreign Secretary.

Memos would have passed between their offices, decisions reached, and signed off, and once again, he'd been deliberately left out of the loop and marginalised. Parker was already acutely aware, politically, he was living on borrowed time. In spite of his growing sense of insecurity, his expression gave nothing away when he said, 'I can see you've thought of everything.'

Spencer smiled lamely. 'We try our best, sir.'

'I understand the Foreign Secretary is in discussions with the Americans about tightening the screw on the *Schamhorst*.'

It was Garvan who answered, 'That's probably going to be easier said than done. They run a very tight ship.'

'So, what's the alternative? Sit back and do nothing, is that what you're saying?'

A flicker of irritation crossed Garvan's face. 'No, sir, that's not what I'm saying at all. Sir Spencer will back me up on this, but it's not for the want of trying. I was merely pointing out the *Schamhorst's* network is an incredibly well-organised spider's web of corruption and deceit. I'm sure you're aware Scotland Yard has been working very closely with Interpol, investigating all the ratlines, including the *Schamhorst*. I haven't seen them myself, but I understand the investigating officers have come across some old records, indicating there were transfers of Nazi funds from the Reichsbank directly to the Vatican Bank. The funds were subsequently moved on from Rome to Nazi-controlled bank accounts in Switzerland.'

Parker looked genuinely horrified. 'What are you saying?'

Garvan's expression registered surprise. He thought he'd made it patently obvious. 'I really can't make it any plainer, sir. The reports indicate the Vatican Bank acted as an intermediary to spirit Nazi gold to the Reich's Swiss accounts.' Garvan held his gaze and smiled a slight, almost cynical smile. 'So, with the best will in the world, sir, you can see progress has been, to say the least, a little on the slow side.'

Parker shook his head in despair, sighed wearily, and glanced at his watch. He was already running late, and wanted to start winding things up. He was due to give a speech in an hour at the House of Commons, and wanted time to go over his notes. 'Before we call it day, gentlemen, the Prime Minister has invited you both to a very select dinner party at Chequers next Thursday. The American and West German Ambassadors will be present.'

Garvan shot the Home Secretary a look of incredulity. 'Why me?' he asked.

'Well, you've both done sterling work for the Government, and saved us a good deal of embarrassment all round. As I said earlier, the Americans are delighted by the way Zimmerman's death was handled. This whole mess could so easily have caused disastrous results for their rocket programme. Heaven forbid what would have happened there! The Soviets would have been sitting back, rubbing their hands together. That's the trouble. Public opinion can be very fickle.'

'As you know, sir,' Garvan continued. 'I'm no politician.'

Parker never allowed him to finish. By now, he was well into his stride, and warming to the theme. Spencer prodded Garvan sharply with his elbow and gave him a look. Garvan smiled to himself; he could almost hear Spencer saying, *"Please don't encourage the old bugger!"*

'You'll be there, of course?' he asked expectantly.

'I'll clear my diary, sir.' Garvan then glanced at Spencer to try and gauge his reaction to the invite.

Although Garvan knew he would hate every second of the small talk, it would be impossible to refuse an invite to Chequers, the Prime Minister's official country retreat. As usual, Spencer was giving nothing away and looked his normal, calm, calculating self. Holding the Home Secretary's gaze, he said, 'I'm afraid, sir, I'll have to decline the Prime Minister's kind invitation.'

'What the hell are you talking about, Spencer? You can't refuse an invite from the PM!'

Garvan thought, even for Spencer, he was chancing his luck, and judging by the look of complete horror on Parker's face, he'd finally overstepped the mark.

'It's a little tricky, sir,' he explained.

'Well, how tricky can it be?' Parker fumed.

'I don't wish to appear ungrateful.'

'You're doing a bloody good job of it so far!'

'You see, I've already accepted an invitation from a lady to attend a dinner party next Thursday.'

'But, I don't think you realise how important this dinner is, and what an honour it is for you both to be invited. I'm surprised at you, Spencer, given your tenure as the Director General of MI5 is up for renewal, you would refuse the Prime Minister's invite to dinner with some ruddy woman or other.'

Spencer glanced calmly at Garvan and then at the Home Secretary. 'I realise the Prime Minister may feel let down by my non-attendance at Chequers.'

'"Let down" are not the words I'd use!'

Spencer stretched forward to stub out his cigarette in Parker's ashtray. 'But, you must understand, sir, that an invite to dinner from,' Spencer paused, he really didn't like to say, but equally, he didn't wish to offend the PM. Somewhat reluctantly, he added, 'If you must know, sir, the invite to dinner is from the lady who lives in the big house at the end of the Mall, and can't be lightly refused. Not *even* for the Prime Minister.'

Parker's expression spoke volumes. 'You mean, the Queen?'

'Well, sir, she's the only lady I know who lives in a big house at the end of the Mall.'

Garvan smiled to himself. The bugger had come up trumps, yet again.

*If you liked this book you might also wish to read the other books by the same author; they are all Free on Kindle Unlimited – **FIVE STAR RATED REVIEWS ON AMAZON AND GOODREADS***

Codename Nicolette
Review from Amazon UK
A really absorbing story which screams out to be made into a BBC produced series or British-produced film (to catch the atmosphere of the like of Tinker, Tailor). The author gives the real feel of how we were "up against it" and that the strategies of the intelligence services, when needed most, played a critical part. It looks as though DCI Garvan is in the position to provide further adventures into the doings of the cloak and dagger brigade and I look forward to reading them.

Mission Lisbon the V-1 Double Cross
Review from Amazon UK
This is a very well researched wartime novel with believable characters and a twisting storyline. It is a gripping story of espionage during World War II, and I hope there will be another book in the series as it leaves the reader on a cliff-hanger.

Dead Man Walking - A Spy Amongst Us
Review from Amazon.com
Fans of British WWII espionage intrigue will love Dead Man Walking, A Spy Amongst Us by Toby Oliver. A British cabinet member is murdered, and the evidence points to infamous double agent, Toniolo, as the perpetrator. The author is a master at weaving deception and conspiracy at every turn of the page. It is a fascinating backstage look at the relationship between England, Germany, and the Soviet Union during the war. The author blends meticulously-researched fact with fiction and will keep your interest until the very end. Buy this book if you love spy novels, and you won't be disappointed.

The Downing Street Plot – An Agent's Revenge
Review from Amazon.com

When an undercover CIA operative reveals a KGB plot to assassinate the Prime Minister, Agent Jack Stein reaches out to his old spy buddy, Spencer Hall. When Spencer starts assembling a team that he can trust, he runs into resistance. It seems retired spies want to stay retired. But when the operative relays further intelligence, Spencer discovers that the assassin could be a former co-worker with a grudge.This was an enjoyable spy thriller. The main characters had history between them, but it is all laid out from the start. I really liked Spencer. He was an uncompromising character, and surrounded himself with the same. At times, I felt like I was part of the team, trying to beat the clock. This was an intriguing plot, and it down-played politics, which is always a plus.

Printed in Great Britain
by Amazon